The Future
She Left Behind

Center Point
Large Print

**This Large Print Book carries the
Seal of Approval of N.A.V.H.**

The Future She Left Behind

MARIN THOMAS

CENTER POINT LARGE PRINT
THORNDIKE, MAINE

This Center Point Large Print edition
is published in the year 2018 by arrangement with
The Berkley Publishing Group, an imprint of Penguin
Publishing Group, a division of Penguin Random House LLC.

The text of this Large Print edition is unabridged.
In other aspects, this book may vary
from the original edition.
Printed in the United States of America
on permanent paper.
Set in 16-point Times New Roman type.

ISBN: 978-1-68324-685-5

Library of Congress Cataloging-in-Publication Data

Names: Thomas, Marin, author.
Title: The future she left behind / Marin Thomas.
Description: Center Point Large Print edition. | Thorndike, Maine :
    Center Point Large Print, 2018.
Identifiers: LCCN 2017051064 | ISBN 9781683246855
    (hardcover : alk. paper)
Subjects: LCSH: Domestic fiction. | Large type books. | BISAC:
    FICTION / Contemporary Women. | FICTION / Family Life. |
    FICTION / Romance / Contemporary. | GSAFD: Love stories.
Classification: LCC PS3620.H6348 F88 2018 | DDC 813/.6—dc23
LC record available at https://lccn.loc.gov/2017051064

For Kevin . . . I still believe you're the greatest thing to ever happen to me. I love you.

CHAPTER ONE

A mmonium thioglycolate, also called perm salt, is murder on your hair."

The famous courtroom scene in the movie *Legally Blonde* flashed through Katelyn Pratt's mind as she sat in the Savvy Salon, listening to the stylist lecture her mother-in-law on the dangers of perming her hair too often.

Katelyn set her sketch pad aside and took her iPhone out of her purse. She Googled ammonium thioglycolate: *a pungent, colorless, clear liquid that burns the eyes, nose, lungs, and may explode if subjected to high heat*—that described Shirley Pratt to a T. She tapped the Wikipedia icon and continued to read. *A chemical used in the manufacturing of plastics, bombs, pesticides and dyes.* Dear God. These poisons had been seeping into her mother-in-law's skull for years. No wonder the sixty-four-year-old was a walking, talking, toxic know-it-all.

"When you're finished with my hair, Pam, maybe you could tame that horse mane my daughter-in-law wears on her head."

The zinger rolled off Katelyn's shoulders, and she resumed sketching the flower vase on the table next to her. Shirley detested long hair, and that was why Katelyn never cut hers.

"She's under the dryer."

Katelyn glanced up from her pad and smiled at Shirley's hairdresser. "How long until you finish with her?"

"Forty minutes." Pam's eyes flicked to the styling chair, then back to Katelyn. "If she doesn't give her hair a break from perms, she's going to molt like a bighorn sheep."

That wouldn't be so bad if her mother-in-law shed her horns along with her hair. "I'll mention it to her." But Shirley wouldn't appreciate the advice. The day she'd moved into her son's house—not her son *and* daughter-in-law's house—she'd made it clear that any comments regarding her age or appearance would not be welcome. The same rule, however, did not apply to Katelyn, whom Shirley criticized whenever the urge hit, which was pretty darn often.

"As much as I love taking her money," Pam said, "she won't do me any good if she ends up bald. I don't want to see her in the salon before November."

Five months from now? No way would a woman who refused to leave the house without makeup and a fresh manicure ignore her hair for eighteen weeks.

"I need to run an errand. I'll be back in a few minutes." Katelyn stuffed the sketch pad into her canvas tote bag, then left the salon, ducking her head against the rain. A cold front had moved through St. Louis overnight, leaving early June feeling like late October. She drove Shirley's silver Mercedes to the other side of the strip mall and parked in front of Henderson Drug. When she entered the store, she went straight to the Hallmark aisle. Her husband should be the one picking out a card for his mother, but she couldn't remember the last time Don had been in town for Shirley's birthday.

The pain-in-the-butt's favorite color was blue, so Katelyn selected a gaudy pink card with neon orange and yellow smiley-face flowers. On the way to the register, she passed an umbrella stand and plucked a plastic rain cap from the display. Heaven forbid Shirley get her hair wet and ruin her perm when she left the salon.

While Katelyn waited in the checkout line, she browsed the retail gift cards. She assumed Don would bring his mother a gift from Japan, but Shirley had nothing to open on her actual birthday tomorrow. She selected a fifty-dollar Starbucks card. Gift cards were impersonal, but it was the begrudging thought that counted. Besides, she got credit for baking Shirley's favorite cake this morning—chocolate fudge.

"Hello." Katelyn set her items on the counter.

The teenage clerk ignored the greeting and asked, "Do you have a Henderson Drug card?"

Her discount cards for the various stores she frequented hung on the key chain for her

Hyundai Santa Fe, which she'd left at the house after Shirley insisted Katelyn drive her car today. "Can I give you my phone number?" She recited the digits, then swiped her debit card.

A moment later the teen's robotic voice said, "Thank you for shopping Henderson Drugs. Next, please."

Katelyn returned to the salon in time to watch Pam spray a final layer of shellac on Shirley's café au lait curls. While the two women settled the bill, she texted her son, Michael.

Hi, honey. Grandma Pratt turns 65 tomorrow. Don't forget to wish her a Happy Birthday. Hope U R doing ok. Call me when U have free time. She added a heart emoticon, then hit send. Michael would eventually answer her—he always did.

A long, lonely summer loomed ahead of Katelyn. She'd been looking forward to spending time with the twins before they headed off to college, but the kids had made other plans. Michael had wanted to get a jump on prerequisite classes for his engineering major and had enrolled in summer school at the University of Michigan. He'd moved into his new apartment in Ann Arbor two weeks ago. Melissa had been accepted into Shirley's alma mater, Stephens College, in Columbia, Missouri, and she was traveling in Greece and Italy until mid-July with a group of incoming freshmen.

Shirley fake-patted her hair. "What do you think?"

"Lovely." The hairstyle looked the same as it always did—old-fashioned. Katelyn held out the plastic cap. Shirley put it on, then walked to the door.

"You forgot your purse." Katelyn pointed to the counter and Shirley retrieved her handbag; then they left the salon.

Once they were on their way home, she asked Grumpy Cat, "Where would you like to go for your birthday lunch?"

"Nowhere." Shirley acted as if she didn't care about celebrating her birthday, but Katelyn knew better. If her father-in-law, Robert, hadn't dropped dead from a massive heart attack three years ago, her mother-in-law would be partying in Kansas City with her wealthy friends. But a series of phone calls shortly after Robert's funeral had prompted Don to invite his mother to live with them.

The first call had come from the housekeeper after she'd discovered the gas stove had been left on while Shirley had been out shopping. The second call had come from the bank after Shirley had failed to pay the mortgage two months in a row. And the third call had come from the pastor at Shirley's church, who'd informed Don that his mother had put her credit card in the donation plate during Sunday services. Shirley's slipups had worried Don and he'd insisted his mother sell her home and move to St. Louis. Katelyn remembered the conversation as if it had happened yesterday and not 1,112 days ago.

"My mother's moving in with us," Don said.

Katelyn hovered in the master bathroom doorway, watching her husband pack his toiletry bag. "You mean for a month or two while she house hunts?"

His gaze skipped over her. "It's not like we don't have room for her."

"That isn't the point."

"What is the point, Katelyn?"

"Your mother doesn't like me." Don had joked when they'd dated in college that he'd been attracted to Katelyn because she had nothing in common with his mother. That was well and good when two hundred miles had separated them— not so well and good when they lived under the same roof.

"It's not safe for her to live alone. She could burn the house down if she leaves the stove on again," he said.

"It was one time, Don. Besides, it's normal for someone to be forgetful after losing a loved one. Your father's death was sudden and unexpected. Give her time and she'll settle down."

"I don't want to take any chances with her safety."

"Then move her into an assisted-living facility."

"She's not that bad off yet."

"She's been fine when I've talked to her on the phone."

Don ignored her protests. "The kids will enjoy having her around."

Katelyn left the bathroom and threw herself across the bed. There was no shortage of adjectives to describe her mother-in-law. Opinionated. Bossy. Snooty.

Don sat next to her on the mattress and put on his shoes. "You'll be busy with the twins and that art group you belong to. I doubt my mother will get in your way. Besides, she'll make her own friends and go off with them."

Don had been dead wrong. Since moving in with them, Shirley had made zero friends. None. Nada. Zip. The woman had made no effort to connect with others her age and had even snubbed the ladies' bridge club after Katelyn had begged her elderly neighbor, Mrs. Krantz, to invite her into the group. And as Katelyn had predicted, after a few months of processing her husband's death and the move to a new city, Shirley's memory appeared fine except for the normal signs of old-age forgetfulness like not remembering the date or where she set her purse.

"Your mother's fine," she told Don three months after Shirley had moved in with them. "She baked a cake yesterday for the kids and remembered to turn off the oven. And she's been running her own errands and finding her way back home. She's ready to move into her own place."

"She just got settled with us and now you want to kick her out?"

A thump in the hallway caught Katelyn's attention and she poked her head out the bedroom door, but there was no one in sight. "Will you please broach the subject with your mother and see how she reacts?"

"I'll talk to her when I return from my trip." Don kissed Katelyn's cheek, grabbed his suitcase and left the house. The next day Shirley took the car to run to the grocery store; then two hours later Katelyn's phone rang.

"Is everything okay?" Katelyn asked.

"I don't know where I am."

"Didn't you go to the grocery store?"

"I must have taken a wrong turn."

"Where are you right now?"

"In a parking lot. There's a donut shop and a cleaner's."

"What's the name of the cleaner's?"

"Fresh Press Laundry."

The business was only four blocks from the house. "Stay put. I'll be right there." Katelyn had driven to the shopping center and then made Shirley follow her home. From that day on, her mother-in-law asked to be chauffeured everywhere. When Katelyn suggested seeing a doctor, Shirley had thrown a hissy fit.

The sudden memory loss had Katelyn wondering if the older woman had eavesdropped on her conversation with Don. But then the following week, Shirley misplaced her wallet and appeared genuinely distressed. They'd torn up the house searching for it, but hadn't found it until the following day when Katelyn took an empty detergent bottle out to the recycle bin and discovered the wallet sitting on top of the garbage can. How it had ended up there was a mystery that had never been solved, and Katelyn had been forced to accept that Shirley's occasional forgetfulness wasn't intentional and that her mother-in-law would be living in her home for the foreseeable future.

Once the queen bee knew she wouldn't be thrown out, she'd gleefully assumed the role of the de facto matriarch of the Pratt clan. Katelyn had complained to Don, insisting he put his mother in her place, but Shirley had emerged from those talks believing she still outranked Katelyn—no doubt recognizing that Don had acted as his wife's messenger.

It wasn't until Melissa asked Katelyn why she bickered with Grandma all the time that she realized the twins had been paying attention to the power struggle between their mother and their grandmother. She cared more about what her kids thought of her than of her mother-in-law, so she'd backed off and chosen her battles wisely and when the kids weren't around.

"Let's have your birthday lunch downtown at the Old Spaghetti Factory." Katelyn turned the wipers up a notch.

"I'd rather wait and celebrate when Don returns."

Both Katelyn and Don were only children, and in Shirley's eyes her son could do no wrong. According to her, Don not only walked on water—he'd invented it. Katelyn got along fine with her mother, Birdie, but they weren't close. Often a couple of weeks would go by before one of them called to check in.

"Denny's offers a free birthday lunch," Katelyn said.

Shirley's mouth puckered and Katelyn swallowed a laugh. Her mother-in-law had high standards when it came to food.

She turned off Delmar Boulevard onto Westminster and a block later pulled into the driveway of their 1907 Classic Revival–style home. The four-thousand-square-foot house included a finished basement, four bedrooms and three and a half baths—plenty large enough for five people to wander around without bumping into one another. *Not.* The idiot who'd renovated the place had added a guest suite on the main floor near the kitchen, making it convenient for Shirley to overhear conversations and phone calls. Katelyn parked the car in the circular drive.

"Why aren't you pulling into the garage? You don't have any appointments for the rest of the day." Amazing how Shirley forgot where she set her purse, yet she memorized Katelyn's personal calendar every morning on her way to the coffeepot.

"I might decide to go out later." Katelyn collected the drugstore bag and her tote, then got out of the car and waited for Shirley. "Be careful on the wet steps." She followed behind. "Pam's banishing you from the salon until November."

"Why?"

Katelyn twisted the knife a little deeper. "Pam said your hair's starting to thin at the crown." If she didn't get in a few jabs once in a while, she'd explode and say something she couldn't take back.

They entered the house and Shirley removed the rain cap, then dropped it on the chair next to the door. "You should change your hairstyle to something more age appropriate."

Oh, this was rich. The Betty White look-alike telling Katelyn she needed a makeover.

"You're too old to wear your hair halfway down your back."

"Since when is forty old?" Katelyn hung their jackets in the hall closet.

"The brown color looks nice on you, but the longer length draws attention to your . . ."

Shirley's gaze dropped. "Your hips aren't your best feature."

Katelyn ignored the criticism, because she derived immense pleasure from knowing that Shirley was powerless to force her to change her hair. Every year she considered trying a new style, then nixed the idea, reluctant to give up the one thing that drove her mother-in-law nuts.

CHAPTER TWO

Katelyn breathed a sigh of relief when Shirley retreated to her bedroom. She'd enjoy the peace and quiet while she made the frosting for the birthday cake. The recipe came from her grandmother's cookbook, which Birdie had given to Katelyn on her wedding day. Speaking of mothers . . . She peeked at the calendar on the kitchen desk. Birdie turned sixty on June twenty-first—two weeks from today.

It had been more than three years since Katelyn had flown home to Little Springs, Texas. After Shirley had moved in and turned their lives—mostly Katelyn's life—upside down, it had been all she could do to get through each week, let alone plan the next one. With the kids gone for most of the summer, she intended to ask Don if he'd schedule a week's vacation and entertain Shirley while she visited Birdie.

After collecting all the ingredients, Katelyn combined melted chocolate squares, butter, vanilla flavoring, sour cream, water and powdered sugar into a bowl, then flipped on the mixer. The sound of the beaters brought back memories of her mother baking a cake every Sunday morning and then letting it cool on the counter while they attended church.

Katelyn had grown up a latchkey kid, and because both her parents had worked, she'd spent much of her childhood alone, playing with Mack, the stray Rottweiler that had wandered into the yard one afternoon and had never left. Mack hadn't been allowed inside, but her father had built a house for him to use during the winter. In the summer Mack slept beneath the front porch to escape the heat.

By the time Katelyn had entered junior high, Mack's muzzle had turned white. Her father had predicted the dog wouldn't survive another winter. Mack must have known, too, because he'd died the day before Halloween that year. They'd buried him in the backyard near Birdie's yellow lantana plants. Katelyn's cell phone rang, interrupting the poignant memory, and she shut off the mixer.

Melissa. "Hi, honey. Everything okay?"

"I'm fine, Mom. You worry too much."

Busted. Katelyn admitted she was a helicopter parent and proud of it. After the twins had been born, she'd made a vow to stay involved in their lives and become their champion—unlike her own mother, who'd been too tired from her job to keep track of Katelyn's hobbies. And when Birdie wasn't cashiering at the Buy & Bag grocery store, she could be found working in her garden, not attending her daughter's extracurricular activities. Katelyn might have gone overboard making sure her kids had everything they needed to succeed.

Don's job as the executive vice president of logistic operations for NicorTrune—a company that produced chemicals, fibers and plastics used by other manufacturers—required him to spend several weeks a month overseas, and she'd felt compelled to double down on her efforts to make up for his absence.

"I wanted to wish Grandma an early happy birthday, because I can't call tomorrow."

"Why not?"

"We're touring Pompeii and I'll be gone the whole day."

"Grandma's napping, but I'll tell her you wished her a happy birthday. How are you doing? Are you getting along with the other girls? What are you eating?"

Melissa laughed. "Which question do you want me to answer first?"

"I don't care. Just keep talking. It's good to hear your voice."

"I'm having a great time and so far the weather's been decent."

It didn't sound as if Melissa missed home at all. As soon as the thought entered Katelyn's mind, she chastised herself. It hadn't been that long ago that she'd been as eager as her daughter to venture out into the world.

"OMG, Mom, the guys over here are hot."

"No hot guys for you, young lady."

"Has Jared called?" Jared and Melissa had

dated their senior year but decided on an amicable breakup when Melissa left for Italy. Katelyn understood only too well the difficulties of letting go of a first love.

"Jared hasn't phoned. Is he supposed to call?"

"I thought . . . Never mind. If he stops by, tell him I'm having a great time abroad."

"Do you want me to tell him the boys over there are hot, too?"

Melissa groaned. "How's Michael?"

"Fine, I guess. He hasn't called home yet for money."

"Is Dad around?"

"He returns from Japan on Friday."

"Tell him I said hi."

"I will. How are you doing with your money? Do you need more?"

"I have plenty. Mom?"

"What?"

"Don't say no right away."

Uh-oh.

"Sara Kerns invited me to stay with her after we return to the States in July."

Melissa had met Sara during the orientation meeting for the trip and the two had become fast friends. "Doesn't Sara live in Georgia?"

"Near Savannah."

"Is Jared the reason you don't want to hang around St. Louis the rest of the summer?"

"Maybe. It'll be so awkward, Mom."

Katelyn understood. When she'd broken up with her high school boyfriend, Jackson, during her first semester of college, she'd avoided going home, wanting to spare them both the awkwardness of running into each other.

"Sara's family owns a horse farm and you know I've always wanted to learn to ride."

"I offered to set you up with lessons when you were ten, but you changed your mind." Katelyn had taken Melissa to a horse stable on the outskirts of St. Louis, but the huge animals had scared her and she'd asked to take dance lessons instead.

"Sara said they have a really old mare that I can learn to ride on."

Katelyn hated not seeing Melissa until school began in late August, but she didn't want to stand in the way of her daughter chasing her dreams. "Are you sure you don't want to come home?"

"Positive. And Dad won't care, because he's gone all the time. Please, Mom."

"As long as it's okay with Sara's parents, you can stay with them."

Melissa squealed. "It's going to be the best summer ever."

"I'll change your plane ticket when—"

"I can do it."

Katelyn bit back a sigh. She'd been looking forward to taking her daughter shopping for school clothes and spoiling her with a girls' day at the spa before she left for college. Melissa had begun getting her hair highlighted in ninth grade and mani-pedis had become a monthly habit. Michael always had the newest video-game system and cool athletic shoes. Katelyn had wanted only to give her children what she'd never had. The twins knew they were spoiled, but so were their friends at school. Fortunately, they'd never abused their parents' generosity or seriously rebelled.

"I gotta go. Tell Grandma I miss her."

"Stay safe."

"I will. Love you."

"Love you, too, honey." As soon as Katelyn set the phone on the counter, she received a text message from Michael.

I'll wish Grandma a happy birthday tomorrow.

Katelyn wasn't letting her son off the hook that easy. What are you up to? she texted back.

5'11"

Very funny

On my way to the gym. Gotta go.

Call this weekend. Your dad will be home.

K

Love you XXOO

Me 2

In a good mood after both kids had checked in, Katelyn took extra care frosting the two-layer cake before covering it with plastic wrap and returning it to the fridge. After she cleaned up the mess, she decided to throw a load of laundry into the washing machine, but the sound of the doorbell interrupted her.

A pair of blue eyes rimmed with pale blond lashes stared back at her through the peephole. The man wore a dark suit, and behind him a nondescript green sedan sat in the driveway next to the Mercedes. She opened the door. "May I help you?"

"Are you Katelyn Chandler-Pratt?"

"I am."

He handed her a manila envelope. "This is for you."

"What is it?"

"Papers." He backed up.

"What kind of papers?"

"Legal papers."

"I don't understand. Are we being sued?"

"Only you, ma'am. Your husband wants a divorce."

· · ·

Katelyn stood in the kitchen, shoveling chocolate cake into her mouth, her gaze fixated on the table where the manila envelope rested. She swallowed a gulp of milk and washed down the frosting that stuck to the sides of her throat.

The kitchen lights flipped on and Shirley gaped at her from the doorway. "Is that my birthday cake you're eating?"

"Yes." Was this her second or third piece?

"It's almost six o'clock." Shirley glanced at the stove. "Did you have dinner already?"

"This is dinner." She finished the last bite, then sucked the frosting off the end of the fork. Ignoring her mother-in-law's openmouthed stare, she helped herself to another slice, albeit smaller.

"Aren't you going to save some of that for tomorrow?"

Katelyn's gaze shifted to the table—her brain barely registering the chocolate melting on her tongue.

"Is this what's got you eating like an ogre?" Shirley snatched the envelope and waved it in the air.

Katelyn shoveled another bite into her mouth. She'd stop gorging herself as soon as she felt sick. Right now she was numb from the shoulders down and in serious danger of devouring the entire cake.

"What is this?" Shirley moved closer, invading Katelyn's space.

"A legal document." After the messenger had driven off, Katelyn had stood in the entryway, waiting for him to return, certain once he reached the corner, he would realize he'd delivered the envelope to the wrong address. When the doorbell never rang, she'd done what any reasonable woman in her situation would do—she'd eaten chocolate.

"Steven Long . . ." Shirley tapped a fingernail against the return address. "The name sounds familiar."

"Don's lawyer."

"Don isn't thinking of taking early retirement, is he? The kids need to graduate college first." A pencil-thin eyebrow arched. "Aren't you going to open it?" Shirley tapped the envelope against Katelyn's leg. "Before your pants become too tight."

Katelyn shook her head, too dazed to feel the insult.

"I'll open it." Shirley slid her nail beneath the flap and tore the seal.

The coldness that had filled Katelyn the past few hours was beginning to ebb and her stomach ached. "Don's not retiring."

Her mother-in-law unfolded the pair of reading glasses hanging from a fake pearl chain around her neck and put them on. " 'Regarding the marriage of Donald Pratt, petitioner, and Katelyn Pratt, respondent . . .' " Shirley sucked in a noisy breath and looked at Katelyn. "This is a dissolution-of-marriage notification."

Katelyn pulled out a chair at the table and sank onto the seat.

"I don't understand."

Shirley didn't understand? Shoot, Katelyn had been blindsided. Her mother-in-law left the room and returned a minute later with her cell phone. "This must be a mistake."

Shirley's reaction surprised Katelyn. Years ago she'd been less than enthusiastic upon hearing the news that her son would be marrying a lower-class girl from Texas.

"Donald, this is your mother. Call me as soon as you get this message."

Katelyn wanted to laugh but feared a sob would escape if she opened her mouth. Shirley riffled through the legal papers, then set a smaller envelope with Katelyn's name scrawled across the front in Don's handwriting onto the table.

"Open it," Shirley said.

"Later." After she finished processing the news that her husband was tossing her aside.

Shirley helped herself to a piece of birthday cake, then sat across from Katelyn.

"While you were napping, Melissa called to wish you an early happy birthday."

"Some birthday this is turning out to be."

"I'm sorry my getting dumped has ruined your celebration."

"The reason Don wants a divorce doesn't matter." Shirley pointed her dessert fork at Katelyn. "You can fix this."

How could she fix anything, if she didn't know what was broken?

"I told you to cut your hair years ago."

"A man doesn't divorce his wife over a hairstyle." But in the back of Katelyn's mind she worried that Shirley was right—not about the long hair, but about Katelyn's appearance. Maybe her husband wasn't attracted to her anymore.

She thought back to the last time Don had been home. Every night he'd retreated to his office, claiming he had work to catch up on, and she'd gone to bed alone. In the morning he'd already been dressed and downstairs eating breakfast by the time she'd woken up.

"I'm sure this is nothing more than a midlife crisis." Shirley's smile wobbled. "The cake is very good, by the way."

Katelyn felt it coming . . . the slow clenching of her stomach muscles, her mouth watering and her eyes stinging. She bolted from the kitchen and stumbled into the half bath outside Don's office, then dropped to her knees and shared Shirley's birthday cake with the porcelain god.

Chocolate cake would never taste the same after today.

CHAPTER THREE

It was past midnight.

Shirley had holed up in her room hours ago with a second helping of cake. Katelyn preferred to drown her sorrows in a hundred-dollar bottle of Nosotros.

Now that she was up to her eyeballs in courage, she set her empty wineglass on the bedroom dresser and picked up the white envelope with her name on it. Almost two decades of marriage had warranted only a single sheet of notepaper—typed, not handwritten.

Katelyn, I'm unhappy.

Why hadn't Don said something to her before now?

Our marriage hasn't been good for a long while and since the kids are moving on with their lives, I want to move on, too.

Snapshots of their life together flashed through Katelyn's mind as she searched for a moment, a conversation or a look, that had hinted at her husband's unhappiness. His phone call the previous week had been like all the others. . . . *How's Mother? The kids? You? Work is busy. Gotta go.*

She couldn't remember if either one of them had said "I love you" at the end of the conversation. And when was the last time they'd made love? A month ago? Two?

Maybe their marriage wasn't as warm and fuzzy as other couples', but what did they have to be unhappy about? Don made more money in a year than they could spend. They had two great kids. And they had their health.

> I've listed the house with a real estate agent. The For Sale sign goes up tomorrow.

He wasn't wasting any time.

> Take whatever furniture you want, but leave me a few pictures of the kids. Steven will arrange to put what's left into storage. I paid off the Santa Fe. It's yours now.

She picked up the wineglass—a gift Don had purchased for her in Belgium a year ago—and hurled it at the fireplace. The glass shattered against the white marble, the shards raining down on the carpet.

31

I'll cover the cost of the divorce and the kids' college tuition. I think you'll find the settlement more than fair.

What was almost nineteen years of marriage worth?

I leased an apartment for my mother at the Garden Oaks Retirement Estates off of Delmar Blvd. The rent is paid through the end of the year. I've arranged for a caretaker to chauffeur her on errands and to doctors' appointments. This is the best I can do for her until I figure out my living arrangements.

Three years ago a retirement home hadn't been good enough for his mother, but now that Katelyn wouldn't be around to babysit the woman, it was suddenly okay to shove her off on someone else? Then again, why did she care? Her mother-in-law wasn't her problem anymore.

The movers arrive two weeks from Saturday to pack her things. I'd appreciate it if you'd help her get settled into the apartment. I left the contact information for the caregiver service with the leasing agent.

Don wasn't just dumping Katelyn; he was dumping his mother, too. As much as Shirley got on her nerves, the woman didn't deserve this coldhearted treatment from her son.

And what about Michael and Melissa? He could have found a better way to spring this divorce on the family. She doubted the twins had a clue that their father was unhappy. Because Don traveled so much, they saw him for only a few days once or twice a month.

I'll let you break the news to the kids.

Screw that. Don wanted the divorce—he could tell their son and daughter.

And, Katelyn . . . there's someone else.

What had begun as a one-bottle wine night had become a two-bottle pity party. She set the letter aside, then took the back staircase to the kitchen. She opened the basement door and descended into the wine cellar, where she selected the last bottle of Nosotros, and then used the opener on the bar to remove the cork before returning upstairs.

She paused in her bedroom doorway, her gaze taking in the lavish furnishings. Floor-to-ceiling pillars separated the bed from the sitting area with a fireplace. Slivers of burgundy-colored glass winked at her from beneath the crystal chandelier hanging from the ceiling.

The Egyptian linens and the shimmering silver duvet had cost a small fortune, as had the sixty-five-inch mirror mounted above the dresser, which morphed into a TV screen at the flick of a switch. Heated marble flooring and matching countertops greeted her each morning in the bathroom, where the walk-in rain shower was wide enough to accommodate a small crowd. The clothes closet was almost as large as the bedroom.

Katelyn recalled the countless nights during her teen years when she'd sat on the front porch of her childhood home, dreaming of a life like this. A life where she and her husband didn't have to worry about which bills to pay first because there was enough money to cover them all. A life where she didn't have to plan weekly meals around supermarket coupons. A life where she had the freedom to come and go without having to wait until her husband arrived home from work with the car. A life where she could buy an object because it was pretty and not because it served a purpose.

When Katelyn had met Don, she'd known he could give her that life. There had been passion in the beginning, when they'd dated—a passion fueled by the excitement of being with someone from a different socioeconomic background. But after they'd had the twins and Don's career had taken off, the excitement in their relationship had begun to fade.

She entered the closet—the only room in the house that showed she and Don came from vastly different backgrounds. The space contained his-and-her dressers, shoe shelves, floor-to-ceiling mirrors, a marble vanity and a TV mounted on the wall.

Don's side was filled with bespoke dress shirts, ascot neckties, Armani suits and Stefano Bemer shoes. Her side had J. Crew blouses, American Eagle jeans, Old Navy T-shirts and cargo pants. Her jewelry came from Charming Charlie, except for her wedding ring and the diamond necklace Don had given her on their tenth anniversary.

She walked over to his prized possession—an Italian silk dress shirt he'd paid five hundred dollars for—and poured half the bottle of wine down the front of it. Then she shut the door, grabbed the corner of the duvet as she walked past the bed and dragged the cover outside onto the balcony facing the street.

She tossed the blanket over the chaise lounge still wet from the previous day's rain, then stretched out and gazed at the shiny specks of light in the sky and sipped the wine.

There's someone else.

Katelyn squeezed the neck of the bottle, wishing her fingers were pressing against Don's jugular. Anger pushed the tears from her dry eyes. She'd devoted her married life to taking care of their children and supporting Don's career as he climbed the corporate ladder, and the past few years she'd put up with his mother. So what if her reasons for marrying him had been rooted in a desire for a better life? Surely all these years of devotion made up for that.

She wrapped the quilt around herself and let her thoughts drift to another man. Jackson Mendoza—her first love. The dark-eyed, dark-haired hometown bad boy from the other side of the tracks had almost derailed her plans to attend college. Jackson had been able to see into her soul . . . feel her passion. Leaving him behind had been one of the scariest things she'd done in her young life. And then during the first semester of her freshman year she'd met Don, a wealthy kid from Kansas City, and suddenly he was her fast train to everything she'd dreamed of having.

As she dozed off, Katelyn realized that when she'd chosen Don, she not only left her best friend and first love behind. . . . She'd also left a part of herself.

Katelyn pressed the phone against her ear. She'd tried Don's number three times in the past half hour, but her calls had gone straight to his voice mail.

"Katelyn."

The sound of his voice startled her and she didn't immediately respond.

"I assume you're calling because you received the divorce petition."

"I did."

"Any questions you have should go through my lawyer."

"You couldn't have told me you were unhappy when you were home last? You waited to spring this on me until you were halfway around the world?"

He cleared his throat—the only indication he was uncomfortable with the conversation. "I've got someone else on the other line."

"I have questions."

"I'm listening." The sound of shuffling papers in the background said otherwise.

"I need to know what kind of access I have to our bank accounts."

"I'll deposit money into the joint account each month to cover the household bills and any expenses you have."

"There's something else."

"What?"

"I intend to hire my own lawyer, and I'm going to ask him to request that you set up a 401(k) for me and make a monthly deposit into the account," she said.

"You're getting half of everything. You'll have plenty of money to put aside for retirement."

"I think it's safe to assume you've been plotting this exit from our marriage for a while. I'm sure by now you've moved all of our assets someplace where the courts won't find them."

Silence.

Now that she had his undivided attention . . . "I intend to be compensated for the role I played in helping you get to where you are at NicorTrune."

"What are you talking about?"

"I was the one who gave up having a career to stay home, manage our household affairs, raise our children and look after your mother for the past three years so that you were free to focus on your career."

"I didn't force you to stay home with the kids."

Okay, that was true, but . . . "Have you forgotten the dinner party I hosted for your boss and his wife ten years ago? How those little place cards I sketched for the dinner table were such a big hit with Sylvia that she asked me to make them for her social get-togethers?"

Katelyn had never told Don that the boss's wife had also asked her to sketch party invitations for all her wealthy friends. She'd bent over backward to please Sylvia, because the woman had promised she'd encourage her husband to look favorably upon Don. "After I agreed to help Sylvia, it wasn't long before you received a promotion to executive vice president."

"I earned that promotion."

Don would believe what he wanted. "The least you can do is make sure our kids have enough money to put me away somewhere nice when I'm too old to remember my name."

"I'll discuss it with Steven," he said. "Is there anything else?"

"Do I know her?" *Damn.* She'd promised herself she wouldn't ask about the other woman. She didn't want him believing she cared one way or another about his mistress.

"You don't know her." He didn't elaborate and Katelyn dropped the subject. "I have to go," he said.

"Since you filed for divorce, you should tell the kids."

"Fine."

"When do you plan to call them?"

"I don't know, Katelyn. I have to go."

She disconnected the call as Shirley walked into the room. *Uh-oh.* Her mother-in-law never showed up at the breakfast table without wearing lipstick. "You look like hell."

"So do you."

Touché. "Sit down." Katelyn poured a cup of coffee and set it in front of Shirley. "Bagel or toast?"

"Toast."

After slathering a piece of wheat bread with butter and strawberry jam for Shirley, Katelyn topped off her own coffee mug, then covertly studied her mother-in-law. She looked every one of her sixty-five years.

"Happy birthday, by the way," Katelyn said.

"There's nothing happy about it." She nodded to Katelyn's coffee mug. "Aren't you hungry?"

"I ate earlier." She'd choked down half a bagel with a glass of water and three aspirin. "I'm sorry Don took you by surprise, too."

"I doubt you're that sorry. I know how you feel about me."

A smile tugged at the corners of Katelyn's mouth. "Kind of like how you feel about me?"

Shirley's lips twitched before she sipped her coffee.

There were many things about her mother-in-law that bugged Katelyn, but she grudgingly admired the older woman's spunk.

"I'm sure if you discuss this with Don, you two can work things out."

Shirley was old-school. She didn't believe in divorce—not because she felt it was morally wrong, but because keeping up appearances was more important than a happy marriage.

"I just talked to Don on the phone, and . . ." It was difficult to say out loud. "He's involved with another woman."

Shirley's mug thunked against the table. "I don't believe it."

Katelyn retrieved Don's letter from the kitchen desk.

After Shirley scanned the note, she flung it down and said, "My son is a jackass."

For once, Shirley was right.

"How dare he cast you aside and stow me away like an antique clock so he can go off and start a new life with his mistress?"

Katelyn had always wanted to find something she and her mother-in-law could bond over—she just never imagined it would be Don's infidelity.

"If he thinks I'll disappear without making a scene . . ." Shirley's mouth trembled. "I changed my son's poopy diapers longer than most mothers." She sniffed. "Did he ever tell you he wasn't potty-trained until he was five and a half years old? I sent him to his first day of kindergarten in a diaper."

Katelyn smiled when she imagined a little boy wearing a diaper that made his pants bulge in odd places.

"Robert would be angry if he knew our son abandoned me."

"If you don't want to live in a retirement apartment, then tell Don you want to move in with him." Katelyn would have loved to eavesdrop on that conversation.

"Did Don say where he plans to live?" Shirley asked.

"No, but the house goes on the market today."

"So soon?" Shirley made a rude noise and took her plate to the sink. "We'll get through this."

Katelyn resisted laughing at the absurd comment—as if she and her mother-in-law were a team. Shirley was the least of her worries. Katelyn was more concerned about becoming a forty-year-old divorcée who had no idea what she was going to do with herself.

CHAPTER FOUR

Late Thursday afternoon a loud thumping sound caught Katelyn's attention. She shut off the kitchen faucet, dried her hands and then went searching for the noise. She found Shirley peeking out the front window. "What's going on?"

"He's destroying our lawn."

Katelyn shoved the drapes aside. A stout man in black slacks and a blue dress shirt stood on a stepladder and pounded a post into the ground. Once he was satisfied it wouldn't topple, he attached the For Sale sign to the hooks on the crossbeam, then admired his handiwork before stowing the tools in the trunk of a red sedan and driving off.

"I'll be in my bedroom packing, if you need me," Katelyn said.

"You haven't mentioned the divorce to the kids, have you?"

"No. Don's going to break the news to them. If you speak with Michael or Melissa before then, please don't say anything." Katelyn walked to the stairs. "By the way, I called my mother an hour ago and told her I was coming for a visit." She intended to tell Birdie about the divorce in person. "I'm leaving on Sunday."

"This Sunday?"

"Yep." Let Don worry about his mother. "If you want, we can take a look at your apartment before I go." Maybe if Shirley saw the place, she'd warm up to the idea of living there—not that it mattered. In a little over forty-eight hours, Katelyn would be free of her mother-in-law and on her way home to Little Springs, Texas.

Friday morning Shirley waltzed into the master bedroom, where Katelyn was sorting her clothes into three piles—storage, Goodwill and her trip to Little Springs. "I spoke to the manager and my unit won't be ready until mid-July."

"How did you get the phone number for the apartment complex?"

"I called directory assistance."

Who used directory assistance anymore?

"Why the delay?" Katelyn asked.

"I didn't care for the flooring or countertops that Don picked out."

Suddenly the room smelled like rotten fish. "You haven't seen the apartment."

"The manager described the place and I told him that I didn't want black granite countertops or beige carpet. I'm having hardwoods and white marble installed in the kitchen and bathrooms."

Katelyn smothered a smile behind a fake yawn. Don's mother was going to make him pay dearly for deserting her.

"Is that broken glass in the carpet?" Shirley pointed to the area in front of the fireplace.

"I haven't had a chance to run the vacuum." She ignored Shirley's raised eyebrow and dropped a blouse into the Goodwill pile. "We have a showing later today."

"It's too soon to sell."

Getting rid of the house didn't bother Katelyn. Don had picked out their home, insisting the elegant dining room with a brick fireplace was the perfect setting to entertain his clients and bosses. All the rooms were beautifully decorated, but they lacked warmth and Katelyn didn't care to stay in a place surrounded by cold reminders of a life that hadn't turned out as she'd planned.

"You can't move," Shirley said. "You'll miss your friends."

"I'll make new friends." Katelyn was on a first-name basis with her neighbors and the people she'd met through her work with the Central West End Association, but her other *friends* were connected with NicorTrune and she saw the women only at holiday cocktail parties.

"The kids won't have anywhere to come back to during their school breaks," Shirley said.

"They can stay with me or Don. Or maybe with you at your apartment."

"Where will you live?"

"I haven't thought that far ahead." She planned to take things one day at a time and not make snap decisions she'd regret later. Her cell phone beeped with a text message and she stopped sorting through clothes.

I have a work emergency. I'm flying to Singapore today.

Katelyn read Don's text twice. *Work emergency? Seriously?* In the past she'd never doubted his reason for extending a business trip, but after he'd confessed to having an affair, she suspected those delayed homecomings had to do with his mistress.

The phone beeped again.

Tell my mother I'll call her soon.

Damn her cheating husband.

"Is that one of the kids?"

"It's Don. He won't be home today. He's flying to Singapore."

"He's supposed to take me out for my birthday dinner tonight."

Who cared about Shirley's birthday? What about Katelyn's trip home to see her mother? She'd like nothing better than to leave Shirley behind at the house on Sunday, but she didn't trust the woman not to do something to endanger herself. But no way was she allowing Don's change of plans to ruin hers.

"Pack a bag, Shirley."

"What for?"

"You're coming with me to Little Springs."

"I don't want to go to your mother's."

Katelyn played the ace up her sleeve. "Would you rather stay here alone?"

Shirley popped off the bed. "How long will we be there?"

"A couple of weeks."

With the help of divine intervention and the patience of a saint, Katelyn hoped she wouldn't be tempted to abandon Shirley on the side of the road before they reached West Texas.

"You're driving too fast."

Oh. My. God. Katelyn muttered the mantra in her head for the hundredth time since leaving St. Louis five hours ago. The needle on the speedometer inched toward seventy. "I'm going five miles below the posted limit." At the rate they were traveling, they'd arrive in Texas in time for Thanksgiving.

Katelyn eased off the accelerator, checked the rearview mirror, then moved into the slow lane. Shirley had insisted on taking her Mercedes because Katelyn's SUV was too high off the ground and difficult for her to climb into. In truth, her mother-in-law just liked calling the shots. Katelyn consoled herself with the fact that it was only a matter of time before Shirley would be out of her life—at least on a daily basis.

Katelyn hadn't expected to make the fourteen-hour trip in one day, but she'd hoped to reach Norman, Oklahoma, where she'd made a motel reservation at a Days Inn, by six p.m. Too many restroom stops had put them behind schedule and Tulsa was only five miles in the rearview mirror.

"I don't know why anyone would want to live in Oklahoma." Shirley stared out her window. "It's ugly and there are too many tornadoes."

If she thought Oklahoma was ugly, wait until she got her first glimpse of West Texas, where trees were scarce, the wind never stopped blowing and dust was a spice in food. "There's beauty in everything, Shirley."

"There's nothing pretty about scraggly trees and dry prairie grass." She shifted away from the window. "I'm looking forward to chatting with your mother."

Katelyn didn't envision the two women talking as much as she did them circling each other like fighting cocks. "How long has it been since you two last saw each other?"

"I don't remember."

"Wasn't it the Christmas before Robert died?" Birdie had flown into St. Louis Christmas Eve Day, and then that evening Don had opened the front door and there stood Robert and Shirley on the porch, arms loaded with expensive gifts for the kids. "Surprise!" they'd shouted, then barged their way inside, interrupting the board game the twins had been playing with Birdie. Shirley had insisted the twins open their gifts from her and Robert right then—the newest version of smartphones. So instead of finishing their game with Birdie, the kids retreated to their rooms and played with their presents. The day after Christmas, Birdie changed her plane ticket and flew back to Little Springs, cutting her visit short.

"When are we eating dinner?" Shirley asked.

"In a couple of hours when we stop for the night."

"I'm getting a headache."

Katelyn squeezed the wheel until her knuckles glowed white. If she didn't stop, Shirley's whining would grow louder. "Keep your eyes peeled for a restaurant." Five miles down the road she passed a billboard advertising a roadside café and took the exit.

"We're not eating here, are we?"

The faded black-and-red sign on the roof advertised EARL'S: HOME OF THE HOME-COOKED MEAL. "What's wrong with this place?"

"The kitchen's probably overrun with roaches."

Dingy white paint covered the cinder block building, but Katelyn could still make out the orange shadow of a Phillips 66 emblem next to the front windows. Someone had converted the gas station into a restaurant. It wouldn't have been Katelyn's first choice to eat here, either, but if food put a cork in Shirley's mouth, then she didn't mind dining with cockroaches. She parked next to the only vehicle in the lot—a rusty pickup with a missing tailgate and four bald tires.

"I refuse to go in there."

"Suit yourself, but we're not stopping again until we reach the motel." No sooner had Katelyn left the car than the passenger door opened and Shirley followed her inside.

The strong scent of lemon cleaner greeted them when they entered the café. "Welcome to Earl's." A redheaded waitress waved. "Have a seat anywhere." She topped off the coffee mug of a young man texting on his iPhone between bites of food, then disappeared into the kitchen.

Katelyn steered Shirley to a booth by the door. Once they sat on the black vinyl cushions, she trailed her fingertips across the scratched Formica tabletop, pleased to find it clean, even though scuff marks and coffee stains covered the vinyl flooring along with a few petrified French fries.

Shirley removed the laminated menu from behind the plastic salt and pepper shakers and held it between her fingertips.

If the situation weren't so ass-backward nuts, Katelyn might have enjoyed baiting her mother-in-law, but there hadn't been anything humorous about the tears that had welled in

Shirley's eyes yesterday when she'd walked into Michael's bedroom and found Katelyn packing his swimming trophies.

"Haven't seen you ladies in here before." The orange-haired waitress with dark eyebrows and poppy-colored lipstick set glasses of water on the table.

"We're on our way to visit family in Texas," Katelyn said.

"Name's Beth." The waitress propped her hands on her ample hips. "Can I get you something besides water to drink?"

"I'll have a Coke," Katelyn said.

Beth swung her gaze to Shirley.

"Decaf coffee."

"Be back in a jiffy with your drink order."

Shirley sniffed. "We'll probably be infected with intestinal worms after eating here."

"Pick a fried food and you'll be fine."

Shirley scowled. "You can't afford to put on any extra weight."

Katelyn's snarky response was hijacked by Beth's timely return with their drinks. "Ready to order?" the waitress asked.

"I'll have the chicken-fried steak." She ignored Shirley's pointed stare and asked, "How's the fried okra?"

"Decent."

"I'll have a side order of that, please."

"Extra gravy?" Beth asked.

"Why not?" Then Shirley could watch Katelyn's thighs balloon up right before her eyes.

"And for you, ma'am?"

"Turkey on wheat, hold the mayonnaise."

"Fries?"

"Heavens no."

"Comin' right up, ladies."

Shirley tore open a packet of artificial sweetener and dumped the white powder into her coffee, then stirred. "Are you sure you've thought this through?"

"Thought what through?"

"Not contesting the divorce."

"Don's already moved on with another woman." Jackson's face flashed before Katelyn's eyes. Where would she be in life right now if she hadn't broken up with him after she went off to college?

"I still think my son is having a midlife crisis."

Midlife crisis or not, he'd cheated on Katelyn, and once a cheater, always a cheater.

"You need to revive your marriage."

"I'm not asking for your advice. I'll figure things out on my own."

"Start by cutting your hair." Not even a bulldozer across the mouth would shut this woman up when she wanted her opinion heard. "And if you insist on walking around in khaki pants all the time, at least wear bright-colored tops and shoes with a heel. You and Don have two

52

wonderful kids, a beautiful home and eighteen years together. That's worth fighting for."

Part of Katelyn wanted to concede those were valid reasons to try to save her marriage, but the words backed up in her throat.

"Every woman needs a makeover when they turn forty," Shirley said. "Forty is the new thirty. It wouldn't hurt for you to have a little work done."

Other than having a tummy tuck five years after the twins had been born, Katelyn had avoided Botox and face-plumping gels, comfortable with the way she was aging. Had Don thought she'd become complacent?

"A mini face-lift will help you compete with younger women."

She shouldn't have had to compete with anyone. Katelyn imagined a tall blonde with firm boobs and a smooth, flat belly crawling beneath the covers with her husband.

"If you take ten years off your face, Don will think twice about looking at other women." Shirley sipped her coffee. "Mark my words, dear—being alone is no fun. At least consider giving my son a second chance. He's been a good provider all these years, and you and the kids have wanted for nothing."

Maybe so, but Don wasn't a man who worked to live; he lived to work. His identity and self-esteem were tied to his career, which had always come first—even before family. And because Katelyn had taken care of the kids, their home and his mother, she'd made it easy for Don to focus on himself. How had she come to believe his happiness was paramount over hers? The Katelyn who'd left Little Springs to find her place in the world wouldn't have let anyone hold her back.

Beth arrived with their food. "Holler if you need anything else."

Katelyn sampled a piece of chicken-fried steak smothered in white gravy. Nothing special. "How's your sandwich?"

Shirley stabbed her fork into the bread—she was the only person Katelyn knew who used a fork and a knife to eat a sandwich. "Not as awful as I'd expect in a place like this."

They ate in silence, Shirley finishing her meal and Katelyn leaving half of hers untouched.

"You didn't like it?" Beth said, picking up Katelyn's plate.

"She's watching her weight," Shirley answered.

"I guess that means you're passing on dessert." Beth winked.

After gorging herself on Shirley's birthday cake, Katelyn was swearing off sweets for a year. "We'll take the check, please."

Beth set the tab on the table. "Drive safe, now."

After glancing at the amount, Katelyn left thirty dollars on the table.

Shirley stared across the room where Beth chatted with the young man, then fished a twenty-dollar bill from her wallet and added it to the bill.

Surprised, Katelyn said, "That's a huge tip."

"Beth is long overdue for a cut and color."

Everything came back to the hair.

CHAPTER FIVE

K atelyn drove away from Earl's and got on the interstate. She'd gone only a few miles when she glanced at the passenger-seat floor. "Where's your purse?"

Shirley stared at her feet. "It was right here a minute ago."

"I bet you left it in the booth at the restaurant." Katelyn swallowed a groan and moved into the right lane, then took the next exit. Why hadn't she noticed that Shirley had walked off without her purse?

Ten minutes later Katelyn pulled up to the diner. "Wait here." She went inside and thanked Beth for stowing the purse behind the counter and then returned to the car and handed it to Shirley.

"Is all my money still there?"

"I'm sure Beth didn't help herself to your cash. Not after you left a nice tip."

Shirley opened her purse and rifled through her wallet.

"Do you have all your credit cards?"

"How many did I have?"

"Two." Don had taken over Shirley's finances and canceled all her department store cards after she came to live with them.

"I have them." Shirley set her purse on the floor.

Crisis handled, Katelyn merged onto the highway, then set the cruise control at seventy and took her foot off the gas.

"Oh . . ." Shirley placed her hand against her stomach.

Katelyn glanced across the seat. "What's the matter?"

"I need to use the bathroom."

"Why didn't you say something when we went back for your purse?"

"My stomach didn't bother me then."

A mile up the road a sign advertising GAS appeared, and for the third time in an hour, Katelyn left the highway.

"This place is out of business," Shirley said.

Katelyn rolled through the four-way stop at the end of the exit ramp and turned into the gravel lot. "There's an Open sign on the door." Years of dirt and grime coated the exterior of the convenience store. Splotches of beige paint had been slapped over the graffiti on the brick. Posters advertising cigarettes, beer and fireworks wallpapered the front window, and a rusted ice machine, leaking water, sat on the cement slab next to the door. As soon as Katelyn parked, Shirley bolted from the car, leaving her purse behind.

Katelyn waited ten minutes; then when Shirley hadn't returned, she locked the Mercedes and went inside to check on her. A bell tied to the door announced her presence.

OMG, as her daughter would have said. Two rows of metal shelving held an array of mystery foods, the endcaps filled with an assortment of toiletries: Aquafresh toothpaste, Lady Speed Stick deodorant, a package of white tube socks, a box of loose plastic combs for fifty-nine cents apiece, Gillette disposable razor blades, VO5 hair spray, Bic lighters and a twenty-four pack of Contempo Rough Rider Studded Condoms.

"I got more choices behind the counter."

Startled, she glanced behind her. A middle-aged man with slicked-back hair and a pockmarked face leaned against the register. Ketchup splatters marred the image of Jimi Hendrix on the front of his gray tank.

"More choices?"

"Love gloves . . . raincoats." When he grinned, the lump of tobacco inside his mouth crawled up his cheek and rested beneath his right eye.

"I'm looking for my mother-in-law." Katelyn's gaze skipped over the aisles, but Shirley's straw-colored head was nowhere in sight.

He jutted his chin toward the Employees Only sign hanging on the far wall. "She ain't too friendly."

Since Katelyn had insisted on eating at Earl's, she felt compelled to defend Shirley. "My mother-in-law has her good points." She looked out the window and stared longingly at the car, hoping they'd make it to Norman before dark;

then she walked to the back of the store and knocked on the door. "Shirley?"

No answer.

"Are you okay?"

The roar of a flushing toilet met her ears. The door opened, and a pasty-faced Shirley—shirttail hanging out of her slacks and beads of perspiration dotting her forehead—glared at her. "This is all your fault."

Katelyn kept her mouth closed because Shirley looked miserable, and escorted the wobbly woman to the front of the store.

"If you hadn't insisted we eat at that filthy—"

"Fresh air will help." She ignored the clerk's grin and hustled her mother-in-law outside. After helping her into the car, Katelyn started the engine and turned on the air. "Hold tight." She went back into the market and picked out a liter of Sprite, a box of crackers with a week-old expiration date and a travel-sized bottle of Pepto-Bismol. "Where's the nearest motel?"

"Stroud is ten miles down the road. The town's got a couple of places." He pushed the items toward her. "You want a bag?"

She shook her head. "How much?"

"Sixteen dollars and twelve cents."

She set a twenty on the counter.

"You want the change?"

"Yes." She dropped the coins into the plastic charity tub next to the register, figuring the money would find its way into the man's pocket the second she drove off.

After Katelyn got behind the wheel, she held out the bottle of Pepto-Bismol.

Shirley took a swig of the medicine, then closed her eyes. "I don't understand why your mother couldn't visit you in St. Louis."

"Because unlike us, she works." Katelyn drove away from the store.

"You should have ordered the turkey sandwich. I think I lost ten pounds in that bathroom."

Not even Montezuma's revenge could curb Shirley's sharp tongue. "We're stopping for the night in Stroud. It's right up the road." Fifteen minutes later she spotted a sign in the shape of a giant pink poodle.

"You've got to be kidding," Shirley said when Katelyn parked in front of the motel office.

"It'll be fine for one night. Besides, you're in no shape to travel."

"It probably has—"

"I'll check for bedbugs when we get in the room." Katelyn unbuckled her belt.

Shirley pressed her hand to her stomach and leaned forward in the seat. "Hurry."

Inside the office a kaleidoscope of pink hues greeted Katelyn. A woman wearing bright pink lipstick, which matched her pink blouse, glanced up from a magazine and smiled. "Welcome to the—"

"I need a room fast. My mother-in-law is ill."

The woman punched a code into a small machine on the counter, slid the key card through and then handed it to Katelyn. "Room three."

"I'll be right back." Katelyn hurried outside, where Shirley leaned against the hood of the car. "Our room is right here." She swiped the card and then opened the door and flipped on the lights. Shirley raced into the bathroom and Katelyn closed the door, giving her some privacy.

"Is your mother-in-law going to be all right?" the pink lady asked when Katelyn returned to the office.

"We ate at Earl's and something didn't agree with her."

The woman grimaced. "A junkyard dog wouldn't eat at that place."

"Don't tell my mother-in-law that."

"Name's Raquel." She came out from behind the counter, exposing her pink-and-gray poodle skirt—circa 1956.

"Nice to meet you, Raquel. I'm Katelyn. My mother-in-law's name is Shirley."

"Where are you ladies headed?"

"Little Springs, Texas."

"Never heard of the place. You grow up there?"

"I sure did. I live in St. Louis now."

"I'm not a fan of big cities. I spent some time in Fayetteville, Arkansas, years ago, and the traffic drove me nuts."

"I doubt you have much traffic in Stroud."

"Fourth of July is pretty hectic here, but that's about it." Raquel wagged her finger at a table next to the door. "Be sure to sign the guest book before you leave. I take all credit cards except American Express." Raquel returned behind the counter and tapped the computer keyboard.

Katelyn scrawled her signature in the guest book using the pink poodle pen, then handed Raquel her Visa card. "Your motel would look right at home on the Las Vegas Strip." The outside of the single-story brick structure had been painted pearlescent pink and the doors magenta. The place screamed *Girls only—boys keep out.*

Raquel smiled. "The computer takes a few minutes to warm up."

"Not a problem." Katelyn examined the collection of ceramic poodles in a display case until a tinkling sound caught her attention. A live standard poodle pranced into the room, wearing a rhinestone collar and a pink tutu. "Aren't you the cutest thing?"

"That's Princess."

Katelyn held out her hand and the poodle lifted her paw for a doggie handshake. "The pink nails are a nice touch."

"She's the motel mascot, so her upkeep is a tax write-off. I spend more money on her pedicures and wardrobe than I do on my own."

"How much for the room?"

"One ten." Raquel printed off a receipt, then returned Katelyn's credit card. "There's a Jacuzzi out back for guests."

"We'll be staying inside for the night."

"If you need anything after hours, I'm in room one."

"Thank you."

"I hope your mother-in-law feels better soon."

"Me, too." Katelyn carried the overnight bags and Shirley's purse into room 3, then returned to the car for the soda, crackers and Pepto-Bismol. After locking the door, she slipped out of her sandals and propped herself up against the pink velvet headboard behind the bed nearest the window. She grabbed the TV remote and a second later her phone chimed with a text message. *Don.*

Why isn't my mother answering her cell phone?

Not caring to go into detail about their dining adventure, Katelyn fibbed. She went to bed early.

Is she ill?

Upset stomach

Tell her I hope she feels better soon.

63

Katelyn didn't answer.

There's an offer on the house.

Already? Who's interested?

Weren't you there when the couple came through at one o' clock?

Busted. Your mother and I left town.

Katelyn's phone rang. "Yes?"

"Where are you?" Don asked.

"Stroud, Oklahoma. We checked into a motel for the night."

"Why is my mother with you?"

"The apartment you leased for her won't be ready until the middle of July or later."

"What are you talking about? I had everything arranged."

"She's not happy with the flooring and the countertops you picked. They're installing hardwoods and marble."

"Unbelievable."

No kidding. The past few days seemed surreal.

"You didn't think to contact me before she made the changes?"

"Why would I do that? Shirley's your mother, not mine." Katelyn flashed her middle finger at the phone. "Besides, I didn't even know she'd called the manager."

"Where are you traveling to?"

"Little Springs."

"Why is my mother going with you?"

"What was I supposed to do with her? Leave her alone in the house and ask the neighbor to come over fifty times a day to see if she left the gas range on?"

"Couldn't you have waited to visit Birdie until I returned to town?"

"No, Don, I couldn't. I'm tired of arranging my life around your schedule. I've been doing it for three years while you've been off screwing *whatever her name is*."

"If you don't want my mother with you, put her on a bus back to St. Louis."

"Will you be there to pick her up at the station?"

Silence. Of course he wouldn't be.

"I didn't call to argue with you."

Maybe that had been the reason for the lack of passion in their marriage—aside from a few differences of opinion, they'd never fought.

"I admit the timing could have been better," he said.

Dumbass. "Is there a right time to tell your spouse you cheated on her?"

"You can't be that surprised, Katelyn. We've both changed. We're not the same people we were in college."

Obviously he no longer cared for the person she'd become—whoever that was.

"Does she have a name?"

"Lauren and I met through an acquaintance."

She heard the toilet flush. Shirley would be out of the bathroom any second. "The kids will want to know about *Lauren* . . . unless you intend to walk out on our children the way you did to me and your mother."

"I'm not walking out on the kids."

Relief filled Katelyn. She didn't want the twins feeling as if their father had rejected them, too. "When will you be back in St. Louis so I can hand Shirley off to you?"

"I don't know. Some problems have come up with one of our accounts and I may have to return to Japan after I leave Singapore next week."

"She's your responsibility, Don. You can divorce me, but you can't divorce your mom."

"I'll compensate you for the inconvenience."

Katelyn gave the phone the bird again. Don didn't have enough money to offset the misery his mother inflicted on a person. "Since we have an offer on the house," she said, "you should tell the kids about the divorce sooner rather than later before their friends ask questions."

"I said I'd take care of it. Have my mother phone me when she has a chance."

Katelyn ended the call before she sprained her middle finger.

CHAPTER SIX

W ho were you talking to?" Shirley asked when she stepped out of the bathroom, her face haggard and drawn.

"Don." Katelyn hopped off the bed and opened the bottle of Sprite. "You need fluids." She unwrapped a plastic cup next to the empty ice bucket and filled it halfway with warm soda, then handed it to Shirley when she sat on her bed.

"This is the gaudiest motel I've ever stayed at."

"It's fine for one night." After learning the name of the woman Don was having an affair with, Katelyn was too distracted to get back on the road and drive to another motel. Maybe Jackson had crossed her mind on occasion through the years, but she'd chosen Don and until now, she'd never had a reason to look back.

Shirley finished the soda, then set the plastic cup on the nightstand. "What did Don want?"

"He was surprised you were visiting Little Springs with me."

"Is he upset that I made changes to the apartment?"

Shirley looked so miserable that Katelyn didn't have the heart to beat her down with the truth. "Of course not."

"I can take care of myself, you know."

Arguing the point would only antagonize her mother-in-law.

"Did you check for bedbugs?"

"I will right now." After Shirley stood, Katelyn loosened the blanket and sheets at the bottom of the bed, then lifted the corners of the mattress. "No bugs."

Shirley pulled the spread back and plucked a strand of dark hair from the pillowcase. "I don't think they washed the sheets after the last person checked out." With a disgusted sigh, she went into the bathroom and then returned with a towel, which she spread across the pillow before stretching out on top of the cover.

"Aren't you changing into your pajamas?" Katelyn asked.

"I don't want my clean clothes touching the bed linens."

Katelyn had seen documentaries on motel room cleanliness. If she told Shirley about the ultraviolet black lights that revealed body fluid stains on bedspreads and carpets, her mother-in-law would sleep standing against the wall. She lowered the volume on the TV and then shut off the lamp between the beds.

"I'm sorry," Shirley said.

Her mother-in-law must be delirious from dehydration, because she never apologized. "Sorry for what?"

"For not ordering the chicken-fried steak."

Oh, brother. Kately carried her toiletry bag and nightshirt into the bathroom and took a shower. When she returned to the bedroom, Shirley's snores drowned out the QVC program promoting turboblenders. Katelyn crawled beneath the covers and watched the perky blonde drop a head of cauliflower into the glass pitcher. When she flipped on the mixer, Katelyn closed her eyes and imagined Don's head being chopped into a million tiny pieces.

"The Red River looks more brown than red," Shirley said.

"The color intensifies when the river floods and washes away the soil." Katelyn slowed the car as she drove onto the bridge that would carry them across the water and a few miles later into the state of Texas.

"The terrain hasn't gotten any prettier since we began this trip."

They'd been on the road a little over two hours, and Katelyn was growing weary of her copilot's grumpy disposition.

"What are those white things floating in the air?"

"Seedpods from the cottonwoods." The fast-growing shade tree was popular in Texas, even though its life span was short.

"What are the bushes with the pinkish white flowers?"

"Salt cedar. Their roots travel beneath the

ground and interfere with watersheds, so most ranchers remove the plants along the streams on their property."

At the end of the bridge, Katelyn said, "The town of Burkburnett is coming up. Do you want to stop and stretch your legs?"

"That would be nice."

Three miles later Katelyn pulled into a Whataburger restaurant and parked.

"I need to use the restroom." Shirley got out of the car, leaving her purse behind. Again.

Phone in hand, Katelyn paced back and forth along the sidewalk outside the restaurant while she checked their route on the GPS app.

When Shirley returned, Katelyn asked, "How's your stomach?"

"Fine."

"It's about an hour and a half to Wichita Falls, then another two hours to McCaulley. Can you make it that long before we stop for lunch?"

"Sure."

They got back into the car, and Katelyn turned south onto Highway 44 and left the small town behind. After several minutes of silence, she glanced across the front seat and discovered Shirley had fallen asleep. Katelyn's fingers relaxed against the steering wheel. The miles flew by, and she used the peace and quiet to figure out how to tell Birdie about the divorce. In the end she decided there was no good way to break bad news. After one p.m., she pulled into a Subway parking lot and nudged Shirley awake.

"Where are we?"

"McCaulley. Are you hungry?"

"Starving."

They washed up in the restroom first. Then Shirley ordered the Black Forest ham sandwich, and Katelyn the club. After they sat down in a booth, Katelyn said, "May I ask you a question?" She'd spent the past few days pondering her life as a wife and mother and had found no answers to how she'd arrived at this point in her life.

"What do you want to know?" Shirley asked.

"You earned a college degree. After you had Don, did you want to stay home with him, or was it something you fell into and didn't know how to get out of?"

Shirley dabbed the napkin against the corner of her mouth. "What do you mean 'didn't know how to get out of'?"

"Never mind." Katelyn regretted bringing up the subject.

"Didn't you enjoy staying at home with Michael and Melissa?"

"I loved spending time with them." She thought back on her career as a stay-at-home mother. The job had required sacrifices that she'd willingly made. She'd enjoyed volunteering for the kids' school activities. But that part of her life had been like a slow-moving fog, and she hadn't realized that with each passing year as the twins grew older, she was surrendering parts of herself.

She'd become so busy baking cupcakes for Valentine's Day parties, chauffeuring kids to sports practices, chaperoning field trips and then taking care of everyone's needs with weekly jaunts to the dry cleaner's and the grocery store—never mind the hours she'd spent sitting in the car pool lane—that she'd given up doing the things she'd once loved and had morphed into a woman her husband no longer recognized. A woman she no longer recognized.

"You're a good mother, Katelyn. You should be proud of that."

"Thank you, Shirley." In all the years they were married, Don had never told Katelyn she was a good mother.

"To be honest," Shirley said, "I had no idea what to do with my English degree except that I knew I didn't want to teach. Once Don was born, I became involved with other young mothers, and my social circle expanded." She shrugged. "I was content with my life."

Content. Katelyn mulled over the meaning of the word. Even after Don had given her the life she'd always dreamed of, she'd never been one hundred percent satisfied.

"But," Shirley said, "I wish I'd taken time to find my own niche."

"What do you mean?"

"My life revolved around Robert and his career. After he died, I was no longer Mrs. Pratt. I was just Shirley."

Katelyn squirmed in her seat, uncomfortable that she had more in common with her mother-in-law than she'd believed.

"Now I'm too old to do anything with myself." Shirley sighed. "What are your plans if you and Don don't get back together?"

That was the million-dollar question. At the moment Katelyn couldn't say what she wanted in life, much less what she stood for, what she believed in, what was important to her or what made her happy. "I'd always intended to get back to painting when the kids didn't need as much supervision."

"What stopped you?"

"Don's career came first." If she wasn't throwing dinner parties for his bosses or clients, she was working with the other executive wives helping with corporate fund-raisers and community events.

"You sound resentful," Shirley said.

"Lots of husbands help with the child-rearing and household chores so their wives have time for themselves," Katelyn said.

"Do those husbands make the kind of money yours does?"

"That shouldn't matter."

"There's a trade-off if you want nice things in life."

"A marriage is supposed to be a partnership."

"What didn't Don do for you?"

"When the kids were still babies, he promised to cut back on his travel and stay home on the weekends." She'd planned to use that time to paint and build up a portfolio of work that she could present to art galleries in the St. Louis area in hopes of getting her foot in the door.

"And you're upset Don didn't follow through?"

"He was my husband. Of course, I expected him to keep his promise."

"Don is a man first and a husband second. A man will always put his own interests before anyone else's. And we women let them, because they buy us baubles, beautiful homes and more clothes than we could possibly wear in a year." Shirley's pointer finger came out. "For a young woman who came from modest means, giving up a few things in exchange for a better life shouldn't be difficult."

Shirley made it sound as if there was no reason for Katelyn to be unhappy. Of course the girl whose father worked as a game warden and whose mother cashiered at a grocery store had not been reluctant to gain life on easy street, but Katelyn hadn't thought she'd have to sacrifice so much of herself in the process. Don had manipulated her into believing his wants and needs were the same as hers, and she'd allowed him to use her for his personal gain.

"Good life or not, if Don was here right now, I'd give him a piece of my mind."

Shirley wrapped the remainder of her sandwich in the paper wrapper, then pushed it aside. "It's a good thing he isn't here, because I'd have a few choice words for him, too."

"Thanks, Shirley."

"For what?"

"For listening to me complain."

"I still believe you and my son should work to save your marriage."

Katelyn was tired of discussing Don. "Let's hit the road." She deposited their trash in the wastebasket, then checked to make sure Shirley had her purse before they got into the car. "What do you say we put the top down on the Mercedes?"

"I don't want to mess up my hair."

"Who cares about our hair?" Katelyn started the engine.

"Maybe that's been the problem with your marriage all along," Shirley said. "You don't care enough about making yourself attractive to your husband."

"Did Robert comment on your looks? Is that why you always put makeup on before you leave the house?"

"A woman is a reflection of her husband."

"In that case, the top goes down." Katelyn hit the switch and the trunk opened to allow the roof to collapse inside it.

Once she entered the highway and reached the speed limit, she glanced across the seat and smiled. Shirley held her hands against her face to block the wind. "Relax. Neither of us has a man to impress anymore!"

Katelyn turned on the satellite radio to eighties music and "Let's Go Crazy" by Prince blasted from the speakers. An hour later they passed a sign advertising a gas station and Shirley pointed to the exit. "I need to use the bathroom."

Katelyn parked in front of the convenience store, then burst out laughing.

"What's so funny?"

The wind had destroyed Shirley's perfectly teased hair. "Your head is covered in lightning bolts."

Shirley lowered the visor and gaped in the mirror. "We can't go into the store looking like this."

"I dare you," Katelyn teased.

Shirley pointed. "You look like Medusa."

"I'll go inside if you go."

They entered the mart, both managing to keep a straight face when the clerk asked if he should call 911. After using the restroom, they purchased fountain drinks and then got back into the car.

"I still think you need a new hairstyle," Shirley said.

"I'll take your suggestion under consideration."

CHAPTER SEVEN

"I think West Texas may be uglier than Oklahoma." Shirley stared out the passenger-side window. "The grass is yellow, and the trees look anorexic."

"The wind sucks the moisture out of everything." Even though as a teenager Katelyn had wanted out of Little Springs, she'd loved following the train tracks, the hot wind stirring the air fragrant with the scent of creosote from the railroad ties. She couldn't even recall the last time she'd gone on a walk by herself and allowed her brain to daydream.

"If you don't mind, I'll top off the tank before we get to my mom's." She flipped on the turn signal and pulled up to a gas pump at the Texaco right off the highway.

"How close is Little Springs?" Shirley asked.

"We're a mile north of town."

Shirley took out a tube of lipstick from her purse and applied a fresh coat to her lips. When they'd stopped for a bite to eat three hours ago, she'd gone into the restroom and tamed her wild hair with water. Katelyn couldn't get a brush through her snarls, so she'd pinned the tangled mass to the top of her head with a hair clip.

"Pay cash." Shirley held out a twenty-dollar

bill. "You know criminals put those credit card readers on the pumps now."

"My mother's never had a problem using her bank card at this gas station."

"You can't be too cautious."

Too bad Katelyn wasn't a smoker—she could use a cigarette to calm her nerves. Now that she was this close to home, she imagined all kinds of scenarios where Birdie and Shirley acted like a pair of Roller Derby queens, fighting for the upper hand when they passed each other in the hall. Five minutes later she hopped into the car and backed away from the pump.

"I wouldn't mind seeing a bit of the town before we arrive at your mother's."

"I forgot you've never visited Little Springs." Katelyn and Don had become engaged the spring semester of their senior year in college, but they hadn't discussed where to get married until he'd landed the job at NicorTrune a few weeks after graduation. It only made sense then to get married in St. Louis. The wedding was the first time her parents had met Shirley and Robert. Before then, Don had visited Texas with her their junior year, and the only time he'd been back was for her father's funeral ten years ago.

"I'll take you on a tour after we get settled in," Katelyn said, "but you can actually see most of the town from our front yard." Her childhood home sat on a hill overlooking Main Street.

Katelyn drove down the highway a quarter mile, then took the overpass and turned right onto a county road. A half mile later she veered onto a gravel path that climbed in elevation to a white clapboard house, where Birdie's blue Ford Taurus sat parked. A pair of oak trees, planted by her father after he'd purchased the place, stood tall along the side of the house. Birdie's passion for gardening had taken over the backyard, which was enclosed by a white picket fence Mother Nature had bleached gray decades ago. Katelyn's father had built an overhang across the back of the house so that Birdie would have a place to sit in the shade and smell her Texas lilac bushes.

Katelyn preferred the front porch, which faced the town, because it had been Mack's favorite place to sleep. Years later she'd sit on the steps alone, study the stars and dream about a life far away from Texas.

Shirley leaned forward, straining the seat belt as she peered out the windshield. "Your mother should fire her lawn service. The grass is a foot high and the bushes are as tall as the porch rail."

"Mom doesn't have a gardener." But it wasn't like Birdie to let the grass grow long. She steered around a pothole in the driveway and parked next to the Taurus. "Be careful walking on the gravel." Birdie had stepped into a rut last year and broken her ankle.

Shirley unsnapped her seat belt, then got out of the car and walked off, expecting her daughter-in-law to carry their luggage. Before Katelyn had a chance to remove the bags from the trunk, Birdie opened the back door and her eyes widened when her gaze landed on Shirley, gingerly stepping on the stone path.

"Surprise!" Katelyn raised her hands in the air and wiggled her fingers. Her mother flinched, her lips pressing together to form an invisible seam across the lower half of her face. *Oh, dear.* Maybe it had been a mistake not to warn Birdie that she was bringing Shirley with her.

"It's been a long time, Birdie," Shirley said when she reached the porch.

C'mon, Mom, crack a smile. A teeny one.

"You're looking . . . healthy." Shirley called anyone who needed to lose a few pounds *healthy*.

Katelyn's mother had always carried extra weight around the middle, but her father had never complained—mostly because Birdie had made his favorite comfort food dishes for supper and after a day trekking through the woods, the extra calories hadn't hurt him.

Shirley climbed the steps. "If you don't mind, I need to use the bathroom."

"I'll show you where it is." Katelyn closed the trunk and dragged their suitcases across the gravel.

"I'm sure I can find it." Shirley stepped past Birdie and entered the house.

"It's good to see you, Mom." Katelyn hauled the luggage up the steps.

Birdie's lips barely moved when she spoke. "You didn't tell me Shirley was coming with you."

"I didn't want you to go to any extra trouble." Not that her mother would have.

Like a bull ready to charge, Birdie blew out a noisy breath as her nostrils flared. "This puts a damper on my upcoming birthday."

"Don't worry." She hugged her mother. "You'll still have fun."

"I doubt it."

Katelyn went back to the car for Shirley's purse.

"Why did you bring her along?" Birdie closed the screen door after Katelyn entered the kitchen.

"I didn't have a choice. Don's out of the country, and I couldn't leave her alone at the house." Even though Birdie knew the circumstances that had prompted Shirley to move in with Katelyn and Don, her mother's feelings toward Shirley hadn't softened.

"How long are you staying?" Birdie asked.

"Until we wear our welcome out." She gave Birdie a second hug, hoping to earn her forgiveness, and this time she felt her mother's arms squeeze back.

"She's never wanted to visit before." Birdie tilted her head toward the sound of running water in the half bath under the staircase in the hallway. "Why now?"

"I'll explain later."

"Mark my words, that woman will be bored out of her mind in less than twenty-four hours."

"I'll entertain her." As long as Katelyn kept her mother and Shirley separated, the two wouldn't come to blows.

"If she causes me any grief"—Birdie shook her finger in Katelyn's face—"I'll pin your address to her blouse and put her snooty butt on the next Greyhound."

Katelyn kept a straight face. "I'll spring for the ticket."

Birdie's expression softened and she caressed Katelyn's cheek. "Why the dark circles?"

"I didn't sleep well last night." She forced a smile. "Do you still have my single bed in your sewing room?"

"Of course. You know I keep that bed in case one of the kids ever wants to come visit with you."

Michael and Melissa hadn't been to see their grandmother in Little Springs for several years. They complained that there was nothing to do and Birdie worked. It bothered Katelyn that her mother hadn't made time for her grandkids. She'd offered to give Birdie money to take the twins places if they came to visit, but Birdie always had an excuse for not being able to take time off from her job.

"I'll sleep in the single bed, and Shirley can have the guest room," Katelyn said.

"I'd better throw something together for supper."

"Don't go to any extra trouble for us."

"You're no trouble, but your mother-in-law is a royal pain in the ass."

Katelyn delivered Shirley's luggage to the guest room upstairs and put her own bag in the sewing room, then returned downstairs to find the older women sitting in the living room locked in a stare-down. "Mom, do you mind if Shirley keeps her purse on the table by the front door?"

"I don't care," Birdie said.

Now when Shirley came downstairs in the morning, she'd see the purse and hopefully remember to take it with her. At home Katelyn had trained Shirley to leave the purse on the kitchen desk.

"I'd like to take a drive and see the town," Shirley said.

Birdie pointed across the room. "Save yourself the trouble and go look out the window."

Katelyn stopped next to the recliner and nudged her mother's shoulder. Birdie grunted, then asked, "How've you been, Shirley?"

"Fine. And you, Birdie?"

"Fine."

Oh, brother. Katelyn sat on the couch. "Mom, you remember Shirley's birthday is close to yours. She turned sixty-five this past Thursday."

Birdie smiled. "I'd forgotten you were five years older than me."

Shirley patted her hair. "Most people assume I'm much younger."

That was true. The differences in the older women were like day and night. Shirley's face showed few age spots, while years of gardening in the sun had freckled Birdie's skin and deepened the wrinkles around her eyes and mouth. Shirley colored her gray hair light blond, which lent her a more youthful appearance, while Birdie chose to wear her natural gray hair cropped close to the head, making her look older. Shirley sported a fresh manicure, and Birdie's nails were short and the cuticles dry from overexposure to hand sanitizer—a hazard of working as a cashier.

A knock on the back door echoed through the house and Katelyn popped off the couch. "I'll go see who it is."

"There's fresh lemonade in the fridge," Birdie said. "Bring us a glass when you come back."

"Sure." She hurried into the kitchen, then skidded to a stop halfway across the linoleum floor when she recognized the shadow standing on the porch.

"Jackson."

He peered through the dirty mesh. "Katelyn?"

She opened the screen door and stepped outside.

Brown eyes surveyed her, starting at the top of

her head and working their way down her body as slow as dripping honey. When he reached her sandals, his gaze shot back to her face and the right side of his mouth curved in a lazy smile—the same grin that long ago had sucked the air from a much-younger Katelyn's lungs and left her woozy.

"It's been a while," he said.

The last time they'd seen each other was at her father's funeral, but they hadn't spoken. He'd sat in the back pew, and they'd only made eye contact at the end of the service before he'd slipped out the side door.

Jackson looked older, but there were still traces of the young man she'd fallen hard for in his dark gaze. Silver strands mixed with black along his temples gave her beloved bad boy an almost respectable air. Faint lines bracketed his mouth and crossed his forehead. The once clean-shaven teenager now sported a neatly trimmed goatee, which made his face appear leaner and his cheekbones more chiseled. He still wore his jeans slung low on his hips, the faded denim ripped along the pocket, the hem ratty.

She closed her eyes as the smell of sandalwood wafted beneath her nose, a nice change from the cloying scent of Shirley's old-fashioned Chantilly perfume. He grasped her upper arm. "Are you okay?"

"I'm fine." She drew in another deep breath and his aftershave messed with her head again.

He loosened his grasp, his fingers gliding down her arm, leaving a trail of heat in their wake. "How long are you staying?"

"Until my mother and mother-in-law come to blows."

"Are your kids with you?"

Twenty-two years had passed since she left Jackson behind, but she could still read his mind—he wanted to know if Don had come with her. What would he say if she told him that her husband was dumping her? "Michael's taking summer school classes at the University of Michigan, and Melissa's traveling abroad with a group of incoming college freshmen."

An awkward silence stretched between them before he nodded to the lawn mower next to the porch steps. "I fixed the motor for your mother."

"How much does she owe you?"

"Nothing."

She shifted from one sandal to the other, trying to find her balance beneath his steady stare.

He backed down the steps, never taking his eyes off her. "You look good," he said, then turned away and headed for his pickup.

When his comment finally sank in, Katelyn swallowed a gasp and fled inside to check her reflection in the bathroom mirror. She groaned. It looked like she was wearing a squirrel's nest on top of her head, and whatever makeup she'd begun the day with had been dissolved by the wind after driving with the top down.

It figured that the first time she ran into her ex-boyfriend, she'd look as if she'd been spit out of a funnel cloud.

"Who was at the door?" Birdie hollered from the living room.

"Be right there." Katelyn went into the kitchen and poured two glasses of lemonade. "Jackson," she said, handing each of the mothers a drink. "He returned your lawn mower."

"Who's Jackson?" Shirley asked.

"A high school friend." Ignoring the twinkle in Birdie's eye, Katelyn changed the subject. "Is that why the grass looks as if it hasn't been cut in over a month?"

Birdie was too smart for her ploy. "I thought for sure Katelyn would marry that handsome devil."

Handsome wasn't the right adjective to describe Jackson Mendoza. *Sexy* popped into her mind, followed by *hot,* and *tasty*—the word her daughter used to describe cute guys. "I'll mow the lawn after supper."

"No, you won't," Birdie said. "I like cutting the grass. I'll get it done in a couple of days."

Katelyn walked over to the the staircase. "I think I'll unpack." She could use a few minutes to figure out why her anger toward her soon-to-be ex-husband had mysteriously vanished when she'd gazed into Jackson's eyes.

CHAPTER EIGHT

M ore potato salad, Shirley?" Birdie held out the bowl.

"Good heavens, no. It's high in cholesterol and bad for the waistline."

This was the third instance when Katelyn's mother-in-law had commented on the fatty ingredients in the meal Birdie had put on the table.

"There are pills you can take for your cholesterol," Birdie said. "Besides, who cares about our waistlines at our age?"

"I'll have another spoonful." Katelyn reached for the salad.

Shirley made a *tsk-tsk* sound. "Now is not the time to let yourself go."

Birdie's gaze swung to Katelyn. "What's she talking about?"

"Nothing." Katelyn shot Shirley a warning glare, hoping she'd keep quiet about the divorce.

"Do you have plans for your birthday, Birdie?" Shirley asked.

"I do." Birdie tapped the end of her fork against the table and gave Katelyn *the look*—a squinty-eyed stare that insisted they'd talk later.

"Mom's friends have a party for the birthday girl at their weekly bridge game," Katelyn said to break the silence.

"I've never played bridge. Robert and I mostly socialized at cocktail parties and of course we attended community fund-raisers each year."

When Birdie didn't invite Shirley to her birthday celebration, Katelyn kicked her shin beneath the table.

"Ouch!" Birdie rubbed her leg. "You can come to my party if you want."

"Thank you, but"—Shirley dabbed the edge of the napkin against her mouth—"I wouldn't fit in with your friends."

Birdie rolled her eyes. "You'll fit in fine. All of our husbands are dead."

Shirley ignored the comment and patted Katelyn's arm. "You should make your mother the chocolate fudge cake you baked for my birthday."

Birdie talked around the food in her mouth. "I can't remember the last time my daughter baked a cake for me."

"Katelyn uses sour cream in the frosting. It's delicious."

Birdie smirked. "My mother's recipe."

Katelyn felt a headache coming on.

"We polished it off in two days."

"What happened to counting calories?" Birdie asked.

"Katelyn ate most of it. If I recall, you also drank two bottles of wine that day."

"I'm full." Katelyn set her napkin on the table.

"Of course you are." Shirley stared at Katelyn's empty plate. "You ate for two tonight."

Birdie crushed her napkin into a ball and Katelyn lurched across the table, grabbing the paper projectile before it beaned her mother-in-law in the face. "I put fresh towels for you on your bed, Shirley." Katelyn cleared the dishes, carrying her mother's arsenal of weapons to the sink first.

"Do you need any help?" Shirley asked on her way out of the kitchen.

"No, thanks. I have everything under control." That was the furthest thing from the truth. If Katelyn didn't tell her mother soon that Don had filed for divorce, Shirley would blurt out the news.

"I believe I'll turn in early. It's been a long couple of days," Shirley said.

As soon as the stairs creaked, Birdie whispered, "What happened to taking a tour of the town?"

"She probably forgot. I'll drive her around tomorrow." Katelyn opened the pantry. "Want me to make a pot of coffee?" Her mother drank decaf after supper.

"I'd rather you tell me what the heck is going on." Birdie covered the leftover potato salad with plastic wrap and stored the bowl in the fridge.

There was no sense delaying the conversation. A good night's rest wouldn't change Katelyn's situation or make it easier to explain. "How about peppermint schnapps instead of coffee?"

"Oh, Lord. This can't be good." Birdie bumped Katelyn aside and found a bottle of Hiram Walker in the back of the pantry. "Bring the glasses."

Katelyn would rather chat on the front porch. The back porch was her mother's domain and she'd always felt trapped sitting behind the house without a view of the town.

"Leave the light off so the bugs don't come calling." Birdie poured two fingers of liquor in each juice glass.

"Thanks." Katelyn sipped the alcohol, the taste bringing back memories of eating the tiny candy canes her mother had hung on the Christmas tree each year. "How come you never fixed up the front of the house?"

"What do you mean?"

"The front porch would look cute with a couple of chairs and a potted plant."

"Why would I do that?"

"So you could sit out there once in a while." *And not hide from the world back here.*

"I like the back porch. It faces west and I can watch the sun set."

"Seriously, Mom. Why haven't you decorated the front of the house all these years?" Katelyn couldn't even remember a holiday wreath on the door.

Birdie tossed back the remainder of her

schnapps. "Because I don't want to sit out there and stare at the place I work every day."

Katelyn couldn't recall her mother complaining about her job before. "I thought you liked cashiering at the Buy & Bag."

Birdie shrugged. "It's a paycheck."

"Why didn't you quit years ago and find a job doing something else?"

"We only had one vehicle, and it was easy to walk down the hill to the store." What about after Katelyn's father had died? Birdie could have landed a new job then.

"Have you thought about retiring?"

"Not all women are blessed with a husband who makes lots of money."

Ouch. "Dad left you a life insurance policy."

"Fifty thousand dollars is a drop in the bucket. I put that in savings to cover my funeral expenses and to help settle my estate when the time comes."

"If you're having financial trouble, you should have told me."

"I'm making ends meet."

Birdie was too stubborn for her own good. Once Katelyn received the lump sum settlement from the divorce, she could pay off her mother's house and lighten her load. Maybe then Birdie would cut back on her hours at the store.

"And it's silly that you send me a thousand dollars every year for my birthday," Birdie said.

Silly or not, her mother cashed the check within a week of receiving it. "I miss Mack." Katelyn stared at the yellow lantana patch covering the dog's grave, wishing her childhood buddy sat beside her now. She'd welcome one of his slobbery kisses.

Birdie poured herself a second shot of schnapps. "Are we through beating around the bush?"

There was no good way to ease into the subject. "Don filed for divorce."

"*Don* did?"

Katelyn tore her gaze from the yard. "You sound surprised."

"I always thought *you'd* be the one to leave him."

"Me?"

"Don's gone more than he's home with you and the kids. That's no marriage."

Katelyn shoved her fingers through her hair, knocking the clip loose. "I admit it hasn't always been easy parenting by myself, but Don's been a good provider." She vacated her chair and sat on the porch step. "The divorce seems surreal, because we rarely argued."

"It's difficult to fight with someone you don't know."

Katelyn hadn't shared any intimate details of her marriage with her mother, but obviously Birdie had seen through her daughter and son-in-law's relationship.

"What do the kids think?" Birdie asked.

"They don't know yet. I'm making Don tell them."

"And Shirley?"

"She wants Don and me to reconcile."

Birdie grabbed the bottle of liquor and joined Katelyn on the steps. "Shirley never thought you were good enough for her son. I'm surprised she agreed to come home with you."

"I'm the lesser of two evils. She'd rather be with me than be left by herself." Katelyn drained her glass, then wheezed. "There's another woman."

"There usually is," Birdie said.

Don's infidelity was a slap in the face. The spark might have flickered out of their marriage, but until now she'd respected her husband. "We have over eighteen years together."

"You mean eighteen years mostly apart," Birdie said.

Birdie's jabs at Don were justified. He hadn't been a very good son-in-law. There were things around the house that Birdie could have used a man's help with after Katelyn's father had died, but Don would rather pay a professional to do the work than take the time to travel to Texas and help his mother-in-law.

"He put the house up for sale, and we've already received an offer. And he wants Shirley to move into a retirement apartment."

"He's not letting any grass grow under his feet."

"I'm guessing Lauren—his new lover—isn't keen on Shirley living with them."

"I don't care for the way Shirley criticizes you." Birdie sniffed. "Maybe she's kept her figure all these years, but her hair is ridiculous. It looks like she's walking around with a wild boar on top of her head."

Katelyn laughed.

"You need to stand up for yourself, daughter."

"I do when it's important, but some things aren't worth protesting."

"Why didn't you tell me you were having marital problems?"

"I didn't know Don was unhappy."

"You mean you ignored all the signs."

Katelyn opened her mouth to refute the charge, then snapped it closed. Was she guilty of voluntary blindness? Her mind raced through the past year, dissecting Don's calls, his visits, his body language. He used to hug her and give her a long good-bye kiss. The last time he'd left on a business trip, he'd kissed her on the cheek.

Birdie stabbed her finger in the air. "Don is a pompous ass."

Katelyn agreed, but no matter how big of a buffoon her husband was, she appreciated the privileged life he'd provided her and the kids. A life Katelyn's father, working as a park ranger, could never have given Birdie in a million years.

"Remember when you brought Don home to meet me and your father?" Birdie said. "I invited him to sit down and he brushed his hand across the sofa fabric as if our furniture would dirty his clothes."

Don's obvious discomfort around Katelyn's parents had put a damper on the visit, and they'd left early, using the excuse of having to prepare for exams.

"So did you come home for my birthday or because you needed a shoulder to cry on?"

"Can I say both?"

Birdie whisked a strand of Katelyn's snarled hair out of her eyes. "I'm sorry you have to go through this."

She rested her head against her mother's shoulder. "Besides Shirley's snootiness, why do you dislike her so much?"

"I'm jealous of her."

"I know she's lived a life of leisure, but—"

"It has nothing to do with her wealth." Birdie sat up straight, forcing Katelyn to lift her head away. "I've been a widow seven years longer than Shirley, yet you and Don never invited me to move in with you."

"You didn't leave the stove on and go out all day."

"It shouldn't matter that my memory isn't short-circuiting. Did you ever think I might have been lonely?"

The thought had never crossed Katelyn's mind. "All your friends are here."

"Maybe I wouldn't have wanted to live with you all year-round, but I would have enjoyed spending a month each summer with you and the kids."

"I invited you to fly up every Christmas."

"I didn't care to spend the holidays with your in-laws."

"I said I was sorry that Shirley and Robert showed up unannounced that one time." Katelyn couldn't believe her mother was still miffed about the incident.

"You should have asked them to stay at a hotel, but instead you moved me out of the guest suite."

A lump formed in Katelyn's throat, blocking her airway.

"Remember when I broke my ankle last year?"

"Don and I said we'd cover any medical bills that your insurance didn't pay for."

"I didn't want your money. I wanted you," Birdie whispered.

"I offered to fly home, but you insisted your friends were taking good care of you."

Birdie poured herself a third shot and tossed it back, then thunked the glass against the step. "I only said that after you made excuses about how you needed time to find rides for Melissa and Michael to their after-school activities."

"I was thinking out loud, not making excuses."

"Don should have taken a week off to stay at home with Shirley and the kids."

Shame filled Katelyn. "You're right. I'm sorry." She reached for the bottle of schnapps. "Shirley will be out of the picture soon."

"Putting that woman in an apartment of her own is the first smart thing Don's done in years."

Katelyn steered the conversation in a different direction. "I didn't know Jackson was in town."

"He moved back a few years ago."

"You never told me."

Birdie's chest expanded, then slowly deflated when she released a loud breath. "You stopped coming out here after Shirley moved to St. Louis, so I didn't think it mattered if you knew or not." Birdie bumped Katelyn's arm. "Aren't you going to ask if he's married?"

"I didn't see a ring on his finger when he dropped off the mower."

"So you looked."

"Of course I looked." Katelyn's smile faded as she studied her wedding band. Until now she'd forgotten she still wore the symbol of love, commitment and loyalty. She twirled the platinum circle embedded with diamonds around her finger. Should she take it off or leave it on until the divorce was final? She pushed the thought to the back of her mind and said, "Jackson's still as sexy as ever."

Birdie tipped her head back and laughed. "Even on a good day, Don can't hold a candle to Jackson's looks."

Katelyn sighed. Her life was a mess right now. The last thing she needed was to become involved with her old flame. But having a friend to talk to would be nice. Jackson had always been a good listener. Her gaze swung to the Mercedes. "I'll try to keep Shirley out of your way."

Birdie put her arm around Katelyn's shoulder and squeezed. "I'm sorry about the divorce, but I'm glad you're here." She kissed the top of Katelyn's head, then went into the house, leaving the bottle of schnapps behind.

As soon as the door shut, the tears she'd held at bay since leaving St. Louis leaked from Katelyn's eyes. Birdie wasn't a woman who wore her feelings on her sleeve—most strong women weren't—but this was the first time after Katelyn left for college that her mother had come close to admitting she missed her daughter.

CHAPTER NINE

Y ou're beating the hell out of that muffler."
Jackson pushed his creeper out from
beneath the van he'd been tinkering with since
lunchtime. "For a man of God, you use the word
hell out of context a lot." Jackson sat up and
reached for the can of Dr Pepper he'd set by the
rear tire.

"And you drink too much of that stuff. Soda's
not healthy for you."

Neither was alcohol. "Better than the alter-
native." He noted the dark circles beneath the
seventy-year-old preacher's eyes. The loss of
his wife this past winter weighed heavy on Vern,
and his stooped frame stole an inch from his
five-foot-ten height.

Vern made himself comfortable on the gold
plaid sofa Jackson had purchased from Gifford's
Resale next door. He'd put the couch in the
garage so Vern would have a place to sit and
shoot the breeze when he stopped by every day.
"You get into it with Abby again?" Jackson
asked.

"I don't understand how my daughter got to be
so opinionated."

The few times Jackson had run into Abby
after she'd arrived in town to keep an eye on

her father, he'd gotten the impression she was a woman who spoke her mind—like the preacher. "What's Abby upset about now?"

"She says I smell."

Jackson grinned. "Did you run out of Old Spice?"

"Abby hid my cologne and won't give it back unless I shower before bed. How can I stink that bad when I sit around all day?"

Vern didn't know that Jackson had been the one to beg Abby to return to town a month after her mother's funeral, because he'd been terrified his sponsor would pick up the bottle again. Abby had taken a leave of absence from her job in Dallas and moved back to Little Springs to pull Vern out of his depression.

"Missed you at the meeting this morning." Vern cleared his throat, the gravelly sound echoing through the cinder block garage. "Thought it might have to do with Katelyn being back in town."

Vern knew Jackson better than Jackson knew himself. "Nope," he lied. He'd skipped the Friday AA gathering because he hadn't been able to focus since Katelyn had arrived on Monday. Every time he walked past the open bay doors, he glanced outside, hoping to catch a glimpse of her driving by or eating at Mama's Kitchen across the street.

"I'm running behind on this repair job."

Jackson held the old man's stare. Seeing Katelyn at Birdie's house had shaken him. She'd looked as pretty as his memory of her. The angles of her face were sharper, more defined. She still had brown hair, but the strands were mixed with gold highlights now. Faint lines fanned from the outer corners of her eyes—eyes that were missing the spark he'd been drawn to back in high school. Katelyn had grown into a sophisticated, beautiful woman no one would ever guess had come from this Podunk town.

"Yesterday Sadie had breakfast at Mama's Kitchen, and since Ginny runs the place, she hears all the latest gossip. Birdie told her that Katelyn answered the door when you returned the lawn mower."

"I've got to get this van put back together by tomorrow," Jackson said, hinting again that he didn't care to discuss Katelyn.

"What did you two talk about?"

He wasn't surprised Vern wouldn't let the subject drop, because Jackson had spilled his guts to him years ago and had confessed how messed up he'd gotten after Katelyn had ended their relationship.

"Sadie said Katelyn brought her mother-in-law with her and Birdie's not happy about that."

Jackson guzzled the rest of the soda, then climbed to his feet and pitched the can into the trash. He glanced out the open bay door, his gaze traveling down the street to the Buy & Bag, where Birdie worked. She'd stopped by the garage two weeks ago and asked him if he'd take a look at her broken mower. He'd been happy to help, but it hadn't been easy resisting the urge to ask about Katelyn.

"Can the church count on you to set up the tents for the Fourth of July chili cook-off?" Vern asked.

"Sure."

"Gary mentioned a band from Odessa might play before the fireworks."

"You've got too much time on your hands, old man. You need to get back to preaching." After Elaine had been diagnosed with cancer, Vern had turned the pulpit over to the much younger Reverend Billy Ray Sanders and his wife, June. The handoff was supposed to have been temporary—until Vern regained his enthusiasm for God's word—but so far his excitement extended only to attending Sunday services as a parishioner at the Grace Community Church.

"Might get a trim today," Vern said.

"You keep getting a haircut at Sadie's and you'll turn into a Chatty Cathy like all the grayheads at the beauty shop." Vern went to the salon once a week, not because he needed to, but because he missed having a woman fuss over him—his daughter, Abby, badgered.

"We could use another judge for the cooking

competition. Ginny thinks she's an expert on chili recipes."

Jackson would not be attending the festivities. He moved away from the door and stretched out on the creeper, then pushed himself under the van.

"You're stronger than you think, son."

Jackson was stronger, but he didn't want to test that strength. "You know crowds aren't my thing."

"You've been sober for a long time. Maybe you've gotten over your fear."

"Back off, Vern." Jackson would love to partake in the town's celebration, but being around people made him nervous and fed his insecurities.

It hadn't been easy making friends growing up in Little Springs. No one had wanted to hang out with the offspring of the town drunk. The kid whose mother had ditched him and his father in search of a better life. The only time Jackson had had friends as a teenager had been when he'd brought booze to a party. This Fourth of July he'd stick to drinking Dr Pepper and watching the fireworks from the window of his apartment over the garage.

Vern's cell phone played Willie Nelson's "Always on My Mind"—the ringtone he'd told Jackson that he'd assigned to his daughter's number.

"You gonna answer that?" Jackson asked.

"Nope."

He pushed himself out from beneath the van. "If you don't, Abby will call me."

Vern shrugged.

Stubborn geezer. Willie's voice cut off and a moment later Jackson's phone chimed. "Hello, Abby."

"Is he with you?"

"He's watching me work on a car."

"I didn't mean to hurt his feelings." Her voice wobbled.

Afraid he'd get caught in another father-daughter squabble, Jackson said, "He's heading over to Sadie's for a haircut. Then he'll be home."

"Okay, thanks."

"You bet." He disconnected the call and shoved the phone into his pocket. "Your daughter loves you."

"I know."

Abby had been a freshman in college when Vern took over as the minister of the only church in Little Springs. She hadn't grown up in this town and she'd confessed to Jackson more than once that she was going stir-crazy here. "Maybe it's time for Abby to return to Dallas." He popped his head out from beneath the front fender. "Can you keep away from the bottle if she leaves?" Jackson swallowed hard at the thought of Vern falling off the wagon. The old man had been like a father to him.

"I only had a few drinks after Elaine died. Haven't touched another drop since and I don't plan to."

"Then let Abby go. I know you like having her around, but she misses her job." She'd confided as much to Jackson a month after she'd arrived on her father's doorstep.

Vern stood. "You're one to lecture about letting go when you haven't forgotten Katelyn after all these years." He walked out the bay door without saying good-bye.

Jackson had never forgotten Katelyn—not even the dark years of drinking had erased her from his memory. As much as he'd love to spend time with her while she was in town, he worried that dredging up old memories would trigger the insecurities that had caused him to drink in the first place. He'd been sober for a little over three years now and owned a business. The thought of jeopardizing all that should be enough to convince him to keep his distance from her.

In the grand scheme of things, what did it really matter if he was lonely?

CHAPTER TEN

I can't imagine what people do here all day." Shirley paced in front of the window like a caged animal late Friday afternoon.

"The same thing they do in other small towns," Katelyn said.

"I don't see why *you* have to clean right now."

"Mom's house is small—it won't take long to tidy up." Her mother had made her feel like crap for not taking care of her when she'd broken her ankle, and all week Katelyn had been looking for ways to make it up to her—cleaning, doing laundry and knocking down cobwebs on the porches.

"I'd be happy to pay for a professional cleaning service to come in after we return to St. Louis," Shirley said.

"That's nice of you to offer, but there's no need to waste your money." Katelyn ran the dust rag over the coffee table, then wiped off the fingerprints on the empty candy dish. She hadn't gotten much sleep this week. Each night she'd lain awake until after midnight ruminating over her conversation with Shirley at the sandwich shop on the drive to Little Springs.

Katelyn had been so busy being nice, pleasing Don, going along with things, because she thought she was getting something better in return, when in reality she hadn't only sacrificed parts of herself when she'd married Don; she'd neglected her relationship with her own mother.

Granted their mother-daughter bond wasn't the kind found in storybooks, but Katelyn respected Birdie. Years ago when she'd told her parents she intended to go out of state to college, her father had balked, wanting Katelyn to remain close to home. Her mother had been the one to insist Katelyn follow her dreams no matter how far away from Little Springs they took her.

Katelyn couldn't control Don's feelings for her and his desire for a divorce, but she did have control over her relationship with her mother and she wanted them to grow closer.

Shirley stared out the living room window. "It's odd that there's only one hill in town."

"The hill is man-made from leftover construction dirt after the highway went in decades ago."

"This house is sitting on a toxic dump site?"

Why did Shirley have to be so dramatic all the time? "The ground isn't contaminated, but my father once uncovered a wheelbarrow and a pair of men's boots when he dug the storm shelter on the side of the house."

"The workers should have leveled the land so the hill wasn't so high."

"No one expected a tourist town to pop up

between Odessa and Pecos." Little Springs had sprung up when the United States Army Corps of Engineers had dug Catfish Bay in 1956 to help with flood control. Bait shops and food shacks for fishermen were the first to open their doors. After the Fish and Wildlife Department made improvements to the lake—campsites, picnic areas and a swimming beach—families descended on the area, and local businesses like the Buy & Bag and Little Springs Bait & Hardware opened to cater to the growing tourist population.

"You missed a spot." Shirley peered at a smudge on the table next to the leather recliner.

"There's an extra cleaning rag beneath the kitchen sink, if you'd like to help."

"I don't want to get oil on my slacks." Shirley turned back to the window. "What is there to do here for entertainment?"

"Eat and socialize." Katelyn exchanged the furniture polish for glass cleaner and edged her mother-in-law out of the way.

"I don't see any restaurants."

"The two-story powder blue house is Mama's Kitchen. Ginny offers a lunch special every day."

Shirley's stomach growled. "What's the menu like?"

"Mostly comfort food." Katelyn smiled. "The *not*-heart-healthy variety."

"Your mother's grocery store isn't very big,"

Shirley said. "Where do the ladies shop for cosmetics?"

"The toiletry section in the store carries makeup and skin-care products, but if you're looking for higher-end items, you have to drive to Dillard's at the Music City Mall in Odessa."

"What's the building with all the garbage sitting around it?"

"Gifford's Resale. Gary buys other people's castoffs, calls them antiques and sells them to tourists."

"It's a junk shop, then."

"One person's junk is another's treasure."

"I thought there wasn't a gas station in town."

"There isn't." Katelyn's gaze zeroed in on the brick building next to Gifford's Resale. "That's an auto repair shop." She'd spent hours inside the garage after school, sitting on the floor with her back propped against the wall. She worked on her sketches while Jackson had changed the oil in cars.

"I suppose there's no theater nearby."

"There's Sadie's beauty shop. That's where you can catch up on all the drama in town."

Shirley's breath fogged up the glass Katelyn had wiped clean. "Where's the salon?"

"Sadie lives behind the park. You can't see her place from here."

"There's no other beauty shop in town?"

"Nope."

"Is she any good?" Shirley fluffed her hair.

"You just got a perm." *Wait a minute.* Katelyn didn't have to care anymore if her mother-in-law went bald.

"What's the hairstylist's name again?"

"Sadie."

Why Shirley obsessed over her appearance when she hadn't shown any interest in dating or finding a companion to spend her twilight years with was a mystery to Katelyn. "I need to run the vacuum. Why don't you sit on the back porch and enjoy the garden?"

"Does your mother own an ironing board?"

"Of course she has an ironing board." Shirley acted as if Birdie lived in a sod house with dirt floors.

"Birdie must have forgotten where she put it," Shirley said, "because the clothes she wore to work this morning looked like they'd been left in the dryer for days before being taken out and folded."

Ignoring the snooty comment, Katelyn said, "Check behind the door in the sewing room. The iron is on the dresser."

After Shirley went upstairs, Katelyn put away the cleaning supplies and then went to the kitchen pantry to retrieve the vacuum, but instead took the bag of Cheetos from the shelf and sat at the table.

She propped her feet on the chair across from her and stuffed her face, wondering if there was such a thing as a mother-in-law whisperer. Katelyn had told herself that she'd allowed Shirley to cocaptain the household after she'd moved in with the family because she hadn't wanted to subject the twins to their constant bickering. But on some conscious level she'd suspected that her mother-in-law had seen through Katelyn and guessed she'd married Don as much for the lifestyle he could give her as because she'd been in love with him—if not more so.

She licked her orange fingers, then returned the bag to the shelf and studied the food selection—mostly canned soups. She checked the freezer, which was stocked with hot dogs and single-serve pizzas. Nothing Shirley would eat.

After Katelyn ran the vacuum, she'd take Shirley on a field trip down to the grocery store and pick up the ingredients for lasagna—one of Birdie's favorite meals.

"You know what they say about small stores." Shirley unsnapped her belt after Katelyn parked the Mercedes in front of the Buy & Bag.

"What's that?"

"The food isn't fresh. Make sure you check the dates on everything you buy."

Katelyn swallowed a sigh and said, "Don't forget your purse." Shirley grabbed her bag and followed Katelyn into the store.

The layout of the market hadn't changed much since she'd worked there in high school. White walls, and the same signage with the Buy & Bag logo—a green *B&B* inside a white circle—hung above the aisles, listing the food products. A handful of green shopping carts and green handbaskets sat inside the store near the doors. Katelyn picked up a basket, then glanced at the empty registers. "Mom must be on her break or stocking food in one of the aisles."

Shirley selected a box of Entenmann's blueberry muffins off an endcap as they passed by. "Where's the deli?"

"In the back." She took the muffins and dropped them into the basket.

"Katelyn?" Birdie walked toward them.

"Hi, Mom. I thought I'd make lasagna for supper tonight."

Birdie's eyes lit up. "That sounds great."

"Katelyn's lasagna isn't very good," Shirley said. "We should grill chicken breasts instead."

Birdie stiffened. "What's wrong with my daughter's lasagna?"

"She puts too much cheese in it."

"What recipe are you using?" Birdie looked at Katelyn.

"Yours."

"Then I'm sure it's fine," Birdie said.

"Katelyn's meat loaf is good, but sometimes it's a little dry."

"If you don't like my daughter's food, why don't you do the cooking?"

Katelyn opened her mouth to call a truce, but a male voice interrupted her.

"Look who came back to town."

"Hello, Walter." Katelyn smiled at her former high school classmate and now the manager of the store. Walter's hairline had receded another inch since she'd last seen him and his cute wife at her father's funeral. She held out her hand, but he ignored the gesture and hugged her. The scent of cheap cologne, cigarette smoke and mint chewing gum threatened to gag her. When she pulled away, her hair snagged on his eyeglasses, pulling them down his nose.

"Sorry," she said, tugging the strand free.

He adjusted the glasses and smiled, showing off the gap between his front teeth. "You look great."

"Thank you."

Katelyn motioned to Shirley. "This is my mother-in-law, Shirley Pratt. Walter and I graduated from high school together. He's the manager of the Buy & Bag."

"Welcome to Little Springs," he said, then looked back at Katelyn. "How long will you be in town?"

"Not long," Shirley answered for Katelyn.

"We should go out for a beer and talk about old times."

What old times? They'd run with different

114

crowds in high school and Katelyn didn't know his wife—he'd met her in college. "How's your wife?"

He frowned. "We divorced a while back."

"I didn't know. I'm sorry to hear that."

"Tell me, young man," Shirley said, "how's your meat department?"

"Fresher than most chain grocery stores." Walter offered his arm. "Would you like me to show you our best cuts?"

"Please." Shirley walked off with him.

"Don't say it, Mom."

"Say what? That your *monster-in-law* is rude and obnoxious?"

"Yes."

"How can you stand being around her? I'd rather someone stab me in the chest with a butter knife than wake up to her each morning."

Katelyn plucked a box of lasagna noodles off the shelf, then added two jars of store-brand tomato sauce to the basket. "Do you have fresh basil at home?"

"What do you think?"

Katelyn headed over to the produce section to pick up basil and thyme and then added a tomato, an onion and a carton of mushrooms to the basket, while her mother hovered over her shoulder.

"I have a package of hamburger and a box of Texas toast in the freezer," Birdie said.

"Then I think I have everything." On the way up to the registers Birdie stopped when the front doors opened and an elderly woman entered the store.

"I didn't think you were coming today, Clara." Birdie looked at Katelyn. "Clara usually does her shopping in the morning." She turned back to the blue-haired woman. "You remember my daughter, Katelyn, don't you?"

"Of course. Hello, dear."

"Nice to see you, Mrs. Smith."

"What's on your list today?" Birdie grabbed a handbasket, then took Clara's elbow, and the women walked off.

Katelyn placed her items on the checkout counter and glanced around.

A pretty woman walked out of the aisle across from the register. "Sorry," she said. "I was straightening the shelves."

"No worries."

"I'm Layla." She began scanning the items in the basket. "You must be Birdie's daughter."

"Katelyn." She admired the cashier's bold eye makeup. On any other woman the black liner, false lashes and sparkling lavender shadow would look trashy.

"Your mom talks about you all the time. You have twins that recently graduated from high school."

"I do. A boy and a girl."

Layla set the empty basket aside. "Birdie says you're a really good artist."

Katelyn was momentarily speechless. Neither of her parents had shown much interest in her art before she'd left for college.

"You won some kind of scholarship."

"I did." Katelyn moved to the end of the counter and bagged her groceries.

Layla searched a laminated produce card until she found the code for the basil. "What's it like . . . being an artist?"

The question stumped Katelyn. "I haven't painted anything in years." She'd forgotten small towns were filled with nosy people. "I've been busy raising my kids."

"Birdie told me, but I forgot their names."

"Michael and Melissa."

"Your mom has their senior photos up in her locker. Melissa's pretty. She looks like you." Layla batted her eyelashes, hinting that Katelyn should return the compliment.

"You have gorgeous hair."

The younger woman fluffed the ends. "Sadie custom-mixes my color."

"Maybe Sadie would fix your hair, Katelyn." Shirley approached the register and smiled at Layla. "You're young enough to wear long hair, dear, but my daughter-in-law is forty and women that age should wear their hair shorter."

"Men like long hair," Layla said.

Shirley scoffed. "I suppose that depends on what kind of men you're trying to attract."

Katelyn made a mental note to speak with Layla before she left town and apologize for her mother-in-law's rudeness. Better yet, she should take out an ad in the next edition of the *Springs Jotter* and apologize to the whole town.

Layla winked. "I bet your husband likes your long hair."

If Birdie hadn't told her coworker that her son-in-law had filed for divorce, then Katelyn wasn't going to mention it. She swiped her bank card through the machine and Layla handed her the receipt.

"I'm not sure about this sirloin." Shirley set the meat on the conveyor belt.

"Walter knows his meats," Layla said.

Shirley opened her purse. "How much did the stylist charge to do your hair?"

"A hundred and ten with tip."

"Are we still talking about hair?" Birdie and Clara arrived at the register.

"I'd be happy to treat Katelyn to a new makeover," Shirley said.

"Maybe my daughter doesn't want to change her looks."

"I'm only trying to help her situation." Shirley removed a fifty-dollar bill from her wallet.

Layla took the money. "What situation is that?"

"My son filed for divorce and I think Katelyn should fight to save their marriage."

So much for keeping her business private.

"My daughter changing her appearance isn't going to fix their marital problems," Birdie argued.

"She could also afford to lose ten pounds."

Layla's sparkly eyes widened.

"Why should Katelyn change anything about herself when your jackass of a son cheated on her?"

"One little indiscretion shouldn't ruin a marriage."

"Have you considered that my daughter might not want to save her marriage?"

"That's ridiculous," Shirley said.

"Oh, really?" Birdie looked at Katelyn. "Do you want to stay married to Don?"

Katelyn spoke to Shirley. "You have to bag your own groceries here." Then without another word Katelyn took her food and left the store.

CHAPTER ELEVEN

"Where's Katelyn?" Shirley's voice echoed into the opening of the attic, where Katelyn was searching through boxes of mementos Sunday evening. She wanted to find the teddy bear Jackson had given her the night before she'd left for college. *To hold if you get lonely and miss me.*

"I don't know." Birdie's voice drifted from the kitchen. Her mother knew exactly where Katelyn was—she'd sent her up to the attic to look for the stuffed animal.

"It was very rude of you to bad-mouth my son in public," Shirley said.

"But it's okay if you offend my daughter?"

Katelyn crept closer to the attic door. The two women were still arguing about the grocery store incident two days later.

"I was offering constructive criticism."

"This is my home, Shirley. If you can't be respectful of my daughter . . . there's the door." Birdie had put on her boxing gloves.

"I'm not condoning my son's behavior, but I can understand where he might have been tempted to stray."

A deathly silence followed Shirley's statement and Katelyn put one foot on the top step of the ladder, prepared to intervene if her mother went ballistic.

"Cheating is cheating." A loud squeak echoed below. Birdie had opened the pantry door—was she searching for the schnapps?

"I've told Katelyn for years to try a new hairstyle. Something classy. Maybe a sleek bob."

"And what have you told your son to do to improve himself?" A loud thud—like the sound of a liquor bottle banging against the countertop—followed Birdie's question. "The last time I saw Don, he was sporting a spare tire around the middle, and his hairline had receded another inch."

Go, Mom.

"Don works long hours so he can provide for his family. He doesn't have time to exercise like Katelyn does."

"My daughter doesn't have time to exercise, either. She's too busy babysitting you."

Laughter bubbled up inside Katelyn and she pressed her hand against her mouth to keep it from escaping.

"I beg your pardon."

"You should be begging Katelyn's pardon for being a burden on her the past few years."

Birdie had gone for the jugular.

"I have not been a burden."

"How can you say that when my daughter has to chauffeur you around town and watch your every move because you're growing forgetful?"

The spat was turning ugly. Katelyn descended the ladder and walked into the kitchen. "What's going on?"

Birdie pointed a finger at Shirley, who stood next to the back door, looking poised to run. "Ms. Prissy Pants is slandering you."

Shirley's pencil-thin eyebrows arched. "Slandering?"

"You didn't think I knew what the word *slandering* meant, did you?"

"Mom, take it down a notch. It's been a long day and we're all tired."

"I am tired." Birdie stamped her foot. "Tired of watching you let your mother-in-law run your life."

"A life *your* daughter could only dream of before she married *my* son."

Steam spewed from Birdie's ears. "Is that what you dreamed of, Katelyn—big houses, expensive cars and fancy vacations? I thought your dream was to be an artist."

"I need a drink." Katelyn poured a splash of schnapps into a glass and finished it off in one swallow. The way things were going with this visit, she'd need to make a liquor run and stock up on the happy juice.

"If Katelyn hadn't married Don, she'd still be stuck"—Shirley spread her arms wide—"in this awful place."

"Stuck?" Birdie glared.

Shirley spoke to Katelyn. "I think we should leave."

Birdie called Shirley's bluff. "Go right ahead. No one's stopping you."

Katelyn was torn. She felt sorry for her mother-in-law because Shirley was still reeling from Don casting her aside, and at the same time she was grateful to Birdie for defending her.

"Let's call a truce. No more talk about the divorce while we're here." Katelyn glanced between the mothers. "Agreed?"

Shirley grimaced.

"Fine." Birdie fetched a third glass from the cupboard and poured an inch of liquor in it, then handed it to Shirley before refilling her own glass and Katelyn's. "To keeping our mouths shut." Birdie tossed back her shot. Katelyn followed suit; then Shirley plugged her nose and took a sip.

"Oh, for God's sake, are you a teetotaler?"

Shirley wheezed. "I prefer a nice glass of chardonnay."

"I don't drink expensive wine. You'd better get used to hard liquor."

Shirley shuddered.

"Gary Gifford makes white lightning for the holidays. I could see if he has any jugs left in his shed from last Christmas."

"Mom, I don't think Shirley—"

"Your mother-in-law can decide for herself what she wants to drink."

Truce or no truce, Katelyn didn't dare leave the two women alone again. "I can't find the box of books I left behind when I went off to college. Will you help me look?"

Shirley set her glass on the counter. "If you want to talk about me behind my back, say so. I'll be in my room."

"Katelyn's room."

Shirley paused in the doorway. "Pardon?"

"It's Katelyn's room, not yours," Birdie said.

Shirley walked off without a word.

Katelyn waited for the stairs to stop creaking before she spoke. "You were a little rough on her."

Billowing tendrils of smoke still leaked from Birdie's ears. "Do you need my help in the attic or not?"

"I do."

Birdie climbed the ladder, then crouch-walked across the space and sat on a crate of vintage *Field & Stream* magazines. "It's hotter than Hades up here. If you want to look through all this crap, you should come back in October and do it."

"Mom, you need to lay off Shirley."

"She's your mother-in-law, not mine."

"It's not like you to be mean."

Birdie grimaced. "You're *my* daughter. I'm the only one who should get to cut you down."

"Gee, thanks."

"You know what I mean."

"I appreciate you sticking up for me, but give me some credit for having learned how to handle Shirley after all these years."

"Maybe so, but I wish you wouldn't allow her to run roughshod over you."

"Half of what Shirley says goes in one ear and out the other."

"What happens when it doesn't?"

"I get even."

Birdie snorted. "Yeah, right."

Katelyn lowered her voice. "Promise never to tell a soul, not even the ladies in your bridge group?"

"Not tell them what?"

"Last year the president of the community arts organization called the house to tell me that he was nominating me as his successor. Shirley answered the phone and said I wasn't interested in the position and that they should offer the job to someone else."

"That was bitchy."

"I didn't find out about the call until one of the members mentioned it at a meeting and said what a shame it was that I had turned down the job."

"How did you get even with Shirley?"

"I made her favorite meat loaf recipe with canned cat food."

Birdie whooped. "There's hope for you yet, daughter."

"I still feel horrible about it."

"She got off lucky with cat food. I would have used arsenic."

"Seriously, Mom. Can you please try to be patient with Shirley?"

"She shouldn't even be here. She's Don's responsibility, not yours."

"Once she moves into her new apartment, Don will have to step up," Katelyn said.

"I'll believe it when I see it."

"If you want us to leave, I understand."

"No." Birdie wiped the sweat from her brow. "I'll try to watch my temper."

That was all Katelyn could ask of her mother. "We should sort through this stuff and purge the attic." She nudged a cardboard box with the toe of her sandal. "I think it's safe to shred your 2001 tax returns." She opened the box and pushed aside the balled-up newspaper. "Wait a minute. These aren't tax returns."

Katelyn pulled out her sketch pad from junior high school and flipped through the images. "You saved all my projects?"

"You sound surprised."

"I didn't think you and Dad cared that much about my art."

Birdie sat up straight. "Why would you say that?"

"You two never came to any of the shows at school."

"Your father and I both worked."

"You could have asked for the time off." Katelyn had been the only student without a parent in attendance when her drawing of Mack received first place in the senior art competition.

"Jackson was there."

Katelyn's boyfriend had always been there. She closed the sketch pad, slamming the door on the memories of the promises she and Jackson had made to each other their senior year. Promises Katelyn had turned her back on when she'd left for college. She dug through the box and found a charcoal drawing of the railroad tracks across town.

"When I saw that, I knew for sure you were leaving." Birdie flashed a tired smile. "I didn't blame you for wanting to go far away to college, but I do regret not spending more time with you growing up."

Katelyn hadn't been the best daughter after she'd gone off to school. Maybe they both should call it even and forget the past.

"Shirley's right about one thing," Birdie said.

"What's that?"

"Don's job allowed you to stay home and be involved in the kids' lives." Birdie pursed her lips and stared, eyes unblinking.

Yes, Katelyn had been involved in all of the

twins' activities, but that hadn't been the plan in the beginning. After marrying Don, she'd become pregnant right away and then taking care of two babies had exhausted her, leaving little time to nurture her creative side. When Michael and Melissa entered kindergarten, Don's career had taken off. He'd begun traveling more, leaving her as the sole caretaker. Each year Katelyn planned to start sketching, but when she set up her easel and opened her paints, she couldn't muster any enthusiasm.

Katelyn glanced up and found her mother studying her. "What?"

"You don't seem all that broken up over your impending divorce."

"It hasn't sunk in yet."

"You're not in love with Don, are you?"

"No." In the beginning Katelyn had believed she loved Don, but now she admitted that love had been rooted in what he'd represented more than the man himself.

"Prissy Pants thinks there's still a chance you and her son will reconcile."

"She'll accept the truth once she speaks with Don."

Birdie sucked in a deep breath. When she exhaled, her shoulders slumped forward. "Life is going by too fast, and I'm on the downhill side."

"You're turning sixty next week, not eighty."

"I know, but you live so far away, and my

grandkids are off to college. I hardly ever see them."

"Now that I don't have Shirley to take care of, you and I will do more things."

"Sure." Birdie seemed unimpressed with Katelyn's pledge. "Where will you live?"

"I don't know."

"You could move back to Little Springs. Or Odessa if you want to be in a larger town."

Katelyn rebelled at the suggestion. Why would she want to return to the place she'd been eager to escape growing up? "Wherever I land, I'll have a room for you when you come to visit."

Birdie rubbed her fingers, her knuckles popping. "I need a favor."

"Anything."

"Will you take my shifts at the store while you're here?"

"And leave you alone with Shirley?" Katelyn laughed. "I'd have to spend my entire share of the divorce settlement to pay a lawyer to defend you against murder charges."

"Prissy Pants is a pain in the ass, but I wouldn't touch a hair on her head."

"Stop calling her names."

Birdie grinned. "Her cheeks turn red when I insult her. The woman can dish it out, but she can't take it."

"Which is why *you* shouldn't be saddled with her all day."

"At least I don't let her walk all over me."

Katelyn ignored the dig.

"The truth is," Birdie said, "I could use a break from Abby and Layla. All those girls do is bitch about their lives."

Katelyn attempted to decipher the truth behind her mother's words. Did she really need time away from her coworkers, or was she worn-out after years of standing on her feet in front of a register?

"Walter said it was okay."

Birdie must be serious about taking a breather from her job if she'd already spoken to her boss. "What would you and Shirley do all day?"

"I'll introduce her to the Little Springs Ladies' Society and show her how we do culture in West Texas."

As much as Katelyn worried about leaving Shirley at Birdie's mercy, this was a chance to do something for her mother—a step toward renewing their mother-daughter bond. Honestly, it would be nice to spend a few hours a day away from her mother-in-law. A win-win for everyone, except maybe Shirley.

"When do I start?"

"Tomorrow morning."

CHAPTER TWELVE

Fifty-three cents is your change." Katelyn dropped the money into the older man's trembling palm, then folded his knobby fingers over the coins to keep them from spilling onto the floor.

"*Gracias.*"

She smiled and watched him shuffle out the door.

Abby Wilkes set aside the magazines she'd been stocking in the display case at the front of the store. "I think Mr. Flores has a crush on you."

"Mr. Flores is old enough to be my grandfather." Katelyn glanced at the clock on the wall. Two p.m. "Is it always this slow on a Monday?" In high school she'd worked weekends during the summer and the store had been crowded with campground people staying at the lake.

"Mondays are the slowest," Abby said.

Katelyn took a swig from the bottle of water beneath the counter. "How long have you worked here?" She couldn't remember if Birdie had mentioned Abby during any of their phone conversations, which covered the kids, the weather and not much else.

Abby waved a hand in the air. "I don't know if

Birdie told you, but my mother passed away right before Christmas. I took a leave of absence from my job in Dallas to come stay with my dad." She expelled a deep sigh. "But I didn't expect to still be here six months later."

"I'm sorry about your mother."

"Thanks."

"What do you do in Dallas?"

"I'm a public relations manager for Milligan Natural Gas."

"Corporate America is stressful." Not only for the employee but for the employee's family.

"I love working under pressure." Abby's eyes lit up. "I'm an adrenaline junkie. Deadlines fuel my creativity."

Katelyn envied her coworker. It had been so long since she'd experienced a hunger to nurture her passion. Only when she'd painted had her body, mind and spirit felt in tune. Colors appeared richer, sounds stronger, touches warmer. It had been ages since she'd felt her fingers tingle with the urge to pick up a paintbrush.

"I'm dying a slow death in this town. If I don't escape soon, I'll tie myself to the railroad tracks and put an end to my misery."

Katelyn laughed. "Have you told your father you miss your job?"

"If I mention returning to Dallas, he has a fake panic attack. When I call his bluff, he gets tears in his eyes and then I feel horrible."

"How long has your family lived in Little Springs? I don't remember the Wilkes name."

"My parents moved to town right after I left for college and Dad took over as minister for Grace Community Church. I've never lived here, only visited."

"I can see how life in a town of less than three thousand people would be difficult after living in a large city."

"It's not that I just miss my job, but I feel like my life is slipping away. I devoted my twenties to my career and have no regrets, but I'm thirty-three now and I'd like to marry and have a family. When I tell my father that, he thinks I'm still twelve and says I have plenty of time."

"You might have to show a little tough love and leave." Who was she to give advice on handling parents? She'd allowed Shirley to bulldoze her for years while ignoring Birdie's needs.

"I was hoping it wouldn't come to that," Abby said.

"Would your dad be willing to move to Dallas?"

"I can't ask him to leave. His support group is here."

"Support group?"

"My father's been a recovering alcoholic since I was in kindergarten. When my mother died, he fell off the wagon."

"That's awful. I'm sorry."

"I don't think he has the urge to drink anymore, but he's using the threat to keep me here."

"Parents can be stubborn. So can in-laws."

"I'd put up with an interfering mother-in-law any day in exchange for finding a decent man to marry." Abby lowered her voice. "Did your husband really file for a divorce?"

The Little Springs gossip brigade was in full swing. Thanks to Birdie and Shirley's spat in front of Layla in the store last week, everyone in town knew Katelyn had been dumped. "Yes, the rumors are true."

Abby's gaze shifted to the register, then back to Katelyn. "You're not planning to work here the rest of your life, are you?" She winced. "I'm sorry. That was rude of me to say when your mother's been an employee for years."

Katelyn waved off the apology. "I'm not sure what I'll do." She'd barely had a moment to herself to think about anything since she'd arrived in town.

"Layla said you went to college on an art scholarship."

The romantic in Katelyn had once fantasized about living in Paris and being a street artist in Montmartre, sketching tourists as they meandered by. She thought of the art pad she took with her everywhere. Why hadn't she ever turned one of her doodles into a painting? "I haven't gotten my easel out in years."

"You should paint while you're here. I'd love to see one of your pictures."

People who weren't artistic thought it was easy to create. That after you dabbed the end of a brush into a glob of color, a masterpiece would magically appear on the canvas. "I'm out of practice," Katelyn said.

"I'm sure it'll come back to you."

"Maybe." Inspiration was an important part of the creative process, and Katelyn's life had revolved around the kids, her mother-in-law and Don's career for so long that she'd lost touch with the things that used to fuel her creativity—long walks along the train tracks, hours of people-watching and plenty of alone time.

Abby turned her head to the side, her blond bob swinging across her face. "Maybe Walter will inspire you."

"Pardon?"

"Haven't you noticed the boss always has his eye on you?"

Katelyn's gaze shifted to the manager's window and Walter ducked his head.

"I think he wants to ask you out on a date."

"No." Not Walter Davis.

"I'm right, aren't I, Layla?"

Their coworker approached the checkout, her voluptuous bosom and full hips sashaying in rhythm with her wavy black hair. The twenty-nine-year-old batted her false eyelashes. "Right about what?"

"Walter told you that he was thinking of asking Katelyn out."

"Oh, yeah." Layla smacked her gum, drawing attention to her pouty mouth and red lipstick so shiny it looked like she'd kissed a puddle of baby oil. "Walter wants to take you to the new steak house in Odessa." She glanced at his office. "He said you were good friends in high school."

"Not really." Katelyn couldn't remember if she'd ever said hi to Walter when they'd passed in the halls.

"I might have told him that you were happy about your divorce." Katelyn's mouth dropped open and Layla rushed on. "I had my roots touched up the other day." She fluffed her hair. "Sadie said you were relieved that your marriage was over."

Birdie was putting her own spin on Katelyn and Don's situation, because she was happy Don and his mother would be out of the picture soon. Still, Birdie had no business gossiping about her daughter.

Layla and Abby exchanged glances. Then Layla said, "Is it true he cheated on you?"

The nosy question reminded Katelyn of why she'd wanted to go away to college and leave her hometown in the dust. "Yes, there's another woman."

Abby tugged the sleeve of Layla's work smock. "He's late."

"Who's late?" Katelyn asked.

"Brian, the Entenmann's delivery driver. He has a crush on Layla, but she's playing hard to get."

"Why?" As long as everyone was sticking their nose into Katelyn's business, she'd join in the gossiping.

"Layla's waiting for her prince to drive his white pickup through town and sweep her off her feet." Abby laughed.

"Princes are in short supply when you have a twelve-year-old son." Layla thrust her lower lip out.

"And," Abby said, "she's attracted to hot guys with lots of muscle."

Layla shrugged. "What can I say? I like six-pack abs."

"Unlike other men around here"—Abby's gaze flicked to the office window—"Brian still has all his hair."

Katelyn laughed. "Is there anything you like about Brian, Layla?"

"He asks about my son, Gavin, when he comes into the store."

"And he always tells Layla how nice she looks," Abby said.

Don had hardly ever complimented Katelyn on her clothes or her looks.

"But Brian's a deliveryman," Layla whined. "I want a man who makes enough money to help pay my bills."

Katelyn didn't know what to say, because she'd snagged a rich prince for herself. *And look where that got you.*

"Here he comes now. Pretend we weren't talking about him." Abby went back to stocking magazines. Katelyn remained at her register and Layla beat a hasty retreat down the bread aisle. As soon as Brian pushed his dolly of baked goods into the store, Walter emerged from his office.

"Brian, did you catch the Astros game Wednesday night?"

"Couldn't believe they came back in the ninth inning to clinch the win." Brian had sun-bleached hair and an all-American smile that belonged on a package of beef franks. His blue eyes swung to the register and Walter said, "This is Katelyn. Birdie's daughter."

He parked his dolly and shook her hand. "Brian Montgomery."

"Nice to meet you," she said.

"Katelyn's taking her mother's place for a few days."

"Nothing's wrong with Birdie, I hope."

The boy-next-door was kind, too. Layla needed to give this man a closer look. "She's taking a mini vacation from the job," Katelyn said.

Brian's gaze skipped around the store. Katelyn

tilted her head toward the bread aisle, and he and the dolly of pastry cakes made a beeline in that direction.

Walter pushed his wire-rimmed glasses up his nose and inched closer to Katelyn. He wore gray slacks, a white dress shirt and a red-and-gray-striped tie—a little overdressed for a small-town grocery store. "Can I talk to you a minute?" he asked.

Hoping to distract him from asking her out, she said, "It's really nice of you to allow me to work my mother's hours while I'm in town."

"Birdie's my best employee." He straightened the plastic-bag caddy at the end of the counter. "I thought that since you'll be in town for a while . . ."

Darn it.

"There's a new steak house in Odessa. Maybe Birdie told you about it."

"No, she hasn't mentioned the restaurant."

His brow glistened with sweat. "If you weren't busy one night this week . . ."

Walter's gaze swung past Katelyn. "Jackson."

The once infamous Little Springs bad boy set a twelve-pack of Dr Pepper on the check stand. "Walt." Jackson dipped his head at Katelyn.

"I was telling Katelyn about the new steak house in Odessa. You been there yet?"

Jackson shook his head.

She scanned the soda. "Five fifty-three."

Jackson put his credit card in the machine, selected the cash-back option, then entered his PIN.

The till popped open, and Katelyn handed him two twenty-dollar bills but held on to the money when he attempted to grab it. His eyes twinkled when she sent him a silent plea to save her from Walter. She released the money and he grabbed the soda.

"You'll have to let me know how the steaks are," he said, and walked off, Katelyn's gaze admiring the way his worn jeans hugged his backside. When he reached the exit, he glanced over his shoulder and grinned. *Rat.*

"Does that mean you'll have dinner with me?" Walter asked.

"I appreciate the invite, but I'm afraid I wouldn't be good company."

His gaze dropped to her ring finger. "It doesn't have to be a date."

Maybe Walter thought she didn't want her marriage to end because she still wore her ring. Jackson's pickup sped through the parking lot and turned onto Main Street. Did he wonder why she still wore her wedding band?

"We don't have to talk," Walter said. "We'll eat and leave."

"Walter?"

"What?"

"I'm not going to go out with you."

"Sure. Okay. Maybe another time." He hurried into his office and closed the door.

Abby wheeled the cart of magazines back to the storeroom, then returned to the registers. "I heard you broke Jackson's heart after you went off to college."

"For someone who never lived in this town, you sure know a lot about what went on decades ago."

"My father gets his hair cut a lot."

If only humans were bald . . . there would be no need for hair salons or beauticians and everyone's secrets would remain safe.

CHAPTER THIRTEEN

Walter thinks you snubbed his invitation to dinner because of Jackson." Layla stepped behind Katelyn's register.

"That's not true. I don't like steak." Three hours had passed since Jackson had left the store, and Katelyn figured Layla would ask about him.

"Jackson hasn't come into the store in a while." Layla winked. "Maybe he still has a crush on you."

Jackson had always been a private person and he wouldn't appreciate her sharing their history with others. "We're too old for crushes."

"Maybe, but you're not too old to have sex with him."

Katelyn fumbled the role of nickels she was emptying into the money drawer and two of the coins spilled onto the floor. No matter how intriguing a fling with her old flame sounded, she didn't need another complication in her unsettled life.

"Don't worry about Walter. If you decide to hook up with Jackson while you're here, the boss will have to deal with it."

"I'm not getting together with anyone." Maybe saying it out loud would make it so.

Layla peeked over her shoulder at Walter's

office. "You do know that he divorced his wife, Missy, because she had a one-night stand with Jackson."

No wonder Walter's greeting had been cool toward Jackson. A sliver of jealousy pricked Katelyn. She'd rather not put a face to the women who'd shared Jackson's bed. "Brian seems like a nice guy."

Layla laughed. "Okay, I'll stop talking about Jackson." She expelled a loud sigh. "Brian's nice, but he's not exciting."

"What happened with Gavin's father?"

"Mike comes around once in a while. Mostly when he's broke or needs a place to stay." Layla's smile didn't reach her eyes. "I was crazy for him, but he could never hold down a job, so I filed for divorce. Mike didn't even put up a fight."

Shirley thought Katelyn should fight for her marriage. Maybe if Don hadn't had an affair, she'd consider counseling, but not after he'd cheated on her.

The office door opened and Walter said, "It's almost five, Katelyn. Time to cash out." He watched her transfer the money from her drawer into the bank bag; then he took it back to his office and deposited it in the safe.

"Enjoy the rest of your day," Layla said.

"See you tomorrow." Katelyn cut through the produce department and entered the employee lounge located in the back of the storeroom.

Five lockers, a card table and chairs, an old fridge and a microwave sat in the corner next to the loading-dock door. She punched in the date of her parents' anniversary on the keypad, then opened her mother's locker and hung up her smock. She caught her reflection in the magnetic mirror on the inside of the door and studied her drawn face. Stocking tomato soup and scanning groceries for twelve customers shouldn't be that taxing, but she looked exhausted.

And to think her mother had done this job for decades.

She dabbed a little color on her pale lips, powdered her nose, then removed the elastic band that held her hair in a ponytail and tossed it onto the shelf before grabbing her purse and closing the locker.

She'd walked down the hill to the store earlier in the day, leaving the Mercedes at the house in case Shirley talked Birdie into taking her somewhere. She flipped the light off, then left through the back door. She'd made it to the bottom of the ramp before she saw Jackson's pickup and stopped short. He leaned against the passenger-side door—arms crossed over his chest, boots notched at the ankles. His red T-shirt matched the color of the truck. His lips spread into a lazy grin and her pulse kicked up a notch.

"What are you doing here?" she asked.

"I thought you might want to take a ride."

His words sent her reeling back in time to the spur-of-the-moment drives they'd taken in Jackson's old Mustang.

She walked over to him and smiled. "Remember the drive we took on Highway Twenty-nine and we ended up at the abandoned mine?"

"All I wanted to do that afternoon was make out with you in the cave, but you had to draw it on your sketch pad first."

Jackson had always been patient with her when she'd wanted to draw, sitting next to her quietly, studying her—like he was doing now. "You were a good sport."

"The waiting usually paid off," he said, then opened the door and stood back.

What could it hurt to climb in, buckle up and pretend she was eighteen again? She glanced at her mother's house on the hill, where Birdie and Shirley waited for her to get off work. A gust of wind stirred the scent of Jackson's cologne, propelling her forward into the passenger seat.

He walked past the hood of the pickup and got behind the wheel, then drove around the corner of the building and cut through the parking lot. Walter stood at the front window next to the "Get It While It's Hot—Glacier Bag of Ice $2.99" sign. The boss's mouth dropped open when he recognized Katelyn in the front seat of Jackson's truck.

"We're going to be the topic of conversation at Mama's Kitchen tomorrow," she said.

"Like old times." He flashed a smile and hit the gas as they headed out of town.

"How about the railroad tracks?" What would he think of her wanting to visit their special place? She reached into her purse for her cell phone.

"I heard about your divorce," he said.

"And I heard you cheated with Walter's wife."

His mouth twitched. "Welcome back to Little Springs."

They drove in silence, the truck whizzing past an abandoned mobile home park with a handful of dilapidated trailers propped up on cinder blocks. Past acres of scrubland fenced in by barbed wire. Past an abandoned car with its hood missing and weeds growing up through the engine.

He slowed the truck and moved onto the shoulder, then turned down a familiar dirt road. The same path she'd walked with Jackson numerous times. "What happened to that house?" She pointed to the charred remains.

"Meth lab blew up."

"Little Springs has a drug problem?"

"The meth cooks weren't from here. No one knew they'd been using the abandoned house until it caught fire."

"Back in high school, it was beer and pot. Kids

146

today are taking prescription drugs and sniffing bath salts," she said. "Do you have any kids?"

"Not that I know of."

His flippant response surprised her. How many casual affairs had he had since their breakup? She'd slept with only two men in her lifetime, and one of them was sitting next to her.

Jackson slowed the pickup as he navigated the potholes in the road. "When was the last time you came down to the tracks?"

"The night before I left for college." When she'd brought Don home to meet her parents, she'd thought about visiting this spot, but hadn't wanted to bring her fiancé to the place that held special memories of another man. "What about you?"

"I came out once after I moved back." He stopped the truck, shifted into park and then turned off the engine. "I had to know if the tree was still here."

Their tree. The live oak they'd spent hours sitting beneath, talking. Kissing. The place where they'd said their final good-bye.

"How did you end up with Walter's wife?" she asked as they hiked along the path leading to the tracks.

"There's not much to the story." He took her hand and helped her step over a fallen branch. His grasp was as secure as she remembered, but his skin was rougher, the calluses thicker—as if her fingers held a coarse sanding block. Years of manual labor had left his knuckles covered in scars. After she cleared the branch, he released her hand and she curled her fingers into her palm, to keep the warmth of his touch from escaping.

"I see the path hasn't completely disappeared," she said.

"We weren't the first or the last teenagers to discover this spot." They walked through a wooded area filled with oak trees and pine, weeds, sparse grass and leftover trash from numerous drinking parties. As they emerged from the woods, memories of Jackson trying to impress her pulled her back in time.

She spotted the huge oak they'd carved their initials in and walked up to it. After a few seconds of searching, she found the *JM + KC* and traced her finger over the outline of the heart encircling the letters.

"Let me check for snakes."

She smiled. "I swear to you I saw a snake that day. I wasn't imagining it."

"When you screamed, I thought you'd found a dead body."

Jackson had gone to his car to fetch her sketch pad from the front seat. A minute after he'd left, a Western diamondback had slithered across the ground in front of Katelyn's foot and she'd shrieked like a banshee. Jackson had raced back to the tracks and when he'd burst through the trees, his tan face had been paler than his white T-shirt. He'd never said the words—in fact, the whole time they'd gone steady, he'd never confessed his feelings for her. But when she'd seen the abject fear in his eyes that afternoon, she'd known that he loved her.

Jackson kicked up a cloud of dust. "All clear."

Katelyn sat with her back against the trunk. "My mother never told me that you'd moved back to Little Springs."

"It took a while to find my way home." He joined her on the ground.

"Where were you all these years?"

"I worked the oil fields in North Dakota for a while. Did construction in California and Nevada. I was in Odessa when I ran into Vern and he told me Al planned to retire to Florida. I made Al an offer for the garage and he accepted."

"You own Al's Auto?"

"Mendoza Auto." He grinned. "Didn't you notice the new sign?"

"Sorry. I guess I wasn't paying attention when I drove through town."

"I'll never be rich, but I get enough business from folks in Pecos and Odessa to pay the bills."

"What happened to your father?" She knew his mother had run off when Jackson was a young boy.

"Dad left town a year after we graduated from high school. He hooked up with a woman named

Rosa and moved to Reno with her. I visited him once in a while, and we spoke on the phone every month. He passed away five years ago."

"Of what?"

"Cirrhosis of the liver."

Katelyn wasn't surprised. Everyone in Little Springs had known that Ricky Mendoza had had a drinking problem—it was the reason Jackson had never invited her over to his house. He'd worried his father would say or do something to embarrass her.

"Was your relationship any better with your father before he died?"

Jackson picked up a stone and threw it at the tracks. "He quit drinking before he passed away and apologized to me for being a crappy dad. I appreciated that."

Katelyn gathered her courage and said, "I owe you an apology, too."

"For what?" He brushed a speck of dirt from his jeans.

"I should have called you instead of writing to you," she said.

"It's not a big deal."

"You deserved better than a Dear Jackson letter."

"I've been treated worse."

She sprang to her feet and paced in front of him. "Don't make this easy on me."

"We've all done things we wish we hadn't."

"Like sleeping with Missy?" She groaned out loud and turned away from Jackson. What was the matter with her? She was acting like a jealous girlfriend.

"It was only one time."

"Once is enough to break up a marriage." How many times had Don slept with Lauren or whomever else before he'd decided to divorce Katelyn?

"I wasn't the first guy Missy cheated with, but Walter made sure I was the last."

"What happened?"

"I ran into her at Logan's Bar in Pecos. She made the first move." He raised his hand. "I realize that's no excuse, but I was drunk off my ass and I didn't care what the hell I did that night."

Didn't care? She stared at him, speechless. That wasn't the Jackson she'd dated in high school.

"You don't know, do you?" he asked.

"Know what?"

"I'm an alcoholic."

CHAPTER FOURTEEN

Jackson resisted squirming under Katelyn's steady stare. "I'm Ricky Mendoza's son. You can't be surprised." His father had drunk a twelve-pack each night before bed, then risen at five a.m. for work. He'd been a high-functioning alcoholic who hadn't seen the end coming until it was staring him in the face.

"You never drank around me." She sat back down.

"Your old man would have decked me if I'd showed up at your house wasted."

"How old were you when you began drinking?" Katelyn asked.

"I snuck my first beer when I was twelve."

"Did you drink a lot with your friends in high school?" Katelyn asked.

He lifted his shoulders as if he could shrug off the weight of their conversation. "I didn't have any friends."

"What about that Craig guy that used to hang out at the garage when you worked?"

"Craig stopped in when he wanted me to buy beer for him and his buddies." As soon as word got around that Jackson could charge beer to his father's account at Lenny's Liquorland in Pecos, he'd suddenly become everyone's friend. And because his father had taken numerous gambling trips to New Mexico, Jackson had been willing to do anything to keep from going home to an empty house—even party with kids who'd ridiculed him behind his back.

"Have you made many friends since buying the garage?"

"Before I joined AA, I stopped drinking on my own a few times, but eventually I'd end up at a bar with a buddy, thinking I could quit after one beer. Or two. Or three." He shoved a hand through his hair. "Having friends and staying sober didn't mix."

She slipped her hand into his as if she didn't trust him not to take off. "What made you finally give up alcohol?"

"Vern caught me the second time I ran into Missy at the bar."

"The minister was in a bar?"

"Walter went to Vern and asked for help finding Missy after she'd been gone for two days. The pair of them split up looking for her." Jackson stared into the distance, silently cursing himself for seeking out Katelyn. He'd thought they'd discuss her artwork, maybe her kids, his buying the garage, and then they'd wish each other a good life and go their separate ways. He hadn't expected to discuss his drinking or sex life.

"So Vern found you two in a bar?"

"He drove Missy home, then suggested she and Walter try marriage counseling."

"What kind of counseling did Vern recommend for you?"

"AA." He looked away from their entwined hands and thought of the nights he'd battled the urge to get out of bed at two a.m., drive to a bar and buy a drink to satisfy his craving. Those nights rarely happened now, but when they did, he'd close his eyes and imagine Katelyn holding his hand like she was doing now, and then the gnawing hunger would subside.

A tiny line formed between her eyebrows. "Talk about being a shitty girlfriend. I didn't even know my boyfriend was a drunk."

"If you'd found out I went home at night and got wasted with my old man, you'd have wanted nothing to do with me." He wished she'd quit staring at him with that wounded-puppy look on her face. "When I had a hangover, I skipped school the next day."

He pressed the pad of his thumb against the corner of her eye and caught the tear that escaped. "I'd promised myself I'd cut back on my drinking after you'd left for college. But then I got your letter." He released her hand and stood up. "I didn't give a damn after that."

"I should have called you or waited until I came home for a visit."

"You wrote that you wanted to focus on your art."

"I did."

"Did you break up with me because you met Don?"

"No. Don was in my English comp class the first semester of college, but he hadn't asked me out yet."

"Did you love him?" His gaze dropped to her ring finger. She still wore her wedding band and he wasn't sure what that meant.

"In the beginning, I did." She blew out a noisy breath. "I knew he could give me the life a small-town girl could only dream of."

And Jackson couldn't.

"I grew up a latchkey kid," she said, "watching my parents barely scrape by. I didn't want to turn into my mother, working at the Buy & Bag for the rest of my life. Don's family was wealthy. I knew we'd have their support if he and I fell on hard times."

"What happened to the perfect life he gave you?"

"I never said it was perfect." A whistle blast sounded and she scrambled to her feet and looked down the tracks. A locomotive's head-light as bright as the afternoon sun headed their way.

Katelyn turned back to Jackson. "Don cheated on me."

As much as it had hurt him to lose Katelyn, Jackson had always wanted her to be happy and he hated that her husband had been unfaithful. "Don's a fool."

She laughed, and the light returned to her eyes. In that instant she looked eighteen again. He stuffed his hands into his pockets to keep from reaching for her. It would be too easy to pretend they were still high school sweethearts.

The ground beneath their feet vibrated and Katelyn raised her voice to compete with the *clackety-clack* of the steel wheels grinding against the rails. "I've missed this."

"Missed what?" he shouted.

"Counting the boxcars."

Sixteen cars passed and then another whistle rent the air when the train crossed the bridge a quarter mile up the tracks. The rumbling sounds faded, leaving behind only the lingering scent of diesel.

She returned to their tree and sat. "Are you in a rush to leave?"

He shook his head and joined her on the ground, his shoulder bumping hers. "Have you ever been married?" she asked.

"Nope."

"Ever come close?"

He shook his head. Drinking had always been his mistress.

"Why didn't you try to change my mind when I broke up with you?"

He'd driven as far as Fort Worth the day after

he'd received the letter, but then he'd gotten cold feet and turned back. "Could I have changed your mind?"

She shook her head. "I would have picked Don eventually."

She'd made the right choice at the time. Jackson's drinking would have torn them apart.

"I'll never regret my marriage, because I can't imagine my life without Michael and Melissa."

"I never remember you as a mother—only as the young girl who took her sketch pad everywhere she went."

She patted his thigh. "Did any of your dreams come true?"

"Owning the garage is something I never pictured myself doing when I was younger." Jackson was very careful about what he wished for. His drinking had set him up for failure more times than success. "I try not to think about the future too much." It was safer living day to day.

Katelyn's gaze slipped to Jackson's mouth and he swore he heard her breath catch right before he brushed his lips across hers. He pulled away, but almost kissed her again when he read the disappointment in her eyes. "We needed to get that out of the way."

She laughed.

"Have you kept up with your art all these years?" he asked.

"I doodle here and there, but I haven't turned any of my sketches into paintings."

"Why not?"

"I got bogged down with everyday life." She leaned her head against the tree. "Those first baby years were tough. It was all I could do to find the energy to make it through the day, let alone find time to draw. When I finally caught my breath, Don began traveling more for work. The years flew by, and then, when the kids didn't need as much supervision, Don's father died and my mother-in-law moved in with us." She blinked. "Why are you looking at me like that?"

"Like what?"

"Like I'm a stranger."

"Art was your passion. It's what took you away from here." Away from him. "The Katelyn I knew would never have set her sketch pad aside for that long."

She opened her mouth, then snapped it closed.

"You used to talk about wanting to see your work hanging in art galleries," he said.

"I did say that, didn't I?"

"So what are you waiting for? Start sketching while you're visiting your mother."

"Inspiration doesn't flick on and off like a light switch. I can't just sit down and decide to draw a picture of"—she pointed to the tracks—"a train."

The wind kicked her hair off her shoulders, and

Jackson tucked a strand behind her ear. "You've got a gift. You shouldn't keep it from the world."

She stood. "I'd better get home before my mother and Shirley start a brawl."

They retraced their steps to the pickup. "What does your mother-in-law think about the divorce?" he asked once they buckled their seat belts.

"She wants Don and I to reconcile."

His fingers tightened around the gearshift in protest. "Any chance you might?"

"No. My marriage is over."

He glanced at her ring finger. "Good."

"Good?"

He nodded. "You can do better than Don."

And Katelyn could do better than him, too.

Jackson returned to the garage after dropping Katelyn off at Birdie's house. Vern was sitting on the couch, waiting. His AA sponsor looked worried.

"How'd it go?"

"Fine." Jackson wasn't surprised that Vern knew he'd gone off with Katelyn, given the town residents' gift for gossip.

"You're not thinking of picking up where you two left off while she's in town, are you?"

"We're catching up on old times, that's all."

Vern popped off the couch and paced across the floor. "You should keep your distance from her."

Maybe Vern was right. Today proved Jackson still cared about Katelyn, and that scared the crap out of him. He couldn't afford to allow anyone or anything to upset the status quo, because this time if he took a drink, he wouldn't lose only himself again—he'd also lose the garage.

It had taken Jackson a year of sobriety to accept that he alone was responsible for his drinking. He'd used alcohol not because Katelyn had dumped him, but because he couldn't change who he was—the kid from the other side of the tracks. With Vern's encouragement he'd returned to Little Springs to face his past and had carved out a niche for himself. So what if Katelyn's visit to town reminded him that his niche was lonely?

Alone was safer.

"Slow down before you wear a path in the cement floor," Jackson said. Something more than Jackson and Katelyn's meeting was bothering the old man. "What's wrong?"

Vern rubbed his hands over his face, then expelled a loud breath. "Abby says I should start dating."

"Do people your age date?" Jackson grinned.

"I'm old, but I'm not a corpse."

"Do you want to date?"

"Even if I did, there's no one to ask out. Elaine was friends with all the women in town."

Jackson glanced at the clock. "What do you

say we forget about women and grab a burger at Marty's up the road?"

"Sure." Vern's shoulders sagged.

The old man looked defeated. Jackson hated to see his sponsor so down, but better he focus on Vern's and Abby's problems than obsess over how good it had felt to sit with Katelyn beneath their oak tree, surrounded by her sweet scent and even sweeter memories.

CHAPTER FIFTEEN

Where are you off to this early?" Katelyn glanced suspiciously between Birdie and Shirley when the women waltzed into the kitchen at eight o'clock Tuesday morning. Katelyn and her mother-in-law had been in Little Springs over a week and this was the first time both mothers appeared in good spirits.

Shirley looked as if she was dressed for a day of shopping at Neiman Marcus: teal slacks, ivory blouse and sling-back sandals. Birdie wore her usual black cotton capri pants, Birkenstocks and a green Buy & Bag T-shirt.

"We're heading over to Sadie's," Birdie said.

Katelyn dumped the toast crumbs from her plate into the sink. "Neither one of you needs a haircut."

"It's the monthly meeting of the Little Springs Ladies' Society." Birdie rummaged through her purse.

"You mean the Widow-makers' Club," Katelyn said.

"Why would you call it that?" Shirley asked.

"Because once a woman joins, her husband expires shortly after." Katelyn looked at her mother. "You said Harriet's husband kicked the bucket a week after she came to her first meeting."

Shirley's eyes widened.

"Sadie's ex-husband died after she began going to the meetings, and he lived in Kansas at the time," Katelyn said.

Birdie stopped digging in her purse and looked at Katelyn. "I forgot about paying dues. Do you have ten dollars I can borrow? I didn't have a chance to drive over to the Texaco yesterday and use the ATM."

"I've got money." Shirley glanced around the kitchen. "Where's my purse?"

"Did you check the table by the front door?" Katelyn asked.

Shirley left the room, then a moment later called out, "It's not here."

"I swear I set the purse there last night before she went to bed," Katelyn said.

"I moved it," Birdie whispered.

"Why would you do that?"

"To see if she's faking her memory loss."

Katelyn groaned. "Where did you hide her bag?"

"I set it on the couch."

"Look on the sofa, Shirley," Katelyn called out, then scolded Birdie. "That wasn't nice."

Shirley returned to the kitchen with the purse, then removed her wallet and handed Birdie the cash.

"I'll pay you back," Birdie said.

"Nonsense," Shirley said. "It's the least I can do in return for your hospitality."

Hospitality? Sunday night the women had been ready to kill each other. And yesterday, after Jackson had dropped her off at the house, she'd caught the two arguing over Birdie's cooking. Shirley, in her typical way, had hinted that Birdie might shed a few pounds if she substituted low-fat versions of sour cream, butter and cheese in her recipes. Then the conversation had shifted to politics and Katelyn had escaped from the kitchen and fled to her room, where she'd stretched out on the bed and thought about Jackson—how familiar and strange it had felt being with him.

"You're not getting a perm today, are you, Shirley?" Katelyn asked.

"No, she's not," Birdie answered. "We ran into Sadie at Mama's Kitchen yesterday and she suggested a keratin conditioning treatment for Shirley's hair."

Her mother-in-law patted her frizzy curls. "I told Birdie she could take a decade off her looks if she colored her hair."

Birdie glared. "I said I'd think about it."

The grannies were getting along too well. It was only a matter of time before one of them imploded. "I'll come with you to the beauty shop," Katelyn said.

"What about work?" Birdie asked.

"I don't have to clock in at the store until ten."

"Let's go, then." Birdie walked out the back

door, Shirley dogging her heels. Katelyn grabbed her purse and followed the new *besties*.

They piled into Birdie's Taurus, Katelyn sitting in the backseat. She searched for a tube of lip gloss in her purse, but froze when her fingers bumped her sketch pad. How many countless afternoons had she sat by the tracks, waiting for a train to blow by? She'd daydreamed of jumping into an empty boxcar and riding to the next town and then the one after that and the one after that . . . until she found a place where the lights were brighter, the sounds crisper and the rhythm of life richer.

Katelyn had left Little Springs believing that her artistic talent would guide her down the path to a life where she would want for nothing. Then she'd married Don and there was no longer a sense of urgency when she sat down to draw. Although she'd still possessed a desire to paint, the driving need to hone her craft had faded over time, leaving her unmotivated.

Her fingers curled into her palms. Whom was she kidding? The sketch pad she carried in her purse was meant to cajole her into believing she hadn't abandoned her artistic self, but it couldn't be further from the truth. Was the young girl who'd left Little Springs eager to make her mark on the world one sketch at a time still inside her?

"Here we are." Birdie pulled up to a metal storage shed, squeezing between a sedan and a beat-up Chevy truck missing its tailgate. The sign hanging across the front of the shed read SADIE'S HAIR SALON~I DIPPITY-DO FOR YOU.

"I didn't know she moved her shop out to the backyard," Katelyn said. The last time Sadie had trimmed her hair had been before her father's funeral and Katelyn had sat in a styling chair on the back porch. The porch was still there, as were the washer and dryer and the worn leather recliner that Sadie liked to sit in at night and smoke her cigarettes.

"Wait until you see the inside of the shed," Birdie said. "Sadie's got it fixed up real nice."

Katelyn held the door open for the mothers and then followed them into the salon.

"'Bout time you ladies showed up." Sadie's bright pink lips stretched into a smile. "It's been too long, honey." She hugged Katelyn. The beauty shop owner was an older version of Layla—big boobs and lots of makeup. If not for the deep parenthesis lines bracketing her mouth and her platinum blond hair, people might mistake her and Layla for sisters. "I'm so glad you've come back to Little Springs." The stylist made it sound as if Katelyn had moved home for good.

"This is real nice, Sadie." The scent of spearmint and eucalyptus permeated the air, a nice change from the chemical odors Katelyn breathed in at the Savvy Salon back in St. Louis.

Her gaze skipped around the room. A zebra-print rug covered the cement floor, and a pair of black-and-white striped chairs, a black faux-leather couch and a black lacquer coffee table covered with gossip magazines composed the waiting area. A styling chair sat across the room next to a standing dryer.

"Got that on eBay." Sadie pointed to the zebra head hanging on the wall. "Goes with the color scheme."

"Is this your daughter, Birdie?" a lady wearing a bright yellow outfit asked.

"This is Katelyn and her mother-in-law, Shirley Pratt." Birdie waved a hand at the couch, where the lady in yellow sat next to a woman who wore the same polo shirt and Bermuda shorts but in blue. "Etta and Faye. They're twins. Etta wears yellow and Faye likes blue."

"Nice to meet you, ladies," Katelyn said. "Have you lived in Little Springs long?"

The blue twin spoke. "We moved here five years ago from El Paso. Etta and I are retired librarians."

"We live in town but spend a lot of time at the Sutton farm raising organic vegetables," Etta said.

"Neither of us has ever been married," Faye said. "We chose to devote our lives to literacy."

Etta beamed. "We're the book-club coordinators for the ladies' society."

Book club? Katelyn couldn't recall ever having seen her mother read a book. Etta must have guessed her thoughts, because she said, "It's a work in progress."

Birdie waved at one of the few African-Americans living in Little Springs. "You remember Harriet. Her husband, Zeke, worked with your dad at the lake."

"Hello, Harriet."

"Glad you found your way home." Harriet adjusted the rainbow-colored silk scarf around her neck, the silver bangles on her wrist clanking loudly before she folded her hands in the lap of her colorful bohemian skirt.

"This is Nanette, Clara Smith's daughter," Birdie said. "She's a nurse at the health clinic in Pecos. She moved here after Clara drove her car through the front window of Gifford's Resale last year."

Nanette smiled. "Don't worry. I've taken away my mother's car keys."

The sly old lady must have a second set hidden somewhere. Yesterday Clara had driven her Lincoln to the grocery store and left it parked in the crosswalk in front of the entrance, keys in the ignition and the motor running. Walter had rushed outside to move the car.

"And Mavis." Birdie pointed to a short, stocky woman who could pass for a drill sergeant. "You remember meeting her son, Scott, at your father's funeral."

No, Katelyn didn't. "What's Scott been up to?"

"The usual. Nothing." Mavis's loose jowls reminded Katelyn of a bulldog.

Nanette offered a sympathetic smile. "Scott's been diagnosed with adult ADD."

Mavis bared her teeth. "Also known as good-for-nothing lazy-ass syndrome."

"And last but not least is Doris." Birdie smiled at the frail-looking woman perched on the end of the couch.

"We're celebrating Birdie's birthday tomorrow at Doris's house." Faye's gaze swung between Shirley and Katelyn.

"Don't worry," Birdie said. "I plan on bringing Shirley. But Katelyn's working."

"I'll stop by the party when I get off," Katelyn said.

"While you all discuss plans for Birdie's party, I'll start Shirley's keratin conditioning treatment." Sadie patted Katelyn's head. "Your hair could use a little TLC, too. An avocado mask would bring back the shine."

"Sure. Why not?" Katelyn said.

It took five minutes to wash and rinse Katelyn's hair and apply the mask. After Sadie covered the wet strands with a plastic cap, Katelyn took her avocado-smelling head back to the couch and eavesdropped on the women's conversations. Without being conscious of her actions, she opened her doodle pad and began sketching. Her pencil flew over the paper, fast and furious, each stroke fueling a slow-building fire in the pit of her stomach. After several minutes she flipped the page and began another drawing, feeling the heat in her gut spread into her chest, then break off and trail down her arms and legs.

With her eyes glued to the group, her hand moved of its own will across the paper. It had been ages since she'd experienced the thrill of capturing and preserving a living, breathing moment in time.

Katelyn flipped to a clean page and studied Nanette. This woman was the peacekeeper, jumping in when tempers flared. Her eyes moved to Mavis's face—her mouth turned down at the corner, but the twinkle in her eyes convinced Katelyn that her grouchy personality was mostly an act. Etta and Faye liked to toss around big words and show off their education. Harriet was the observer—her eyes didn't miss a thing, not even Katelyn sketching. She contributed little to the conversation, but when a debate needed to be settled, Harriet had the final word. Doris smiled and giggled, finding everything amusing. And then there was Birdie.

Katelyn's mother made sure everyone had what they needed. When Harriet squirmed in her seat, Birdie handed her a throw pillow to help support her back. When Faye fanned her face with a magazine, Birdie fetched a bottle of water from the mini fridge behind the door. When Doris made a move to stand up, Birdie offered her hand.

As Katelyn watched Birdie look after the other women, it occurred to her that she and her mother shared the same need to take care of others. Yet Birdie insisted Shirley wasn't Katelyn's responsibility, which only supported Katelyn's belief that her mother was jealous of the attention her daughter showed Shirley. Katelyn had a lot to make up for once her divorce from Don was final.

Her hand wasn't even tired when Sadie interrupted her a half hour later. "Time to rinse." Katelyn followed her to the sink next to the styling chair, where Shirley flipped through a magazine.

"What's this I hear about you getting divorced?" Sadie asked.

Before Katelyn opened her mouth to respond, Shirley spoke. "I told Katelyn that marriages are full of little ups and downs." Shirley set the magazine aside. "Katelyn will work things out with my son."

Did Shirley really believe that?

"In this day and age if a woman wants to keep her husband's attention, she needs to take care of herself." Shirley pointed at Katelyn. "You're still attractive for your age, but you could use a little snip here and there."

"Nonsense." Sadie turned off the water and wrapped a towel around Katelyn's head. "Your daughter-in-law is beautiful." Sadie propped her hands on her hips. "Has your son kept himself up all these years?"

"Don's very well-groomed and his wardrobe is impeccable."

"So in other words," Sadie said, "he's put on a few pounds, too."

"It's hardly noticeable," Shirley said.

Katelyn bit her tongue to keep from adding a comment about Don's receding hairline.

"However things work out, I hope you're happy." Sadie fluffed Katelyn's damp hair. "Want me to blow-dry it?"

"No, thanks." She wrapped an elastic band around the strands. "I'm heading straight to work from here."

"I've been begging Katelyn to try a new hairstyle for years," Shirley said. "Don't you agree, Sadie, that long hair should only be worn by younger women?"

"Are you saying that my hair doesn't look good on me?" Sadie pointed to her blond locks.

Katelyn intervened before Shirley dug herself a deeper hole. "I'm not *that* old," she said.

"Your mid-forties are right around the corner. It takes a few years to experiment with styles before you find one that's classic and time-less."

"I do believe a woman's hair says something about her." Sadie pinched a strand of Shirley's hair between her fingers. "How long have you been wearing your hair like Betty White?"

Shirley gasped, and Katelyn coughed to cover her smile.

"Don't get excited. Betty's hair has made her millions over the years, but believe me, it's not going to make you any money."

Katelyn expected Shirley to march out the door, but her mother-in-law surprised her by asking, "How would you cut my hair?"

Sadie picked at Shirley's bangs. "I'd get rid of the curls. Spike the ends up. Maybe change the color and add a few darker highlights so you don't look so washed-out."

"I vote to lose the curls, too." Birdie's voice carried across the room.

Mavis walked over to the styling chair. "If you get rid of the curls at the back of your neck, you could get a tattoo like mine." She turned around to show Shirley.

"What is that?" Shirley asked.

"A turtle," Mavis said. "What did you think it was?"

"It looks like a toddler scribbled on your skin with Crayola markers." Shirley made a move to escape the chair, but Mavis blocked her exit.

"Ladies," Katelyn said, "will you give me a minute with my mother-in-law?"

Sadie led Mavis back to the group.

"Curls are classic," Shirley said. "I don't

understand why Sadie wants to get rid of them."

"You're the one who's always telling others how to wear their hair, but when someone suggests a new style for you, suddenly they don't know what they're talking about." Katelyn pointed to the women. "Sadie's only two years younger than you."

"Really?"

"Yep, but you'd never guess, would you?"

Shirley shook her head.

"It's not having long hair that makes Sadie look younger—it's how that long hair makes her feel when she looks in the mirror."

"What do you mean?"

"Sadie's hairstyle makes her happy, and when she's happy, she smiles a lot. When she's smiling, people don't see the wrinkles around her eyes—they see the twinkle in them."

Shirley's gaze followed Sadie around the room.

"I think Sadie believes a sassier haircut and a bit of color will make you smile more."

Shirley studied her fingernails, then pulled in a deep breath and looked past Katelyn. "Sadie, come back here and cut off my curls."

Katelyn squeezed Shirley's hand. "I have to get to work." She collected her things, then walked over to her mother and whispered, "If Shirley hates the haircut, call me and I'll find somewhere else to sleep tonight."

CHAPTER SIXTEEN

Katelyn cut through Sadie's yard, stopping to sniff a yellow bloom on the rosebush along the side of the house. In Victorian times the yellow rose symbolized jealousy and infidelity, but on this sunny day Katelyn chose to believe in its modern-day representation of joy, friendship and affection.

With the lingering scent of citrus in her head, she continued down the sidewalk, her gaze swinging from side to side, seeing her hometown in a different light. She passed the park where she'd hung out with friends, and noticed the black-eyed Susans were still there baking in the hot sun.

Across the street an ugly gray cat licked its paw as if it didn't have a care in the world. She cut through the parking lot of the shopping center, where a man's shoe rested next to the Dumpster behind the hardware store. Who had left it behind? For the second day in a row the same motor home sat in front of the Buy & Bag. Did it belong to a family? A retired couple? How many miles across this country had the RV traveled?

Why had Katelyn believed there'd been nothing of value to sketch in Little Springs? All kinds of ideas came to mind as she hurried to the grocery store, and she scolded herself for making excuses not to draw.

The Entenmann's delivery truck sat parked by the loading dock in the alley and as she walked by, Brian stumbled out of the vehicle, shoving the tail of his blue short-sleeved shirt inside his navy shorts.

"Didn't you deliver a bunch of Whoopie Pies yesterday?" Katelyn asked, noticing the way he avoided eye contact with her.

Right then Layla stepped into view and smoothed her hands down her wrinkled work smock.

Keeping a straight face, Katelyn held the back door of the Buy & Bag open and whispered, "You'll want to fix your false eyelash." The long black fringe stuck to Layla's eyebrow. "It looks like you've got a centipede crawling across your face."

Layla checked her reflection in the mirror inside her locker.

"Dare I ask what you two were doing in the back of the delivery truck?"

"We had our first kiss."

"That must have been some kiss if it knocked your eyelash off."

Layla smiled. "He'll get better with practice."

"I thought you were waiting for your knight in shining armor to whisk you away from Little Springs."

"I am."

"Then why are you and Brian kissing?"

"Abby's right. He's a nice guy." Layla flipped her hair over her shoulders. "Brian is Mr. Right Now. I'm still waiting for Mr. Forever."

"You're using him?" As soon as the words left Katelyn's mouth, she wished she could call them back. She was a hypocrite—love hadn't been the sole reason she'd married Don.

"I made it very clear that we can only be friends," Layla said.

"You two ready to clock in?" Walter poked his head through the doorway. "Abby could use some help. We're backing up at the registers."

Layla shook her head after Walter disappeared. "Backing up means three people waiting in line."

"Are you going to introduce Brian to Gavin?"

"I invited him to Gavin's soccer game tonight." Layla raised a hand. "I know I said Brian is Mr. Right Now, but I don't think Mr. Forever will find me anytime soon. No matter what happens between me and Brian down the road, he's the kind of guy who'd make a great friend, and I see him hanging out with me and Gavin a lot." Layla closed the locker. "Why don't you bring Birdie and your mother-in-law to the game? Abby will be there with her father."

"That sounds like fun." Maybe Katelyn would find inspiration for a future painting.

• • •

"Isn't it too hot to sit outside and watch a soccer game?"

Katelyn ignored her mother's burning stare and wished she were strangling Shirley's neck and not the steering wheel. Shirley hadn't stopped complaining since they'd left the house twenty minutes ago. "The sun will set soon." Because of the heat, summer sports events were held at night beneath the lights.

She turned into the community center in Pecos. For a small-town soccer game, the lot was crowded. They piled out of the car and Katelyn couldn't help staring at Shirley's hair. The spiked style and the reddish blond color were a shocker.

"You don't like it?" Shirley touched her head self-consciously.

"I do like it," Katelyn said. "I never pictured you as a redhead, but the color complements your complexion."

Shirley's face brightened.

Guilt jolted Katelyn. She'd been at odds with her mother-in-law for years and rarely flattered her. Maybe if she'd made more of an effort to say something nice about her once in a while, the two of them would have gotten along better.

"Ginny says the style makes me look younger."

"She's right." Katelyn ignored Birdie's snort as they walked over to the bleachers. "I see Abby." She pointed to her coworker in the stands.

"Vern's with her." Birdie looked at Shirley. "Vern's a minister. His wife, Elaine, passed away from breast cancer around Christmastime last year."

"Glad you could make it to the game," Abby said when Katelyn stopped at their seats. She smiled at Shirley. "You must be Katelyn's mother-in-law."

"Shirley Pratt."

Vern stood, then offered his hand to Shirley. "Vern Wilkes." He moved down on the bench and motioned for Shirley to sit next to him. "I bet Little Springs is boring as apple pie for someone from St. Louis."

"I wouldn't say boring, but the town is quiet."

"I saw you eating at Ginny's with Birdie the other day," he said, "and you were a blonde. I've always been partial to redheads."

Shirley blushed. "You don't think it's too short, do you?"

"The style is very becoming." Vern leaned closer. "I've also always been partial to sassy women."

Shirley opened her mouth, then snapped it closed. She'd finally met someone who rendered her speechless.

"I can't remember the last time a high-society lady like yourself visited our town," he said.

Shirley sat up straighter and patted the air around her head. It would take time for her to get used to losing her puffy hair.

"I heard you met the Little Springs Ladies' Society this morning," Abby said.

Shirley shot Birdie the evil eye. "I'm lucky I didn't leave Sadie's salon bald."

Vern tipped his head back and laughed. "I appreciate a woman who tells it like it is."

Birdie and Abby quirked their eyebrows at each other and Katelyn sensed the two had hatched a secret plan without speaking a word.

"I'm hungry for a hot dog." Vern stood. "Can I get you ladies anything from the concession stand?" When no one spoke up, he looked at Shirley. "Maybe a soft pretzel?"

"No, thank you."

"You're not worried about your waistline, are you?" he said.

Shirley gaped at Vern.

"You're a little on the slender side." He smiled.

After Vern left the stands, Birdie nudged Shirley. "I told you that men appreciate a woman with some meat on her bones."

"I shouldn't have allowed Sadie to cut my hair," Shirley said. "This style makes me look like a hussy."

"I've had short hair since Katelyn turned three," Birdie said, "and no man has ever called me a hussy."

"That's because you don't wear any makeup. If not for your bosom, men wouldn't know that you're a lady."

Katelyn sucked in a sharp breath.

"You don't think I'm a lady?" Birdie leaned around Abby and raised her voice. "I'll drop my drawers and show you my cooter."

The giggling teenagers two rows away turned to stare and Katelyn wanted to fall through the crack in the bleachers.

"That's disgusting, Birdie," Shirley said.

"Disgusting is you thinking you're better than everyone else."

Abby stood. "I'll see if my father needs help."

At this rate Birdie and Shirley's bickering would empty the stands before the end of the first soccer period.

Shirley poked a finger in her chest. "I'm the only one who has any class in this . . . this . . . shantytown."

What happened to Shirley and Birdie being best buds the past few days? Katelyn handed Birdie a twenty. "Go buy us some nachos."

"Spicy food is bad for my digestion," Shirley said.

"What's the matter? You afraid you might break wind?" Birdie stormed off.

"Your mother can be so crass. It's no wonder you wanted to leave this place."

"Be careful what you say about my mother and my hometown." No one in Little Springs had a pedigree like the Pratt family, but Birdie's neighbors and friends were decent, caring people.

181

Shirley jutted her chin. "I want to go back to St. Louis. Tomorrow."

"On my mother's birthday?"

"She won't care."

Katelyn's gaze zeroed in on Birdie chatting with Vern at the snack shack. Her proud mother would never admit it, but taking a break from the Buy & Bag had lifted her spirits. Since Katelyn and Shirley had arrived eight days ago, Birdie had been acting more energetic and upbeat than at any other time when she'd visited her. The thought of her mother having to go back to work bothered Katelyn in a way it hadn't before. Birdie had held down a full-time job her entire adult life, while her daughter had lived in the lap of luxury.

"I don't care about your mother's birthday party," Shirley said. "I have nothing in common with her friends."

Katelyn stared Shirley in the eye. "I thought you were enjoying getting to know the ladies' society."

"They're unsophisticated and boring."

Birdie and her friends were far from perfect, but Shirley was no prize, either. "They might not use their manners all the time or shop at Dillard's and Nordstrom, but they have each other's back when things go wrong. Where were your friends after Robert died?"

Shirley pretended to follow the play on the

soccer field. "Successful people lead busy lives."

Bull.

Birdie returned with a tray of nachos and convinced Shirley to eat one. Katelyn exhaled a sigh of relief when the two women engaged in a civil conversation. Layla waved at Katelyn from several rows away where she sat with Brian. They made a cute couple—maybe with time Layla would give Brian the chance he deserved.

Speaking of men who deserved second chances . . . Katelyn's gaze skipped across the field and landed on Jackson, who stood behind the perimeter fence. She nudged her mother. "Why is Jackson here?"

Birdie looked across the field. "He comes to most of the games like everyone else in Little Springs."

So why wasn't he sitting in the stands? His baseball cap shielded his eyes from view, but Katelyn sensed he was watching her and not the game. She reached for the sketch pad in her purse. Birdie and Shirley's conversation faded along with the cheers of the spectators. Only the *skitch-skitch* sounds of the pencil dragging across the pad resonated in her mind.

Jackson stood in the shadows, looking lonely and isolated. The tip of her pencil pressed harder against the paper as if sheer willpower could draw him into the stadium light spilling onto the field. Then without warning he turned and walked to his pickup, parked on the side of the road.

Her pencil froze.

Only after the red taillights disappeared from view did Katelyn sense someone else watching her. She glanced through the crowd and her gaze collided with Vern's. His assessing stare carried a message she couldn't decipher.

"What's going on between you and Jackson?" Birdie whispered.

Katelyn looked at her mother. "Nothing. Why?"

"You were down by the tracks with him."

"Are you having me followed?"

"Mr. Petty saw Jackson's pickup parked on the dirt road behind the tracks."

"We were catching up, Mom."

"Exactly how far do you two plan to catch up while you're here?"

Katelyn wasn't used to Birdie poking around in her business. She couldn't very well confess that before she'd drifted off to sleep last night, she'd fantasized about having a hot, messy fling with her former boyfriend.

"Jackson's not the same young man you had a crush on in high school."

"He told me about his drinking."

"Then you know he followed in his father's footsteps."

"Jackson's not like his dad. He stopped drinking." *Cut the guy some slack. He had a tough childhood.*

"Whether he takes a drink or not, he's still an alcoholic," Birdie said. "You should focus on the future rather than relive your past." She tapped a finger against the pad in Katelyn's hand. "This is the first time I've seen you draw since you left for college."

"I don't know what's gotten into me lately, but I have this insane urge to sketch everything I see."

"You always wanted to have your work in an art gallery. Maybe you should turn those sketches into paintings."

"First I need to figure out what I'm going to do after the divorce."

Birdie's smile faltered. "Don't end up like your mother."

"You mean having to get a job and work?"

"No, I mean don't give up on your dreams."

CHAPTER SEVENTEEN

Wednesday morning Katelyn's son phoned as she stepped onto the back porch. "Hi, honey. Did you call to wish Grandma Chandler a happy birthday?"

"Is Dad serious? Are you guys getting divorced?"

Katelyn sat down on the steps. "When did you speak to your father?"

"A few minutes ago."

How nice of Don to break the news to his kids on their grandmother's birthday. "It's true."

"What happened? I thought you two were happy. It's not like you ever argued or anything."

Obviously Don hadn't had the guts to tell Michael that he'd cheated on his mother. "Your father is having an affair."

"No way!"

The outrage in Michael's voice warmed Katelyn's heart. She had no intention of bad-mouthing Don in front of the kids, but their children deserved the truth. "I didn't find out until I received the divorce papers in the mail."

"He didn't talk to you first?"

"No. A courier delivered the legal document to the house." Katelyn stared at her left hand. Her marriage was over even if she hadn't yet signed the papers. But if she took off the ring, would others believe she was looking for another man? Then again, why did she care what anyone thought?

"I can't believe Dad cheated on you. Are you okay?"

"I'm going to be fine. I don't want you to worry about me."

"Dad said the house sold already and our stuff will be moved to storage somewhere."

"I'll keep all of your things, including the bedroom furniture. You can get it whenever you want."

"What are you going to do? It's not like you can go out and get a job somewhere."

Katelyn's hackles rose. "I'm not helpless."

"You've never had a job."

"Your dad will make sure I'm taken care of financially while I figure out my next steps."

"Are you staying in St. Louis or living with Grandma Chandler now?"

"I'm not sure, but I have time to decide. Listen, no worrying about me. I mean it. Focus on your studies and enjoy college."

"Is Grandma Chandler upset with Dad?"

"She feels bad about what's happening."

"Grandma never liked him."

"Did she say that?"

"No, but I could tell by the way she looked at him."

Kids saw a lot more than they let on.

"Dad said Grandma Pratt's moving into an apartment near the house."

"Your father hired a caretaker to check on her every day. She'll be fine."

"She's going to be lonely. She's used to having you around."

"It will be an adjustment for all of us."

"What's Grandma Pratt been up to?"

"Tonight she's going to Grandma Chandler's birthday party."

"What are you doing down there?"

"I've been sketching."

"Cool."

It was cool. "And I'm working Grandma Chandler's hours at the grocery store. She's enjoying a break from standing on her feet all day."

"That sucks."

Katelyn laughed. "It's not so bad. The ladies at the store are nice."

"Dad told me not to talk to or text Melissa until he tells her."

"When does he plan to do that?"

"He didn't say, but she's gonna flip a shit." Michael expelled a loud breath. "Why did Dad have to go and ruin our family?"

"We're still a family, Michael. That will never change. This isn't what I wanted for you and your sister, but we'll get through this. And remember I'm always here if you need to talk."

"My friends will ask why my parents are splitting up. What am I supposed to say?"

Katelyn hurt for her son. "It's up to you how much or how little you tell them."

"It'll be weird seeing you guys separately."

"We'll figure it out as we go."

"Mom?"

"What?"

"Thanks for always being there for me and Melissa."

Katelyn's eyes burned. "I love you, honey." Time to change the subject. "So what's new in your life?"

"I went out on a date last night."

"Tell me about her."

"It was only a first date, Mom."

"What's her name? How did you meet?"

Michael rambled on about a girl named Sloan from Dearborn, Michigan. He'd met her at the pool in his apartment complex. Sloan was really cute. She was a sophomore and a nursing student.

Katelyn thought back to the first time Don had asked her out on a date. He'd turned bright red with embarrassment, which she'd found charming. He'd impressed her when he'd taken her to a swanky restaurant and paid with his own credit card. While they ate dessert, he'd regaled her with stories about the countries he and his parents had traveled to. A week later he'd shown up at her dorm with a beautiful, expensive art easel and he'd won her over.

"Sloan sounds like a nice girl," Katelyn said when Michael paused to take a breath.

"What am I supposed to do this Christmas if I don't have a house to come home to?"

"You'll have an invite somewhere. And remember—home isn't a house; it's the people you love."

"Mom?"

"What?"

"You're really okay?"

"I'm fine." She had to be, for the sake of her kids.

"Text me if you need to talk," he said.

Katelyn smiled. "I will. You want to speak to your grandma now?"

"Sure. I'll wish her a happy birthday."

"Hang on." Katelyn walked across the yard to the shed, where the door stood open. "Mom, it's Michael." She handed off the phone, then returned to the porch. A few minutes later, Birdie hollered for Katelyn.

"Come give me a hand, will you?"

Katelyn returned to the shed and poked her head inside. "Happy birthday."

Her mother ignored the greeting. "Michael's worried about you."

"I hope you said I was okay."

"I told him that you're one of the strongest women I know."

She was strong when it came to advocating for others, but not so much herself. She'd always made sure everyone was taken care of. Now it was her turn to focus on herself so that her kids wouldn't worry about her.

She pointed to the mess her mother was making. "Why are you organizing the shed on your birthday?"

"I'm looking for my guitar."

"What guitar?"

Her mother pushed a box aside. "The one I played when I sang you to sleep at night."

"I don't remember you singing to me."

"I stopped playing when you were three." Birdie leaned over a box. "I can't reach it."

"Let me."

Birdie wiped her face on the hem of her T-shirt. "The guitar case is behind the Christmas bins."

Katelyn lifted the heavy carton and placed it on top of another. Her mother was a pack rat. "What else besides Christmas decorations do you have stored in these bins?"

"Your father's fishing gear, his camping equipment and his bears."

Katelyn's dad had collected little wooden statues of bears.

"I'm keeping his things in case Michael and Melissa want any of them."

"I see it." Katelyn reached behind the sign advertising Santa Claus Lane and grabbed the battered case.

When she handed it over, Birdie left the shed and returned to the porch, where she sat down and pulled out the guitar. Her fingers caressed the strings. "It's a Martin D-35 made in 1976."

"That thing looks huge in your hands," Katelyn said.

"It's a larger guitar than some, but the high and low sounds on it are beautiful."

"Play something."

After a couple of false starts her mother's fingers plucked the strings, and real music filled the air. "That was beautiful, Mom. What's the name of that song?"

"I didn't give it a title."

"You wrote the music?"

"I did."

"How old were you when you started taking music lessons?"

"I taught myself," Birdie said.

Like mother, like daughter. Katelyn had never taken art lessons when she'd been younger.

"I was thirteen when I knew I wanted to sing in Nashville."

Her mother had wanted to escape her childhood home as much as Katelyn had. Birdie had grown up an only child of older parents on a farm near Wallace, Kansas. Grandma Ada had died of a heart attack when Katelyn was seven years old, and on the way out of town after the funeral, they'd stopped at a convalescent home to visit Katelyn's grandfather, who'd suffered a stroke a year earlier. That was the last time she'd seen her grandfather.

"So that's why the kitchen radio is always tuned to a country station."

"When I was a teenager," Birdie said, "I'd try to mimic the songs on my guitar."

"What happened to your dream of going to Nashville?"

"I met your father and became pregnant with you."

Katelyn had known her mother had been three months pregnant when she'd married her father, but she hadn't known what her mother had given up to keep Katelyn.

"Couldn't you have continued singing?"

Birdie quit strumming the instrument. "Your father put in a lot of overtime, but he didn't make enough money for us to afford our own home, so I had to work, too."

"You could have written songs and played in your spare time."

"You mean the same way you've painted in your spare time while raising the twins?"

Touché.

"Is that why you didn't protest when I went out of state to college?"

A watery film covered her mother's eyes. "I wanted you to follow your dream and not end up like me, always pondering what would have happened if I'd kept playing."

Katelyn picked at a piece of peeling paint on the step. She could only imagine how disappointed her mother had been all these years, knowing Katelyn had stopped painting. "It's not too late to play the guitar again."

"I'm sixty." Birdie laughed. "What's a woman my age going to do with a few lovin'-and-leavin' songs?"

"Perform at local bars," Katelyn said.

Her mother plucked a guitar string. "I haven't written music in decades."

"If you need inspiration for a new song"— Katelyn pointed at the back door—"she's sitting inside at the kitchen table, picking the raisins out of an English muffin."

Birdie winked. "Maybe I can come up with a short little get-even ditty."

"Thanks for coming in," Abby said Wednesday evening when Katelyn walked up to the register. "It's been dead as a doornail since seven thirty, but Walter has a rule that two people have to close when he's not here."

"Where's Layla?" Katelyn asked.

"Brian took her and Gavin to the movies in Odessa. Gavin's been wanting to see the latest

194

Star Wars movie and Brian said he wanted to see it, too."

"That's two nights in a row they've been together. Any chance Layla will change her mind about him?"

"I doubt it." Abby reached beneath her counter for the glass cleaner and paper towels. "Speaking of soccer games, my father really enjoyed chatting with your mother-in-law last night."

Vern had entertained Shirley for most of the soccer game with stories about the different congregations he'd been involved with and the quirky people he'd met through the years. "I think Shirley enjoyed herself."

"Will you wipe down the doors while I stock the checkouts?" Abby handed over the cleaning supplies.

"What's Walter up to tonight?" Katelyn asked.

"He wouldn't say, but last month I caught him using a dating site on the office computer. Maybe he's out with one of his connections." Abby opened a box of candy bars and found a spot for them next to the register.

Katelyn wiped the fingerprints off the doors, then restocked the plastic bags at the end of the checkout counters. "Tell me about your father," Katelyn said.

"My mom was his second wife. The first one divorced him when he started drinking. He'd been sober about a year when he met my mother, and she was a decade younger than him when they married." Abby waved a hand before her face. "After Mom died, Jackson phoned and said he was worried about my father."

"Jackson contacted you?"

"He said Dad had fallen off the wagon and that's when he told me that my father was his AA sponsor." Abby shrugged. "All that AA stuff is supposed to be kept secret, but that's impossible to do in a small town like Little Springs."

Katelyn was glad Jackson had Vern looking out for him.

"I arrived here, thinking I'd only stay a few weeks," Abby said.

"But your dad wouldn't stop drinking?"

"No, he's remained sober, but he's lonely. I think he needs a companion. Someone to tell him where to go and what to do like my mother did."

"Has he dated since your mother passed?"

Abby shook her head. "I invited him to live with me in Dallas, but he doesn't want to leave Jackson or the other members of the group."

"What are you going to do?"

Abby replaced an empty candy box with Tic Tacs. "When I threatened to leave town, Dad got teary-eyed and I dropped the subject."

"I wish I could help," Katelyn said.

Abby smiled. "Maybe you can."

"How?"

"After watching Shirley and my father at the soccer game, I'm certain that my dad likes her."

A red flag went up inside Katelyn's head. "Maybe you're mistaking like for amusement." No one *liked* Shirley.

"Nothing ventured, nothing gained," Abby said. "Will you find an excuse to bring your mother-in-law by the house when Dad's home?"

"I don't think this is a good idea."

"Why not?"

"She's not interested in dating." At least not anyone she deemed beneath her.

"Sadie said Shirley's been a widow for three years. She's probably as lonely as my father."

Katelyn hadn't given any thought to Shirley being lonely after she'd moved in with them in St. Louis, but she supposed it was possible even for someone as ornery as her mother-in-law to miss having a companion to do things with. "Your father is a down-to-earth, nice man, but Shirley's . . ."

"Snooty?" Abby laughed. "She's exactly what my father needs to pull him out of his funk." Abby deposited the empty candy boxes in the recycle bin next to Walter's office. "When are you and Shirley leaving town?"

Katelyn hadn't decided yet. "We'd only planned to stay a couple of weeks."

"Then we have to hurry."

"Maybe we should give it a little more thought."

Katelyn still wasn't sold on the matchmaking idea.

"I'm desperate. I've put my life on hold long enough."

"Have you tried using a little tough love with your father and returning to Dallas without him?" Katelyn winced. Where was her tough love when she'd allowed Shirley to tag along on her trip home? "Or you could create a profile for your dad on a dating site."

Abby ignored the suggestion and glanced at the store clock. "It's almost nine. Let's lock up." She handed Katelyn the keys to the front doors. Five minutes later Abby turned on the security lighting and checked the bathrooms to make sure no customers were left inside.

"Got any plans tonight?" Abby tossed her smock into the locker.

"Nothing exciting." She hoped to finish the drawing she'd begun of the Little Springs Ladies' Society meeting at Sadie's beauty shop yesterday. "I'm heading over to Doris's house to stop in at Mom's birthday party."

"I forgot about Birdie's birthday."

"What do they do at these parties?" Katelyn asked.

"I think they play cards and drink sangria."

"Sounds harmless enough." Katelyn grabbed her purse and they left through the back door.

"Fancy car," Abby said when she saw the Mercedes.

"My mother-in-law likes to show off."

"Sure I can't talk you into setting her up with my father?"

"Not a chance." She doubted even a servant of God could survive a date with Shirley Pratt.

CHAPTER EIGHTEEN

Katelyn drove Shirley's Mercedes through town and then turned the corner at Gifford's Resale. Doris's ranch house sat in the middle of the block next to a vacant lot. She pulled up to the mailbox—a metal container covered in a rainbow of colored seashells. The maritime-styled box sat perched on a wooden post cemented into a Home Depot paint bucket. In place of the postal flag, an aqua blue mermaid with sparkly blond hair waited to be raised in the air.

Light poured through the house windows, spilling across the front lawn. A fence with several missing pickets kept Doris's collection of plaster of Paris wildlife from escaping. A family of gnomes watched over the animals, their little faces peeking above the blades of grass. The flock of miniature flamingos shared the flower bed with a mama skunk and her three babies. Not far away a plastic deer missing its left ear rested with a family of raccoons near a tree stump.

Overgrown oleander bushes hid half the porch, and not until Katelyn reached the front door did she notice the miniature garden—an assortment of tin coffee cans containing potted plants. Katelyn knocked. No one answered. She tried the knob, but the door was locked. She walked around the house and discovered the back door cracked open. Raucous laughter met her ears when she stepped into the empty kitchen.

"Your turn to say something nice about the birthday girl." Mavis's deep voice echoed from the living room.

"This is dumb. I want another brownie," Shirley said.

"You have to say something nice about Birdie," Faye spoke up.

Birdie laughed. "Miss Prissy Pants doesn't like me."

Shirley giggled. "I like you, Birdie."

"Liar."

Katelyn crossed her fingers and prayed the two women wouldn't start an argument.

"I like you because you raised a nice daughter who puts up with me."

Whoa. Where did that come from?

"I don't know why Katelyn tolerates all your crap."

"Because she's a good girl like her mother," Shirley said.

"Is that nice enough, Birdie?" Mavis asked.

"I suppose."

"My turn." The voice sounded like it belonged to Harriet.

"Wait," Birdie shouted. "I want to know if Shirley was a good girl or a bad girl before she got married."

The women giggled.

If Katelyn had to guess, she'd say the women were on their third or fourth pitcher of sangria.

"I was a good girl, of course," Shirley said.

After the group's laughter died down, Birdie said, "It's Mavis's turn, Harriet. Then you."

Katelyn peeked around the doorjamb and saw Shirley launch a pillow across the room, knocking Mavis upside the head. "I thought you were athletic." *Athletic* was Shirley's code word for lesbian.

"I'll show you how athletic I am." Mavis attempted to push herself off the couch but fell back against the cushion.

Shirley held up her wineglass. "I need a refill."

Etta topped off the glass.

"Hurry, Mavis," Harriet said.

Katelyn wished she'd thought to bring her purse with her. She'd love to sketch a picture of the drunken grannies.

"What I like most about Birdie," Mavis said, "is that she doesn't give a rat's ass what other people think."

"Hear, hear." Everyone took a swig from her glass.

"Now it's my turn." Harriet shushed the group. "I like Birdie because no matter how tired she is, she's always got a smile for you when you get to the register."

Sadie cleared her throat. "I like Birdie because

she lets me experiment with her hair and if I screw up, she says, 'Don't worry. It'll grow back.'"

"Etta's going to speak for both of us," Faye said.

"We like Birdie because she can tell the difference between us when others can't," Etta said.

"Aw, that's sweet." Nanette clapped. "I like Birdie because she's always willing to watch my mother if I need an afternoon to myself."

"And I like Birdie because she gives me a gnome for Christmas every year," Doris said.

The comment ignited a conversation about this year's Christmas gift exchange, and Katelyn stepped back from the doorway, her thoughts springing forward to future holidays, thinking of where she'd be and whom she'd be celebrating with.

"When did you get here?" Doris pulled up short after she entered the kitchen and saw Katelyn. The slim granny wore a pair of tie-dyed overalls and a matching T-shirt.

"I knocked on the front door, but no one answered, so I came around to the back." She glanced toward the living room. "Sounds like everyone's having fun."

Doris winked. "Your mother-in-law likes my special birthday brownies."

Katelyn's gaze shifted to the baking dish on the

counter with only a sliver of chocolate brownie left.

"Try it," Doris said.

As if on cue, Katelyn's stomach growled. "You sure no one else wants the last piece?"

"We've all had seconds. Shirley's had three helpings."

Maybe Birdie had finally swayed Shirley to stop counting calories.

Katelyn took a bite, chewed for a second and then spit the cake into the sink. "You didn't!" She tasted marijuana.

Doris pinched her fingers together. "A smidgen."

"That was no smidgen."

"Maybe two smidgens." She smiled. "Or three. I might have gotten distracted when I mixed the batter."

Now Katelyn knew why the women were giggling so much.

"Have you played bridge yet?"

Doris shook her head. "We don't really play bridge. We tell people that's what we do."

"Have you opened presents yet?" Katelyn asked.

"We did. Why don't you pour yourself some wine and join us?" Doris said.

Katelyn couldn't afford to drink. She had to figure out a way to get all the ladies safely home—and she knew whom to ask for help. "I forgot Mom's gift." That was the truth. She'd left the birthday card with a check inside on the dresser in her room. "I'll be back shortly."

"Okay, dear."

Katelyn stopped at the door. "Don't let anyone leave until I return."

"I won't." Doris smiled.

Katelyn let herself out, thinking Little Springs needed an Uber driver. She cut across the lawn, walked down the block and around the corner past Gifford's Resale and then stopped at Mendoza Auto. The lights were on in the bay, the door open. Jackson's work boots peeked out from beneath an Impala. She entered the garage and said, "You're working late."

The clanging stopped and Jackson pushed the creeper out from beneath the car. He stared up at her, his mouth firm but his eyes warm—he was glad to see her. She pointed to the smudge on his forehead.

"Did I mention when we dated that I think grease stains are sexy?"

He gifted her with an amused smile, then climbed to his feet. Her gaze traveled over his body before returning to the ripped denim above the knee, which showed a glimpse of muscled thigh. "I liked your torn jeans, too."

"I know." He grinned. "You used to poke your fingers inside the rip and pull the hair on my legs."

She laughed.

He waved at the couch. "Have a seat."

Once she was settled, she said, "You were at the soccer game last night. Why didn't you sit in the stands?" *With me.*

"I had work to do."

"I can tell when you're lying. Remember we dated for almost a year."

"We did more than date." His brown eyes flashed before he went to the sink to wash his hands. Keeping his back to her, he puttered at the bench, sorting tools. She let him think she'd dropped the subject and spent the next fifteen minutes watching him work.

When he finally looked her way, she sent him a sly grin and repeated her question. "Why didn't you watch the whole game?"

"I don't care for socializing."

Katelyn's heart tweaked when she imagined Jackson keeping to himself all these years.

He found another task to do and she rested her eyes. She wasn't sure how long they'd been closed when he spoke again. "You were drawing in the stands."

She smiled at his not-so-subtle attempt to steer the conversation back to her.

"I'd like to see what you were working on," he said.

"I need more practice before I bare my soul to others."

He crossed his arms over his chest and his gaze bored into her as if he tried to see into her heart.

"You never told me you wanted to run your own business," she said.

"I didn't know that's what I wanted to do until years later, after we'd graduated from school."

"It's funny how all along your dream was waiting right here at home for you." She swept her hand in front of her. "And I was so sure my dream was anywhere but in Little Springs."

"What else have you been doing besides raising the twins and taking care of your mother-in-law?"

"I've volunteered at the kids' school and helped my husband's employer with corporate fund-raisers. I've also become an expert on throwing dinner parties."

"Do you like doing that kind of thing?" he asked.

"The dinner parties?"

He nodded.

"At first it was fun. After the twentieth party . . . not so much. To be honest, I hate cooking now. I'm happy eating a cold salad for supper or popping a frozen dinner into the microwave."

"I love to cook."

"You do?"

"After my mother took off, Dad and I mostly ate fast food and frozen burritos."

"Who taught you to cook?" As soon as she asked the question, she wished she could take it back. She didn't want to hear about all the former girlfriends who'd helped him in the kitchen.

"I taught myself," he said, "by watching cooking videos on YouTube."

"What's your favorite dish?"

"I make a mean rosemary braised lamb shank."

"I'm impressed."

He flashed a half grin. "We've both changed."

"That's for sure."

His smile faded. "So tell me a few facts about the Katelyn Chandler who lives in St. Louis."

"Let's see. . . . I discovered I like sashimi."

"Me, too. What's your favorite?"

"It's a toss-up between mackerel and squid. What about you?"

"I like them both. Have you tried puffer fish?"

"Never."

"There's a place in Denver that serves sashimi that's out of this world."

"When were you in Denver?"

"I spent a few years there on road construction projects. It's a beautiful city."

"You've always liked working with your hands, haven't you?"

"I guess we both have that in common—me with a wrench and you with a paintbrush."

Only Jackson had stayed true to his passion, while she'd abandoned hers. "I've traveled overseas several times. Melissa is visiting two of my favorite countries—Italy and Greece."

"I bet your kids are smart like you were in school."

"Michael inherited his father's mind for business. Melissa isn't sure what she wants to major in, but she's leaning toward psychology." Katelyn smiled. "The twins both look more like me than Don."

Jackson walked over to the couch and sat next to her.

She shifted on the cushion, facing him. "Where else have you lived?"

"After Colorado I built homes in California. Then I did a stint cutting lumber in Oregon."

"You've seen more of this country than I have," she said. "I've been to New York three times. I'm not impressed with the city, but I loved Broadway."

"I went to Vegas and saw a comedy club act, but that's about all the culture I can stand."

"How did you find your way back to Little Springs?" she asked.

"I've always wanted to live here."

His answer surprised her. "Why?"

"It's home."

"What about your crappy childhood? Your mom left you and your dad drank. Nothing good happened here."

He picked at the engine grease beneath his fingernails, then looked her in the eye. "You happened to me."

She wanted to ask if he ever thought about where they'd be if she hadn't broken up with him, but she chickened out and changed the subject. "I think you'd like Italy."

"Why's that?"

"The country is old and you're an old soul." She smiled.

He groaned.

"I'm serious. I bet you like working on old cars more than the newer models."

"I do." He rubbed a finger over her wedding band. "What about your soul?"

"It's a work in progress."

"It seems like you gave up a lot of yourself when you married and had your son and daughter."

"I did, but since I've been home, I'm discovering the urge I once felt to draw is still inside me."

He tilted his head, studying her intently.

"Why are you looking at me like that?" she asked.

"You're different."

"No kidding. I'm older."

"I'm not looking at the crow's-feet around your eyes."

She laughed. "Thanks for noticing."

"When you talked about your drawings back in high school, your pupils would get huge." He released her hand and then caressed the skin beneath her eye. "But right now they're small."

"You're crazy." She shifted away from him, uncomfortable that he'd remembered such an intimate detail about her. She checked the time on her cell phone, surprised she'd been at the garage for almost an hour. "I need your help."

"Help with what?"

Katelyn jumped inside her skin when Vern walked through the bay door. The minister's gaze swung between her and Jackson. "Hello, Mr. Wilkes."

"Call me Vern."

"I stopped by to ask Jackson a favor, but I could use your help, too."

"Doing what?" Vern asked.

"Chauffeuring the Little Springs Ladies' Society home. They're celebrating my mother's birthday at Doris's house and they've all eaten brownies laced with pot."

Vern snickered. "The cannabis queen strikes again."

"Katelyn and I can drive Harriet and Mavis home, since they live out of town," Jackson said.

"Vern, if you don't mind driving my mother-in-law's car, you could drop off the ladies who live in town. Then we'll meet you back at my mother's house."

"Shirley's at the party?" Vern asked.

"Yes," Katelyn said.

"Well, then, what are we waiting for?"

CHAPTER NINETEEN

Jackson closed the bay door and the three of them piled into his pickup to go gather the ladies. He parked in front of Doris's house and waited in the truck while Vern and Katelyn went inside. Five minutes later Katelyn escorted Nanette across the street and down the block to her home. Meanwhile, Vern led Harriet and Mavis to Jackson's pickup, then helped the other women into the Mercedes.

"Did you ladies have a nice time?" Jackson looked in the rearview mirror and caught Harriet trying to help Mavis buckle her seat belt.

"We have too much fun celebrating birthdays." Harriet leaned her head against the seat and closed her eyes. Jackson figured she'd be asleep before they left town.

He checked his side mirror and watched Vern get behind the wheel of Shirley's Mercedes and play with the controls. The lights flashed, the windows rose up and down and Jackson heard the radio go on. Shirley sat in the front seat and rocked back and forth to the music. Faye, Etta, Birdie and Sadie were squished together like sardines in the back. Katelyn returned from walking Nanette home, then checked to make sure Doris's front door was locked before climbing into Jackson's pickup.

He pulled away from the curb but stopped at the end of the block and waited while Vern made a U-turn. He wanted to make sure the old man didn't drive the Mercedes into the ditch. When Vern proceeded down Main Street, Jackson headed north out of town. Harriet lived near the entrance to the Catfish Bay recreational area.

"What time is it?" Harriet mumbled.

"Ten thirty," Katelyn said.

Mavis tapped Katelyn's shoulder. "Your mother-in-law isn't such a bad person once she loosens up."

"I'm guessing Shirley's engaging personality was helped by Doris's brownies."

"When's your birthday, Jackson?" Mavis asked. "I'll tell her to bake you a brownie cake."

He grinned. "I celebrated it in May. Maybe next year."

Mavis kept up a steady stream of conversation after they dropped Harriet off and returned to the highway. Five miles farther up the road, Katelyn escorted Mavis to her front door and made sure she was safely locked inside for the night before Jackson drove back to Little Springs.

"Looks like Vern beat us here." He pulled up next to the Mercedes in Birdie's driveway.

"Thanks for your help tonight. I had no idea

my mother and her friends were potheads."

"I don't think they party like that often." He shut off the ignition and studied the shadowy figures sitting on the back porch. "Tell Vern his ride is leaving in five minutes."

Jackson waited while Katelyn spoke to the couple. Voices carried through the dark, but he couldn't make out any words.

As he strained to see through the shadows, he recalled the nights when he'd driven Katelyn home from their dates and they'd sat in his car necking until her father turned on the kitchen light, signaling that it was time for his daughter to come inside.

Katelyn walked back to the truck and poked her head through the open window. "Vern's not ready to leave. He and Shirley are at an impasse."

"What's going on?"

"Vern believes charities serve an important function in society and Shirley believes charity begins at home."

Jackson grinned.

"I can drive Vern back to his house in a little while," Katelyn said.

Jackson didn't want to leave, either. "I'll wait for him."

"It's been a while since we sat on the front porch."

"Lead the way." He followed her to the front yard, and they sat on the porch steps, close enough that he could smell the fresh scent of her shampoo.

"There's iced tea in the fridge, or I can get you a bottle of water," she said.

"I'm good, thanks." He swayed sideways, bumping her shoulder. "Did your father ever tell you about the night he caught me sleeping out here?"

"When did you do that?"

"It was the week before you left for college. My dad went on a bender, and I had to get out of the house. I could have slept on our front porch but . . ." He stared into the distance. "You hadn't left town yet, and I already missed you, so I snuck up the hill and camped out here."

Little had he known that two months later Katelyn would break up with him. When he'd joined AA, he'd worked through all the baggage from his past that had triggered his drinking binges, but his toughest memory to deal with had been Katelyn's breakup letter.

Even though he'd put the memory to rest, he'd never forgotten the afternoon he'd grabbed a six-pack of beer from the fridge and taken the letter down to the tracks to read.

Dear Jackson,

I don't know how to tell you this. I don't want you to be mad at me.

215

He hadn't been mad. He'd been scared. Katelyn had been the best thing going for him, and he'd been terrified of losing her.

I don't think we should go steady anymore. I really like it here in St. Louis and I decided I'm not ever going back to Little Springs.

He'd known she'd been serious, because she hadn't used the word *home*.

I have to find myself. Find out who I'm meant to be. What I'm meant to accomplish in my life.

And he was holding her back.

I want more from life than scraping by like my mom and dad.

All he could give her was scraping by, because that was all he knew.

Please don't be mad at me. We can still be friends.

When he'd gotten to that line, he'd known that he'd lost her for good.

You'll always be my first love, Jackson.

I won't forget you.

And then she'd gone on and made a life for herself without him.

Jackson slipped his hand into hers. "Stay in Little Springs and paint." He wanted a chance to get to know the woman Katelyn had become.

"I can paint anywhere."

"That's true, but maybe you have to go back to the beginning before you can move forward."

Katelyn mulled over Jackson's words. Was he right? Was the answer to why she hadn't pursued her art after marrying Don here in her hometown? A sliver of excitement poked her in the chest, the sting stealing her breath. Her gaze drifted down the hill to Main Street. How many afternoons had she sat on this porch and drawn bits and pieces of the town below? Sketches of her world. Gifford's Resale. And the Fourth of July celebration in the town park, where she'd drawn a clown making a balloon dog for a little girl. The piece had earned a second-place ribbon in an art show her sophomore year of high school.

What would it hurt to stick around Little Springs? With the twins busy for the summer and the house already sold, there was no reason to rush back to St. Louis. She could continue working at the grocery store, and while Katelyn rediscovered her joy of drawing, maybe Birdie would use her free time to get back into her music.

"Jackson, you ready to go?" Vern's voice called out in the dark.

"I'll think about it," she said.

He tugged a lock of her hair. "I don't remember your hair ever being this long when we dated."

"I keep it long because it bugs my mother-in-law."

Jackson's head fell back and he laughed.

"Thanks for the taxi service tonight," she said.

"Anytime." He climbed to his feet and disappeared into the dark, leaving Katelyn alone with her thoughts.

She couldn't argue with Jackson's logic. Little Springs had provided the fuel that had driven her to hone her craft and compete for scholarships that would carry her far away from a life she'd wanted to escape.

Maybe the only way to revive her dream of painting full-time was to reconnect with the girl who snuck down to the tracks every chance she got with her imagination and a sketch pad.

Katelyn dropped the pair of gloves on the ground and crawled to her feet, groaning at the sharp pain in her lower back. She wiped the sweat from her brow and surveyed the garden bed.

"You missed one."

She glanced at the porch, where Shirley stood

in her pajamas, clumps of hair sticking up all over her head. The new, shorter style was prone to bedhead—not a good thing when her mother-in-law was in the habit of washing her hair only on Sunday and Wednesday nights.

"It looks like you got caught in a wind tunnel." Katelyn wiped a hand down her mouth, erasing her smile with it.

Shirley touched the rat's nest on her head.

"That's what too many glasses of sangria and Doris's special brownies will do to you."

Shirley's mouth turned down at the corners. "I don't know why I couldn't stop laughing last night. Nothing anyone said was funny."

Katelyn climbed the steps and collapsed in the chair. "Vern found you amusing."

"I don't even remember our conversation." Shirley sat in the other chair and fanned her face.

"I think you intrigue Vern."

"Why would you say that?"

"Because"—Birdie stepped onto the porch, wearing capri pants and another Buy & Bag T-shirt—"you're the exact opposite of his dead wife."

"What was she like?" Shirley asked.

Katelyn sent her mother a warning glare as she got up from her chair and motioned for Birdie to take her place.

"Elaine was the perfect minister's wife. She was warm and generous, and she played piano for the church choir. She also did a lot of charity work in Pecos."

"Charity . . ." Shirley frowned. "Why does that topic sound familiar?"

Birdie pointed to the yard. "What are you doing in my garden?"

"Pulling a few weeds," Katelyn said.

"I weeded the flower beds two weeks ago."

"It's therapeutic." Katelyn had used the early-morning hour to mull over last night's conversation with Jackson. When she'd racked her brain for a valid reason why she'd abandoned her art after she'd married Don, she recalled the afternoon she'd sent the twins to their first full day of kindergarten.

She'd planned ahead for that day, purchasing a twenty-five-by-thirty-six-inch canvas and six tubes of fresh oil paints along with new brushes and a new palette. As soon as she'd returned home from dropping the kids off, she'd opened the tubes and squeezed out the colors. She'd known exactly what she wanted to paint—the garden in the backyard.

She'd worked for hours without taking a break when the doorbell rang, interrupting her. She'd spent the next half hour chatting with her neighbor and when she'd returned to the easel, tears had welled in her eyes at how amateurish her work appeared. The rosebushes didn't look like rosebushes and the trellis wasn't in scale, making the patio furniture appear as if it belonged in a dollhouse. She'd thrown the canvas and the paints into the garbage and that had been the last time she'd set up the easel.

Thinking back on that day, Katelyn suspected she'd been too hard on herself, demanding perfection from her art because she'd been living the perfect life. Little did she know that her perfect life had been falling apart around her for years and she hadn't realized it. She'd left Little Springs in search of a world that would nurture her talents and make her a better artist, but instead the world she'd chosen had stifled her creativity. Now that she was back home, where everything was imperfect—maybe it was time to turn her sketches into paintings.

"Until last night no one liked your mother-in-law." Birdie's voice interrupted Katelyn's thoughts.

Shirley opened her mouth, then snapped it closed—too hungover to argue.

"But this morning"—Birdie waved her arms—"everyone's calling me and saying she's not so bad."

"Really?" Shirley and Katelyn spoke at once.

"*I* still think you're a snob," Birdie said. "But Doris believes you're only misunderstood."

"I like Doris," Shirley said.

"Etta and Faye said they like your Mercedes and now they want to trade in their Toyota."

"Before this conversation gets out of hand, I have something to tell both of you."

Shirley's face lit up. "You've decided to work things out with Don."

What?

"I knew you'd come to your senses." Shirley stood. "I'll start packing."

"You're leaving already?" Birdie asked. "You haven't even been here two weeks."

"Shirley, sit down." Katelyn pointed to the cushion on the chair. "I'm not contesting the divorce."

"Talk sense into your daughter." Shirley glared at Birdie. "You don't want her to end up in your situation, do you?"

"Watch yourself, Ms. High Society." Birdie glared back.

"I only meant look how hard you've had to work all your life. Mavis said you wished you could retire."

Birdie cast a quick glance at Katelyn. "I was kidding."

Katelyn couldn't tell if her mother was being truthful or not. "Will you two stop bickering so I can make my announcement?" When she had their attention, she said, "I've decided to stay in Little Springs for the rest of the summer."

Birdie clapped and Katelyn was glad the news pleased her mother. "And I intend to keep working at the grocery store." Birdie wasn't an emotional woman, but her eyes glowed as if Katelyn had given her a special gift.

"Why on earth would you want to be stranded here?" Shirley asked.

"The house in St. Louis has sold and the kids are gone for the summer. Why not stay?"

"But I don't want to be here all summer," Shirley said.

"You weren't—" Birdie said.

"Mom . . . ," Katelyn warned, then spoke to Shirley. "I'll drive you back to St. Louis, and Don will help you get settled into your new apartment."

"After all I've done for you through the years, you're going to leave me at that awful apartment by myself?"

Birdie stamped her foot. "All you've done for my daughter, Shirley Pratt, is make her life miserable."

Shirley ignored Birdie. "What am I supposed to do by myself?"

"Maybe Don's new girlfriend will take you to get your hair done," Katelyn said.

"I don't want to get to know my son's new girlfriend." Shirley grasped Katelyn's hand. "Can I stay here, too?"

Birdie's eyes widened. "You hate Little Springs."

"It's not the worst place in the world." Shirley

glanced between Birdie and Katelyn. "And there is the ladies' society."

"Those are my friends, not yours," Birdie said.

"You said they liked me." Shirley stamped her foot and looked at Katelyn. "Tell your mother to let me stay."

"It's up to you, Mom. This is your home."

Birdie propped her hands on her hips. "Will you keep your mouth shut at the supper table and not comment about the food I serve?"

"Yes."

"And will you stop hiding my Birkenstocks?"

"What?" Katelyn asked.

Birdie looked at Katelyn. "She hides my sandals, because she thinks they're ugly."

"They're hideous," Shirley said. "Fine, you can wear your Birkenstocks. I don't care."

"You promise to stop criticizing my daughter and nagging her about her hair?" Birdie asked.

"If Katelyn hasn't changed her hairstyle all these years, then nothing I say is going to convince her to do it now."

"You step out of line once"—Birdie shook her finger at Shirley—"and I'll drive you back to Missouri myself."

Shirley crossed her heart. "I'll be a model houseguest."

"I'd better call Abby." Birdie opened the screen door.

"What's Abby got to do with Shirley and me staying?" Katelyn asked.

"She said she talked to you about her father and Shirley going out on a date and you thought it was a good idea." Birdie looked at Shirley. "Maybe Vern thinks he can save your soul."

"I can't go out with him."

"What's wrong with the man?" Birdie asked. "He's not fat, and he still has all his teeth."

"I'm a widow."

"Vern's a widower." Birdie raised her hands in the air. "I don't see the problem."

"Mom, maybe Shirley's not ready to—"

"Abby said Vern's picking you up at six o'clock and taking you into Odessa to that new steak house."

"But I didn't say yes to a date," Shirley protested.

"I said yes for you." Birdie stepped into the house.

"Wait!" Shirley went inside, her voice carrying through the screen. "Do you think Sadie would style my hair?"

"Get dressed and I'll take you over to the salon."

Good grief. Katelyn's trip home was turning into a three-ring circus. She left the pile of weeds on the lawn and went inside to shower and change. She didn't have to be at the Buy & Bag until noon, and she planned to use the time to work on a sketch.

CHAPTER TWENTY

I'm off to the grocery store, Mom." Katelyn slipped into her sandals and headed for the back door, stopping when her phone went off inside her purse.

It was Melissa. Katelyn took a deep breath and stepped onto the porch. "Hi, honey. How are you?"

"Oh my God, Mom! Dad called me and said you guys are getting divorced."

Katelyn sat in the chair and closed her eyes. "I'm sorry you had to find out during your trip abroad."

Birdie stepped onto the porch and Katelyn interrupted Melissa's rant. "Grandma Chandler's here. Did you want to wish her a happy birthday?" She handed the phone to her mother. While Birdie and Melissa chatted, Katelyn wished she could make things right for her daughter, but nothing she said or did would change the fact that Melissa's parents were breaking up.

"Love you, too." Birdie handed the phone to Katelyn and went back inside.

"Dad said the house already sold."

"It did."

"Where are you going to live?" That Melissa didn't ask about her possessions surprised Katelyn.

"I'm not sure. Right now I plan to spend the summer in Little Springs with your grandmothers."

"Grandma Pratt wants to stay there?"

"She does, and guess what?"

"What?"

"She went out on a date last night."

"No way. With who?"

Katelyn laughed. "A widower named Vern. He's a minister in town."

"Did she have fun?"

"I don't know. She's still in bed."

"I'm going to change my plans and fly to Texas when I return to the States. I don't need to spend the summer with Sara. I can see her horses another time."

"I love you for worrying about me, honey, but there's nothing to do in Little Springs for a girl your age." That was the truth.

"I can be with you."

"I'm working Grandma's shifts at the Buy & Bag, so I'm keeping busy."

"Why would you want to work at a grocery store?"

"To give Grandma a break. I like having someplace to go every day and I'm becoming friends with the ladies at the store."

"Mom?"

"What?"

"When I asked Dad why you guys were getting a

divorce, he said he'd met someone else. Is it true?"

"Yes. Your father is having an affair."

"What a jerk."

Katelyn agreed.

"I'm so disappointed in him."

The hurt in her daughter's voice broke Katelyn's heart, but she understood what it felt like to be let down by your parents. "Your father still loves you and Michael."

"I know." Melissa sighed. "Are you sure you don't want me to fly to Texas?"

"Positive."

"It's been a while since you visited Grandma Chandler."

"I should have come home a long time ago," Katelyn said.

"Dad said he can't make it to my move-in day at Stephens, because he'll be out of town. Do you think you and Grandma Chandler could help me move into my dorm?"

"We'd love to." Birdie would enjoy tagging along for the trip and seeing her granddaughter's college.

"Promise to call me if you need to talk or vent?" Melissa said.

"The same goes for you, honey."

"You're sure you're okay, Mom?"

"I would tell you if I wasn't."

"Say hi to Grandma Pratt for me and make sure she practices safe sex."

Katelyn laughed. "Maybe you should have that talk with her."

"Love you, Mom."

"Love you, too. Be careful and enjoy the rest of your trip."

"I'll text when I get settled at Sara's house in a few weeks."

"Sounds good."

Melissa ended the call, and Katelyn dropped the phone into her purse.

The screen door squeaked open again. "Is Melissa going to be okay?" Birdie asked.

"She's a tough girl."

"Like her mother."

"Like her grandmother, too." Katelyn descended the steps. "What are your plans with Shirley today?"

"As soon as Prissy Pants hauls her butt out of bed, I'm taking her clothes shopping in Odessa."

"Maybe you can talk her into buying something other than those silk blouses she wears all the time."

"Can't promise anything, but I'll try."

"You know, you might want to look at—"

"Don't you start in on me about my capri pants and T-shirts."

Katelyn raised her hands in defeat. "You girls have fun." She cut through the yard and then trekked down the hill to the grocery store.

"You're late," Walter greeted her when she walked through the loading dock door.

"I got caught"—she didn't want to tell him that her daughter had phoned, upset that her parents were divorcing—"refereeing an argument between my mother and Shirley." That wasn't too far from the truth—the older women were always bickering. She shoved her purse inside her locker and slipped on her smock, then headed to the front of the store, Walter trailing behind her.

"You can take a shorter lunch and make up the time," he said, then escaped into his office.

"What was that all about?" Layla asked.

"He wanted to know why I clocked in a half hour late." Katelyn waved off the topic and asked, "How was your date with Brian?"

"I found out his parents live in California and he has a brother in Iowa. He's been to Hawaii and Alaska, too." Layla patted Katelyn's shoulder. "Thanks for covering for me the other night. I appreciate you helping Abby close."

"No problem."

"Was Birdie's birthday bash a success?"

"I ended up enlisting Jackson and Vern's help chauffeuring the group home after the party."

"I heard about the pot brownies."

"I saw the plants in coffee cans on her front porch. It looks like she's growing her own cannabis."

"Ginny said Doris became addicted to painkillers after falling down and fracturing her spine. Someone told her to switch to pot to help with the pain, and she was able to wean herself off the pills."

A whooshing sound caught their attention. The front doors opened, and Layla's son entered the store.

"Hey, Mom." The boy stopped at the register. "Trevor can't do anything today, and I'm bored."

The doors opened again, and Brian walked in with his dolly of pastries. He parked the treats in front of the bread aisle and exchanged a private smile with Layla before looking at her son. "What are you up to, Gavin?"

"I'm bored."

"I might be able to help with that," Brian said. "I could use an extra hand with deliveries today. The job pays twenty-five bucks, plus lunch is on me."

Gavin's eyes lit up. "I can ride in the truck with you?"

"You'd have to help me stock shelves in the stores, but if you do a good job, you can tag along next week, too."

Gavin looked at his mother. "Twenty-five dollars is a lot of money. I could buy the video game FlatOut: Ultimate Carnage after working only a couple of days."

"Yes, you could." Layla sent Brian a grateful look.

"Okay," Gavin said. "I'll help you make deliveries."

"We'll leave as soon as I unload this dolly."

Gavin took off for the bathroom, and Layla said, "How can I repay you for keeping him entertained?"

"Have supper ready for us when I drop him off later." Brian flashed a smile, then disappeared down the bread aisle.

"He's really good with Gavin," Katelyn said, amused that her coworker couldn't take her eyes off the deliveryman.

"I know, but . . ."

"But what?"

"This is going to sound awful, but I wish he had money."

"Money isn't everything."

Layla scoffed. "That's easy for you to say. I heard your husband makes a fortune."

"Soon-to-be ex-husband."

"Still, when the dust settles from your divorce, you'll have more cash than you'll know what to do with."

There was nothing Katelyn could say in her defense. Layla was a younger version of herself—more beautiful definitely—but her eyes shone with a yearning for something more than what life had shown her so far. The same anxious look that Katelyn had seen in her own reflection before she'd left for college.

"I buy lottery tickets," Layla said.

"Have you had any luck?"

"I won five hundred dollars on a scratch-off two years ago."

"That's nothing to sneeze at."

"I used the money to buy school clothes for Gavin. And I let him get an expensive pair of sneakers, which was stupid, because he grew out of them in six months."

"Bye, Mom." Gavin waved as he raced past the registers.

"Behave!"

When Brian met Gavin at the door, the preteen asked, "Are you my mom's boyfriend?"

Brian locked gazes with Layla. "We're friends . . . for right now." He winked, then ushered Gavin outside.

"I can't remember the last time Don looked at me like that," Katelyn said.

"Like what?"

"Like I was his whole world." Katelyn shrugged. "Money makes life easier but not always sweeter."

"Sweetness is overrated. I'm taking my break." Layla walked off.

Katelyn waved at a family of five who entered the store. It would be several minutes before they made it to her register, so she removed her cell phone from her jean pocket and texted Michael.

Everything going okay?

As soon as she put the phone back into her pocket, it vibrated.

Fine. Why?

Just wondering. I've decided to stay all summer in Little Springs. Grandma Pratt is staying, too.

You guys are gonna be bored out of your minds.

Maybe. How are classes going?

Got an A on a quiz. I'm playing hoops with some guys on Friday nights.

Stay out of trouble.

You, too.

Ha. Ha. Love you. XXOO

Me, too. Say hi to Grandma C and Grandma P.

OK. Katelyn put the phone away right as Walter emerged from his office.

"Your mother called and said she's not

returning to work until the end of August and that you're staying on in her place."

Birdie had wanted to be the one to tell her boss. "Is that okay?"

"Sure." Walter lowered his voice. "Don't tell Birdie I said this, but I think she should retire."

"Is she making mistakes at the register?"

"No, it's her attitude."

"What do you mean?"

"She bites my head off whenever I ask her to do something."

"My mother's not rude to customers, is she?"

"Only me."

"I wouldn't take it personally. Mom doesn't like being told what to do."

"But I'm the boss."

"The trick is making her think she's the boss."

Walter grimaced. "I'll enjoy the break from her over the next few weeks. Then when she returns, I'll do what I always do."

"Which is?"

"Steer clear of her."

Katelyn's laughter coaxed a smile out of him.

"If you're staying the summer, does that mean you and Jackson are seeing each other?" he asked.

"There's nothing going on between me and Jackson."

Yet.

CHAPTER TWENTY-ONE

If you keep this up, I won't have one single weed in the whole yard." Birdie knelt on the ground next to Katelyn in front of the azalea bushes by the side of the house.

"I woke early and couldn't get back to sleep," Katelyn said. "I thought I'd make myself useful, since I have the day off from the Buy & Bag." She tossed a dandelion into the pile of weeds behind her.

"Wouldn't you rather sit in church than out here in the hot sun?"

Katelyn smiled. "No one's stopping you from spending your Sunday praising God."

"I usually skip the first service after one of our birthday parties. Better to wait until the gossip dies down." Birdie squeezed Katelyn's hand. "Are you sure you want to take over my job for the rest of the summer?"

"I haven't done a lot for you through the years, Mom. Use the break to relax and catch up on sleep." Katelyn sat back on her heels and removed a gift-wrapped package from her pocket. "I got you something else for your birthday."

"The check was plenty." Birdie tore at the paper. "Guitar picks?"

"If it's not too late for me to start painting

again, then it's not too late for you to start playing your guitar."

"Maybe I will." Birdie set the picks aside. "Thank you." She pointed at the ground beneath the shrubs. "I didn't put mulch down last year."

"Why didn't you ask me to help you in the yard when I was younger?"

"You were always off somewhere doodling in that sketch pad of yours."

Katelyn couldn't remember a time when she wasn't drawing on something—the back of a candy wrapper, a paper lunch bag or her school notebooks.

"Pulling weeds is therapeutic and I needed a lot of therapy after I gave up my music." Birdie reached around Katelyn and tugged a dandelion out of the ground. "I had to have something pretty in my life to replace my music."

"I wish you and I had been closer, Mom."

Birdie brushed a loose strand of Katelyn's hair off her cheek. "I'm glad you're staying."

"Me, too." And Katelyn meant it. Unlike on previous visits home, she felt no restlessness, no gut-tugging urgency to return to St. Louis.

"The other day Etta asked if you'd donate a piece of artwork for the Fourth of July silent auction."

"That's four days away."

"You must have a sketch or drawing you could contribute," Birdie said.

Katelyn had taken her pencil and pad down to the railroad tracks after she'd finished her shift at the store each day last week, but hadn't decided if she'd turn any of the sketches into a painting. "I'm not ready to share my work with the public."

"Why don't you show me one of your sketches," Birdie said, "and I'll tell you if it's good or a piece of crap?"

"You're a musician. How would you know what's good art and what's not?"

"After I saw your drawing of Mack, I knew you had talent."

"The one of him sitting on the front porch?"

Birdie nodded. "The look of love in that dog's eyes stole my breath. Anyone who can capture that raw emotion on paper needs to share their gift with the world."

"I wish you had told me that back then," Katelyn said.

"I'm ashamed to admit I was jealous."

Startled by her mother's confession, Katelyn didn't know what to say. She'd always believed her mom had been too busy with work, and that was why she hadn't shown much interest in her daughter's art.

"I know it sounds horrible for a mother to be jealous of her own child. Any decent parent would wish for their offspring to be successful, but your talent reminded me of my lost dreams." Birdie blinked hard. "By the time I realized how stupid my jealousy was, you were in college."

Katelyn appreciated the confession, but it made her sad that her mother's envy had kept them from having a close relationship. "Thank you for saying that."

"You have incredible talent, daughter. You simply have to believe in yourself."

Believing in herself would take time. But she'd taken a step in the right direction when she'd decided to remain in Little Springs for the summer. And admitting that the place she'd always wanted to escape from was the same place that nurtured her creative side was another step toward finding the girl who'd lost her way.

"What are you doing with Shirley today?"

"I don't know. We're waiting to see if Vern asks her out on another date."

"Melissa thinks I should have the safe-sex talk with Grandma Pratt."

Birdie tipped her head back and laughed. "The ladies' society has it covered."

"Do you mind if I borrow your car to go down to the tracks for a while?"

"Not at all."

Katelyn tugged her gardening gloves off. "Tell Etta I'll give her a picture for the Fourth of July auction."

"That's my girl."

• • •

He was watching her.

Jackson had shown up fifteen minutes ago, when the Pecos Valley Southern Railway rattled by. Like in old times, his quiet presence comforted her. Her pencil stilled against the paper. She studied the image of the graffiti-covered boxcar and the shadowy figure inside, staring out the open door. There was no way to tell if the oval face with large luminous eyes belonged to a girl or a boy.

"That's you, isn't it?"

"You might give someone a warning before you sneak up on them." She shifted in her lawn chair. "How do you know it's me?"

The corner of his mouth lifted in a half smile. "You had that same glow in your eyes when you said good-bye before you left for college."

"I let you down."

"No one let anyone down." He rubbed his finger across her cheek. "We got lost for a while."

How had she gotten lost when she'd left this place to find herself? "I decided to stay here for the summer, but then, you know that already, don't you?"

"Vern told me."

"I don't think your minister friend likes me."

"He can be overprotective."

"I stopped by the garage Friday afternoon, but

it was closed." She'd walked over after her shift at the grocery store to chat with Jackson.

"I was at an AA meeting."

"You meet on Fridays?"

"We try to meet every Friday, but we have a small group, so we change the day of the week if someone can't make it."

She set her charcoal pencil down and gave him her full attention. "Do you find the meetings helpful?"

"Yes and no." He picked up a pebble and flung it across the tracks. "I don't share much, but I did this time."

"You don't have to explain anything to me," she said.

His gaze swung to her. "I panicked when I heard you were staying."

Katelyn stood and set the sketch pad on the seat of the chair. She took Jackson's hand and led him to the shade of their oak tree. They sank to the ground together, backs against the trunk, shoulders touching—as they'd sat all those afternoons in the past. Eyes closed, she basked in the feeling of rightness that filled her. "Why does my staying in town make you uneasy?"

"I was fine with you being here until I kissed you."

Her eyes popped open. "So the kiss was a mistake?"

"No, it confirmed that I want you as much as

I wanted you back in high school." He grinned. "And my gut tells me it's not a good idea to get involved with you again."

Katelyn pulled her hand free from his grasp and cupped her elbows. Jackson was smart to have reservations about her, but it still hurt. "Why is it a bad idea for us to be together?" When his mouth went slack, she pressed him. "I'm not joking. I want to know."

"You just found out your husband cheated on you, and your divorce isn't even final."

"What you're really saying is that you can't trust my emotional state right now."

He touched her ring. "You're still wearing your wedding band."

"I don't know why." She reached to remove it, but Jackson closed his fingers around her hand.

"Take it off when you're ready," he said.

"Don't get me wrong—I'm angry and hurt that my husband cheated on me. But if anything positive has come from his infidelity, it's me recognizing that I was as unhappy and unfulfilled as he was."

"Maybe you're no longer grieving your marriage, but you're going to be making a lot of decisions about your future, and starting a new relationship right now might not be smart."

"You're probably right, but I can't stop living my life." Not when parts of her life had already been on hold for almost nineteen years.

"How are your kids taking the news?"

Katelyn let him change the subject. "They're upset, but college in the fall will help distract them."

"Do they know about me? That we dated?"

"Not yet."

"That's another reason for us not to get involved."

Now that Jackson mentioned it, there was no need to tell the kids unless something serious came of their relationship. The twins needed time to accept their parents' divorce and their father's new girlfriend before Katelyn introduced another man into the equation.

"You've made some good points." Katelyn turned her head toward Jackson, her lips inches from his. "But right now none of them seems to matter." She brushed her mouth against his and he nipped her tongue. She felt his groan before she heard it—a deep rumble that crawled out of his lungs and up his throat, escaping into the air when he pulled away. Jackson frowned.

"My kisses used to make you smile," she said.

"We're playing with fire."

"A simple kiss?"

"You don't do simple, Katelyn."

She climbed to her feet and walked back to the lawn chair.

After she picked up her pencil and began

sketching, he spoke. "I'm glad you're drawing again."

"I'm donating a picture for the July Fourth silent auction. Will you be at the park?"

"I'll be there in the morning to set up the tent and tables, then later that night to take them down."

"Maybe I'll see you."

"I don't think so."

She looked at him. "Why not?"

"I told you I'm not much for socializing."

"You can't live on the fringes of other people's lives forever, Jackson."

"It's been working for me so far."

"Has it?" When he dropped his gaze, she said, "You assume everyone still thinks of you as the son of a drunk."

"That's what I am."

"It's not a question of people giving you a chance," she said. "It's whether or not you're willing to accept yourself for who you are."

"You're one to talk. You've been running away from who you are since you left town." Jackson walked off, leaving Katelyn with a few truths of her own to digest.

CHAPTER TWENTY-TWO

The morning of July Fourth dawned bright and early.

Jackson hadn't gotten a peaceful night's sleep since Katelyn had returned to town. He shouldn't have encouraged her to stick around—heck, she wasn't even trying and she was wiggling her way back into his heart.

The sun peeked over the horizon, lighting the sky with a warm glow. He crossed the street and hiked the half block to the town park, which was the size of three side-by-side house lots. Only a handful of trees, older than the town, stood sentry over the grounds. Ladies from the church had planted a wildflower garden and put a bench from Gifford's Resale in the middle of it. The flowers always looked thirsty and hungover from too much sun.

Vern's and Gary's vehicles sat parked on the street, their truck beds loaded down with tent poles and canvas. Thanks to the Little Springs Ladies' Society for suggesting permanent postholes be placed into the ground, there was no need to dig into the rocky, drought-stricken soil, and pitching the tents would take less than an hour.

" 'Morning, Jackson." Gary lowered the tailgate

on the truck. "Heard we might hit ninety today."

"Wouldn't be surprised." Jackson liked Gary. The fifty-year-old bachelor didn't care for lengthy conversations, the weather being his favorite topic. They dropped the canvas onto the ground near the postholes, then went back to help Vern gather the poles.

A half hour later they'd tied down the canvas flaps and were admiring their handiwork when Reverend Billy Ray Sanders and his wife, June, drove up in the church van with the folding tables.

"Looks like we're right on time." The reverend walked to the rear of the van and opened the back doors. His wife remained in the front seat, talking on her cell phone. June offered a quick wave and a fleeting smile but otherwise ignored the men.

The couple was in their mid-thirties and had arrived a week after Elaine's death to conduct her funeral. The husband-and-wife team had then remained in town and assumed Vern's duties while he mourned his wife's passing.

"We missed you in the coffee room after services last week, Vern," Sanders said.

"I had things to do."

Vern had admitted to Jackson that he avoided the social hour after the Sunday service because it was still too difficult for him to spend long periods inside the church without thinking of his wife. Not only had Elaine played piano for the choir, but she'd also taught Sunday school and a Bible study class.

"Hopefully you'll join us for coffee next time," Sanders said.

"Maybe," Vern muttered.

The reverend had agreed to take over the church for a few months, but half a year had gone by and Vern didn't appear any closer to resuming his preaching duties.

"Help me with this table." Jackson walked off, Vern following. When they were out of earshot of Sanders and Gifford, Jackson said, "The reverend and his wife are ready to move on and help another congregation, but they can't until you agree to take back the pulpit."

"I'm thinking about retiring."

"You tell everyone that, but you don't mean it."

"Sure, I do."

"You'd miss lording it over folks," Jackson said.

"How would you know that? You've only sat in the pews a few times through the years and those were for funerals."

"Others have told me how good you are at saving souls on Sunday."

"Are you mocking me?"

"Not at all."

"If I go back to preaching, will you attend services?"

"The Boss and I hold our weekly powwows beneath the cars in the garage."

"The Boss doesn't drive a car."

Jackson studied the old man.

"What are you gawking at?" Vern asked.

"There's something different about you." His sponsor's brown eyes shone brighter these days and Jackson attributed Vern's renewed energy to dating Shirley Pratt.

"I'm the same as I always was," Vern said.

No sense riling him by suggesting he might be ready to move on after the loss of his wife, but Jackson was confident that the old man was strong enough to stand before his flock and preach the word of God. Vern hadn't had a drink since the night he'd fallen off the wagon. Jackson admitted he might have jumped the gun when he'd asked Abby to return to Little Springs to take care of her father, but he'd been worried he'd lose his sponsor and his best friend. He hadn't considered how it would impact Abby, who'd put her life on hold to take care of her father.

"You've been doing an awful lot with Shirley." Twice Vern had canceled plans with Jackson so that he could show the older woman around the area—whatever that meant. The *area* consisted of a few miles in each direction. How much was there to see?

"What's my spending time with Shirley got to do with anything?"

"Nothing. I figured you'd want to show off to her."

"Show off what?"

"Your fire-and-brimstone speeches."

"Did Abby say something to you about me and Shirley?"

Jeez, he hadn't meant to open a can of worms.

Vern slapped his hand against his chest. "No one will ever replace Elaine in my heart."

"Abby wants you to be happy and I haven't seen you this content in a long time. I think it's because of Shirley."

Vern grimaced. "Shirley and Elaine would never have been friends."

"Probably not."

"Shirley's an opinionated snob who thinks she knows what's best for everyone, me included."

Jackson grinned. "She keeps you on your toes."

Vern's mouth wrestled with a smile and lost. "I like that she's unpredictable. I never know what's gonna come out of her mouth."

Jackson glanced across the park where Gifford and Sanders were putting the tables beneath the tent for the chili cook-off. "What does Abby think of Shirley?"

"She doesn't like her. But that might be because Shirley suggested Abby needed to find a husband before she became an old maid." Vern frowned. "Why are you grilling me with all these questions?"

"I'm not."

"I haven't pestered you about Katelyn."

"There's nothing going on between us."

"That's not what I heard."

"What did you hear?" Jackson asked.

"You two were seen kissing down by the tracks."

Had someone installed cameras near his and Katelyn's secret spot? "It was one little peck."

Vern stuck his foot out. "Pull the other one."

Jackson wished he hadn't confided his deepest fears to his sponsor, but Vern knew exactly how devastated he'd been when Katelyn had broken up with him.

"Katelyn's part of your past. Nothing good will come out of going back there, even for old times' sake." Vern clasped Jackson's shoulder. "You're a different man now that you've stopped drinking."

"Katelyn's not the same person she was all those years ago, either." He shrugged off his mentor's touch. "We're taking things slow."

Vern pointed a gnarled finger. "You and slow don't mix."

"What do you say we call a truce and quit badgering each other about women?"

"Gary's got this under control," Vern said. "I'd better get home. Shirley's coming over to help make my four-alarm chili."

Vern's chili recipe was more like one-alarm, but nobody had the heart to tell him. "I'm heading into Odessa," Jackson said.

"You sure you don't want to come to the celebration this afternoon?"

"I'll be back in time for the fireworks."

Jackson slid behind the wheel of his pickup and set the bakery box on the seat next to him—a peach pie he'd purchased from Mama's Kitchen yesterday. He passed Doris's house, then took the back road to the highway. As he drove across the tracks, Katelyn's image popped into his head. She was even more beautiful at forty than she'd been in high school.

With Vern's encouragement and a whole lot of AA meetings under his belt, Jackson had been able to place Katelyn on his shelf of life experiences and move on. But he hadn't expected to have to move on from her twice in one lifetime.

When he approached the outskirts of Odessa, he took a frontage road and traveled a half mile before pulling into the driveway of a yellow Victorian with black shutters. He drove to the end of the lot, where a small, nondescript guesthouse sat. Joan Kimble stepped onto the back porch of the Victorian after Jackson got out of his pickup.

"Hi, Joan."

"I see you brought another peach pie."

"Wouldn't show up without one."

"Enjoy your visit."

"Happy Fourth of July." Jackson knocked on the front door, then turned the knob and walked in.

"I was hoping you'd bring a pie," Nicole Parker said.

"Hi, Mom." He set the bakery box on the kitchen counter, then gave her a kiss on the cheek before he settled on the couch. Even though he saw her twice a month, she looked as if she aged a year between each visit. "How are you?"

"Fair to middling." She swung her wheelchair around and pushed herself closer to the coffee table. "Joan took me to a doctor's appointment last week and my blood pressure was a little high. Dr. Hamilton changed my prescription."

He never knew what to say when his mother discussed her health. A year ago a car accident had left her paralyzed from the waist down. The crash had killed her second husband—the man she'd married after she'd divorced Jackson's father.

He'd been caught off guard nine months ago when he'd gotten a call from a rehabilitation center in San Diego, informing him that his mother was ready to be released. After the shock had worn off, he'd made the trip to California, thinking all he had to do was find her an apartment and then return to Texas. He hadn't expected to see his mother in a wheelchair.

Since her husband was dead and she had no other kids or family except him, Jackson had brought her back to Texas and moved her into Joan's guesthouse—close enough to Little

Springs for him to check on her but far enough away that she wasn't part of his day-to-day life. Three times a week a visiting nurse came in to help her shower, do laundry and clean the house. His mother paid Joan to do the grocery shopping and chauffeur her to doctor appointments.

Over the past several months as they'd become reacquainted, it was clear his mother remembered the past differently. She hadn't kept in touch with him through the years, but she claimed she'd written numerous letters, insisting Jackson's father must have tossed them into the trash. Jackson didn't believe her, because he'd brought the mail in every day. He figured she told the lie because it made living with the guilt of abandoning her child easier.

At times he questioned his motive for reconnecting with his mother. Vern believed Jackson had forgiven her, but it was more complicated than that. His visits had served as a reminder to avoid personal relationships. His father's drinking had destroyed their family and made his mother turn her back on her only child. Nothing good came from being married to a drunk.

Jackson hadn't had a sip of booze in years, but he still had a lot of living to do, and without a crystal ball to see the future, he had no way of knowing if he'd be sober next week, let alone five years from now. Every day he woke up fighting on two fronts: *remaining* sober and *wanting* to remain sober.

"How's that neighbor of yours who works at the church?" his mother asked.

"Vern?"

"I don't know why I have trouble remembering his name."

"He has a new lady friend."

"That's nice." She stared out the front window.

Jackson hadn't mentioned Katelyn. He didn't see the point when he had no idea what was going to happen between them. He hadn't spoken to or run into Katelyn since he'd interrupted her sketching at their private spot. He'd acted like a jerk when he'd stalked off, after she'd called him out on his antisocial behavior. He'd given up booze, returned to his hometown to run a business—didn't that prove he'd moved on from the past?

But what if Katelyn was right and he was still holding himself back?

"Are you going over to the lake to watch the fireworks?" his mother asked, interrupting his thoughts.

He shook his head.

"Joan offered to drive me into Odessa to watch them go off at the park, but I don't want to get eaten by mosquitoes." She smiled. "How's work?"

"Business is steady."

"If you need a loan, I can give you one." His mother's deceased husband had managed a car dealership and had invested his savings in the stock market. The money, along with a life insurance policy, had left Jackson's mother well-off, but he'd have to be in dire straits before he took her cash.

He searched for something to talk about and when his gaze landed on the stack of books sitting next to the TV, he asked, "What are you reading?"

She rolled her chair across the room and picked up the book on top of the pile. "*The Life and Times of Lily Mills*. It's about an orphaned girl living in New York City during the late eighteen hundreds."

That topic exhausted, he asked, "Is there anything you need me to repair while I'm here?"

"There's a loose shelf in the kitchen cabinet."

"I'll take a look." He searched each cupboard until he found the wobbly shelf, then fetched a screwdriver from the toolbox in his truck.

After tightening the shelf, he checked the others. When he went back into the living room, he found his mother asleep. Without making too much noise, he cut her a piece of pie, placed a fork on the plate, then covered it with plastic wrap and set it on the coffee table before slipping out the door.

CHAPTER TWENTY-THREE

It's getting warm in here." Shirley's voice echoed from the kitchen.

Katelyn stopped at the bottom of the stairs and slipped into her sandals. Earlier in the morning she'd taken her sketch to the park for the silent auction and then she'd worked at the grocery store until noon. Abby had volunteered to take the afternoon shift until Walter closed the store for the day at five.

"It might hit a hundred degrees today. Don't you have a short-sleeve blouse to wear?" Birdie asked.

"I wanted to look nice for Vern when I help him hand out samples of his chili."

"You and Vern are becoming pretty chummy."

"He's a charming man."

Birdie snorted. "You like Vern because he lets you boss him around."

"I am not bossy."

Uh-oh. The old ladies were getting testy with each other.

"Where's my purse?"

"It should be out in the hallway," Birdie said.

Katelyn glanced at the empty table by the door. Shirley's purse had been there earlier in the morning when Katelyn had left the house.

"I put it on the table last night when I went to bed," Shirley said.

"I'm sure it'll turn up somewhere," Birdie said.

"I hope Vern's recipe wins today."

"I doubt he'll win if you helped him in the kitchen."

"I kept him company while he did all the cooking."

"You two are inseparable," Birdie said.

"Is there something wrong with that?"

"No. I'm sure you've been lonely since Robert died."

Shirley huffed. "I might miss my husband more if he hadn't cheated on me ten years ago with his secretary."

Katelyn gasped.

"I didn't know," Birdie said.

"I never told Don or Katelyn."

"I'll pour us a drink." Chair legs scraped across the floor; then Katelyn heard the squeaking pantry door open and close. "Why'd you stay with Robert?"

Shirley coughed. "This stuff is awful."

"Cheap rotgut takes getting used to."

"I stayed because I didn't have a choice," Shirley said.

"Everyone has a choice."

"What would I have done with myself if I'd divorced Robert?"

"Find a job. Or another husband."

Katelyn wasn't surprised by the advice. Her mother was a practical woman.

"I didn't want my friends pitying me or gossiping behind my back."

"You shouldn't care what other people think."

"Easy for you to say when your friends accept you for who you are. The women I socialized with had higher standards."

"Maybe you should have found new friends."

"You should encourage Katelyn to contest the divorce. I think Don is having a midlife crisis and he'll come to his senses soon."

Katelyn waltzed into the kitchen, intent on putting an end to her mother-in-law's fantasy once and for all. "I don't want to work things out with Don." She removed her wedding band in front of Shirley, then opened her mother's junk drawer and dropped it inside. She honestly didn't know why she'd waited until now. She'd been married to Don in her head all these years but not in her heart for a very long time.

Birdie held up her drinking glass, her eyes sparkling with humor. "Care to join us for a cocktail before we leave for the park?"

"No, thank you." Katelyn put the cap back on the schnapps bottle. "And you two need to lay off this stuff." She returned the bottle to the pantry. *What in the world?* "Shirley, why is your purse in here?" The white leather bag sat on the shelf between the potato chips and a box of cereal.

"I didn't put it there," Shirley said.

Katelyn looked at Birdie and her mother shrugged.

"I don't understand why you wouldn't want to save your marriage," Shirley said.

"I'd never be able to trust Don." When Shirley opened her mouth to protest, Katelyn set the purse on the table and said, "I don't love Don. Not the way a husband deserves to be loved."

"Then you shouldn't have married my son in the first place."

"I was scared."

"Of what?" Birdie asked.

Katelyn spread her arms wide. "I was afraid I'd end up back here in Little Springs after I graduated from college. I wanted to move forward with my life. Not backward." She drew in a deep breath. "I cared for Don, but I don't know that I ever loved him."

Shirley's eyes watered and she looked ready to cry. "I need to freshen my makeup before we leave." She took her purse and escaped into the powder room beneath the stairs.

Katelyn felt horrible that she'd upset her mother-in-law. "I can't let her guilt me into trying to fight for a marriage I don't want to be in anymore."

"Shirley's afraid of losing you," Birdie said. "She doesn't want to be alone."

"I've taken care of her for the past three years. It's Don's turn."

"How can he look after her when he travels all the time?" Birdie asked. "Shirley's a pampered princess. Leaving her on her own would be like turning a puppy loose in the woods and expecting it to survive."

"I can't believe you're defending her."

"Me, neither," Birdie said. "But it's possible you might be stuck with your mother-in-law the rest of your life."

"You're joking, right?"

Birdie's eyes shifted to the kitchen doorway. "She's not that bad if you ignore most of what she says."

"Don't tell me you two are becoming friends."

Birdie smiled. "Stranger things have happened in this town."

The silent auction was closing in a half hour, so Katelyn perused the items one last time before putting in a bid on a basket of spa supplies and a makeover from Sadie's hair salon; then she moved on to her sketch, excited to see the highest bid was three hundred dollars. Not bad for a few hours of work.

She studied the drawing with a critical eye.

"What's the matter?" Birdie stopped at her side.

"Something's off in the picture, but I can't figure out what it is."

Her mother narrowed her eyes. "That's you hiding in the boxcar, isn't it?"

"No."

Birdie laughed. "It's you all right."

"It's a pair of eyes. The body's hidden in the shadows. It could be a boy or a girl, depending on the viewer's perspective."

"This viewer says it's you." Birdie wagged her finger. "You had that same wary look in your eyes the night before you left for college."

"I did not." Katelyn took her mother by the arm and led her away from the tables. "I was excited to finally get out of this one-horse town."

"Yes, but you were worried about leaving Jackson behind."

"Maybe."

"You know why you were worried?"

She didn't bother answering, because her mother would speak her mind regardless. "You'd already decided that you wouldn't return to Little Springs after you finished school."

Katelyn didn't want to talk about Jackson. "Did you eat supper?"

"I had some of Vern's fake four-alarm chili an hour ago, but I could use a drink."

They cut across the grass to the concession stand. "Are you and Shirley going home to relax before the fireworks?"

"I hadn't planned on it," Birdie said. "Last year they shot them off at dusk."

"Where is Shirley?" Katelyn asked when they moved forward in the line.

"With Vern. Where else would she be?"

"Abby has her reservations about Shirley." Katelyn purchased two lemonades; then they sat at a table in the refreshment tent. "How are the others in the ladies' society getting along with my mother-in-law?"

"Miss Prissy Pants amuses them."

"Her apartment will be ready to move into soon. If she becomes too big of a pain, I'll drive her back to St. Louis."

"Vern might have something to say about Shirley leaving town."

Katelyn glanced at the chili tent. The happy couple stood side by side, handing out plastic sample cups. "Why haven't you dated since Dad died?"

"I like my own space." She smiled at Katelyn. "And I'm too old to coddle a husband."

"You don't get lonely?" Katelyn asked, then squirmed under her mother's probing stare.

"Are you afraid of being alone?"

"Maybe a little." Katelyn wasn't the kind of woman who needed attention from a man. If she were, she'd have filed for divorce when Don began traveling. "I already miss the kids and they haven't officially started college."

"Michael and Melissa are a lot like you. They're not afraid of leaving home."

"No, they're not."

"Aren't you eager to devote more of your time to painting?"

"Yes." She was excited but also nervous.

"Did you know Mavis played the drums in high school?"

Katelyn shook her head.

"And both Etta and Faye play the piano." Birdie lowered her voice. "And since I play the guitar, we're going to start a garage band."

Katelyn choked on a swallow of lemonade. "No offense, but you're a little old to be playing in a band." Much less in someone's garage.

"Of course we're old, but who cares? Doris is letting us use her place to practice."

"Have you picked a name for your band?"

"Harriet came up with the Hot Tamales."

"Why would Harriet get a say in the name?"

"She's the band manager."

"What about Nanette? What's she going to do?"

"She can play the wood block or the triangle."

Katelyn grinned.

"I've already written a song," Birdie said. "It's called 'No Men Allowed.' "

"Are you going to perform somewhere?"

"Harriet got the okay from Reverend Sanders to play at the congregation's fish fry in September. But we'll need a trial run before that." Birdie stared down the street. "Jackson's watching from his apartment window."

Katelyn followed her mother's gaze down the block to the window above the auto repair shop. She could barely make out his shadow behind the glass.

"He did the same thing last year. Stood in the window, watching the fireworks by himself." Birdie pushed her chair back. "I've got to find the group. The Hot Tamales are sitting together."

"See you later," Katelyn said, tearing her gaze away from the garage. She'd love to ask Jackson to join her for the fireworks, but he'd made it clear that he and crowds didn't mix.

Reverend Sanders's voice came over the loudspeakers, announcing the end of the silent auction, and Katelyn mingled with the group of spectators, eager to find out who'd won her sketch.

CHAPTER TWENTY-FOUR

The Pecos Chamber of Commerce set off fireworks over the waters of Catfish Bay, a mile north of Little Springs. The town had a clear view of the sky above Birdie's house, and the park was crowded with Little Springs residents and families who lived in the outlying areas. The only view better than the one from Jackson's bedroom window was the one from Birdie's front porch.

Jackson searched for Katelyn in the sea of people gathered in the park. He hadn't planned on coming out of his apartment after he'd returned from visiting his mother, but the memory of watching the fireworks down by the railroad tracks with Katelyn her last summer in town had dragged him outside.

He spotted her speaking with Gifford, who held Katelyn's sketch from the silent auction. Jackson balled his fingers into fists. If he'd had the guts, he would have left his apartment before dusk and outbid the junk-store dealer.

Until Katelyn had shown up in town, Jackson had been able to ignore his loneliness and the fact that his best friend was a seventy-year-old minister. He hadn't experienced anything close to an intimate relationship after Katelyn had broken up with him. Booze had been his mistress and on too many nights he'd crawled into bed with a bottle of Jack Daniel's. When the loneliness had grown unbearable, he'd settled for one-night stands or weekend flings with bar bunnies.

Jackson meandered through the crowd toward Katelyn, admiring her aqua sundress, which ended above the knees, the silky material swirling around her legs when she moved. He imagined moving his hands up her legs, beneath her skirt. . . . She turned toward him and their gazes clashed. Her smile widened, propelling him forward.

"I'm glad you came." She squeezed his fingers.

"Guess I'll take this to my store so it doesn't accidentally get ruined," Gifford said.

"See you, Gary." Katelyn's eyes never left Jackson's face.

He led her across the street, where it was less crowded, and they sat on the curb. Katelyn folded the hem of the dress around her knees.

"You look beautiful," he whispered in her ear.

"Thank you." Her cheeks turned pink, reminding him of how shy she'd acted when they'd first dated. "Guess who won the chili cook-off."

"Who?" he asked.

"Vern. I think the judges were terrified of Shirley."

"Speaking of your mother-in-law"—he nodded

to the tent where Shirley and Vern sat—"she doesn't look happy to see you with me."

"Shirley's upset because I took off my wedding band." Katelyn set her left hand on his thigh. The ring was gone.

His fingers entwined with hers.

"I've been ready to move on for a while," she said. "I just didn't know it."

Jackson wished she hadn't sounded so confident. He should leave well enough alone, but he couldn't. And he didn't want to. "Would you like to watch the fireworks from my apartment?"

Her brown eyes warmed, the gold specks glowing. "I thought you'd never ask."

He stood, then tugged her to her feet. If he'd believed kissing Katelyn had been a bad idea, then making love was going from bad to worse. "Do you need to tell your mother you're leaving?" Because once he had her in his bed, he wasn't letting her out of it until morning.

She laughed. "I hope I've outgrown my curfew."

Hand in hand, they walked away from the park and straight into the consequences that lay ahead.

Katelyn smiled at the sound of Jackson snoring. He slept on his back, his mouth half-open with one arm resting on his chest, the other across his forehead—not how she'd imagined them waking after a night in bed together. She'd envisioned him holding her, her leg resting between his thighs, her hand over his heart. Then again, their lovemaking hadn't played out as she'd expected, either.

The first time, Jackson had been careful with her—as if he'd feared one wrong move would send her running down the fire escape. His hands had played over her body with such gentleness that she struggled not to cry. And the look on his face after they'd made love almost broke her heart—it was as if he'd expected her to leave his bed and walk out the door.

She'd put his mind to rest when she'd initiated the second round of lovemaking, and by the time they'd crossed the finish line, the sheets were tangled at their feet and the pillows had fallen to the floor. They hadn't even heard the fireworks outside, because the ones going off in the bedroom had been louder. Afterward they'd showered, returned to bed and eaten Froot Loops out of the box while they watched a Netflix movie that she couldn't recall the name of or how it had ended, because Jackson's kisses and caresses had distracted her.

She had no idea why he'd decided to invite her into his bed, and rather than risk a morning-after apology or listen to his reasons why they shouldn't repeat last night, she padded quietly over to the chair and slipped on her panties and sundress. Sandals in hand, she tiptoed from the room.

At the apartment door she paused to take one last look around. Jackson's home was depressing—a dreary brown love seat and matching chair sat on the gray linoleum floor. The particleboard coffee table was barren, save for a single Route 66 drink coaster. A bookcase filled with car-repair manuals rested in the corner with a lone picture frame on top. She crept closer and examined the strip of black-and-white photo-booth pictures she and Jackson had taken at the carnival in Odessa the summer before she'd left for college.

He looked happy, but her smile wasn't as bright. Her stomach churned now and not from hunger. She could deny it all she wanted, but her mother had been right—a tiny part of Katelyn had always known she wouldn't return to Little Springs once she'd left. Her gaze swung to the bedroom door. Was history repeating itself? Had last night been about making another memory before she left again?

She stepped outside, put on her sandals and descended the fire escape. The sun was inching over the horizon and with luck she'd sneak home without being seen by anyone.

Fat chance. Ginny sat on the porch of Mama's Kitchen, peeling apples for her pies. When Katelyn came around the corner of the garage, Ginny raised her cup of morning joe and saluted her. Katelyn waved and continued on her way.

She had four hours to catch a catnap before she began her shift at the grocery store.

As she cut across the parking lot of the strip mall, a car horn honked. Why was Walter arriving at work this early? He pulled alongside her and lowered the passenger-side window.

"You don't start work until ten," he said.

"I know that." *What a moron.* Didn't he notice that she wore the same outfit he'd seen her in at the park yesterday? She continued walking.

"Then what are you—"

She stopped and he hit the brakes. She leaned through the open window. "Don't ask me where I've been, Walter."

He glanced in the rearview mirror. "So it's like that between you and Jackson now?"

"I'll see you at ten." She climbed the hill to her mother's house and found Birdie waiting on the front porch.

"What are you doing up this early?" Katelyn joined her on the steps.

"I thought it was time I used the front porch."

Yeah, right. "Go ahead and say it."

"Say what?"

"That I'm making a mistake with Jackson."

"Are you?"

"I don't know, but"—she smiled—"I'm not making a mistake taking it one day at a time." Which was a big deal for Katelyn, because she'd always made decisions based on how her actions would reflect on her husband, their marriage or their kids. She hadn't anticipated how liberating it would feel to do what was best for her.

Birdie quirked an eyebrow. "Actually I was about to say you look satisfied."

Oh, man, was she ever.

"After that early-morning stroll along Main Street, it won't be long before the whole town knows you're satisfied."

"You're better-looking than my son. I'll give you that."

Jackson's hand froze in the process of turning a bolt on the sedan he was working beneath. He glanced sideways and discovered a pair of shiny black flats staring him in the face.

"Are you going to hide under there or come out and speak to me?"

He'd rather hide, but Vern would give him an earful if he was rude to Vern's lady friend. Jackson pushed the creeper out from beneath the car, then climbed to his feet. "What can I do for you, Mrs. Pratt?" He doubted Katelyn had told anyone they'd slept together, so he assumed someone had seen her leaving his apartment.

"I'm not pleased that my daughter-in-law has decided not to reconcile with my son." She lifted her chin. "But I still know what's best for Katelyn."

He tugged the rag from his back pocket and

271

wiped the grease off his fingers. "And you're here to tell me that I'm not best for her."

"That's right, young man. Katelyn can do better"—her eyes traveled around the garage—"than a mechanic."

"You're right." No one needed to remind him that he had nothing to offer Katelyn.

"She's become accustomed to the finer things in life."

Jackson couldn't compete with Don's success, and he didn't care to. "Katelyn's a grown woman, Mrs. Pratt. She can be with whom she wants."

"She's built a life for herself in St. Louis."

The old lady was getting worked up over things that might not happen. "I have no expectations of Katelyn." And he hoped she didn't have any of him. "My life is right here in Little Springs. I'm not leaving."

"As long as we understand each other."

"Shirley?" Katelyn walked through the open bay door. "What are you doing here?"

Jackson soaked in the sight of Katelyn, and he didn't care if Shirley Pratt caught his gaze roaming over her daughter-in-law's figure. He hadn't spoken to Katelyn since she'd snuck out of his bed the morning after the Fourth of July celebration two days ago. He'd had forty-eight hours to wonder if she regretted their lovemaking. Forty-eight hours of berating himself for breaking his vow not to cross the line with her.

"I stopped by to ask how much an oil change costs," Shirley said.

Jackson let her get away with the lie.

"I had the oil changed in the Mercedes right before we left St. Louis," Katelyn said.

"I guess I forgot."

Vern entered the garage, his face lighting up when he saw Shirley. "I've been looking for you." He glanced at Katelyn. "You mind if I take your mother-in-law out to lunch?"

"Not at all," Katelyn said.

"My pickup's down the block." Vern pointed over his shoulder.

Shirley pulled the keys from her purse and dropped them into Vern's hand. "We'll take the Mercedes. It's more comfortable."

"You drove here?" Katelyn gaped.

"I parked behind the garage."

Vern jiggled the keys. "Let's go, then."

"Tell Birdie I won't be able to make it to her band rehearsal this afternoon." Shirley grasped Vern's arm and the couple walked off.

Jackson's eyes skimmed over Katelyn twice before returning to rest on her face. He was forty-one years old. He should have morning-after protocol down pat by now.

"That's weird." Katelyn frowned. "Shirley hasn't driven her car in over two years."

"You said she's growing absentminded. Maybe she forgot she didn't like driving." Katelyn's smile appeared genuine and the tension in Jackson's shoulders eased.

"I'm happy she found a new chauffeur." Katelyn pointed to the vehicle in the bay. "Are you busy?"

He braced himself for a the-other-night-was-a-mistake speech. "I can take a break."

She held up the sketch in her hand. It was the picture Gifford had won in the silent auction. "I figured out what's missing in this drawing. I was going to ask if you wanted to go down to the tracks with me."

If he'd known she'd act as if nothing had happened between them, he wouldn't have consumed half a bottle of heartburn medication since they'd slept together. "Sure. I can take a break."

"While you close up, I'll buy sandwiches from Mama's Kitchen and meet you at your pickup in fifteen minutes."

CHAPTER TWENTY-FIVE

Katelyn let out a quiet breath when she and Jackson arrived at the tracks. The five-minute ride to their private hideaway and the short walk along the path through the trees had been made in silence. She handed him the bag containing the salsa turkey sandwiches. "I'll be right back."

She crept closer to the tracks, stopping at the spot where she'd made the sketch. "This is the view I want." She drew an X in the dirt with the toe of her sandal.

"Aren't you going to eat first?" Jackson sat on the ground in front of their tree. She joined him, then took the sandwich and bottle of water he held out to her.

"Thanks." They ate while they talked about the weather and the latest gossip at the Buy & Bag; then she squished her wrapper into a ball. "My mother-in-law didn't stop at the garage to ask about an oil change, did she?"

He shook his head.

"I think Shirley's going to need more time before she accepts that Don and I aren't reconciling."

"She warned me away from you."

Katelyn laughed. "I may have to ask the lawyer

to add her name beneath Don's before I sign the divorce settlement."

"About the other night. I—"

"It's coming." She scrambled to her feet and returned to the spot she'd marked when they'd first arrived.

"Don't you want your sketch pad?"

She shook her head, staring into the distance at the beacon of light heading her way. When the locomotive drew closer, she shut her eyes and concentrated on the tremors in the ground beneath her feet. The tiny pulses of energy traveled up her calves, along her thighs and into her stomach, where they spread through her chest until her entire body quivered with energy.

The whistle blew and she jumped inside her skin but kept her eyes closed. Her heart pumped in rhythm with the steel wheels clanking against the rails. Years ago she'd stood by these tracks and envisioned herself jumping into an empty boxcar as the train sped by. She'd imagined the faraway places she'd see. The strangers she'd meet.

Her heart banged against her rib cage as the locomotive blew past her. She imagined herself catapulting into the empty boxcar and being whisked off to a solitary place inside herself.

As the freight cars thundered past, blowing her hair around her head, the scent of coal and hot iron filled her lungs. After the final car passed, her snarled hair settled onto her shoulders. The noise of the chugging wheels grew faint and the ground settled. She opened her eyes and found Jackson smiling at her.

"What was all that about?" he asked.

She returned to his side. "That was about this." She set the sketch on the ground, then took her charcoal pencil out of her pocket and went to work. She'd asked Gary if she could tweak her picture, and he hadn't objected. "It won't bother me if you talk."

"I'd rather watch you draw."

He was watching *her,* not the pencil moving across the paper. She didn't mind. Her creative side had always felt safe in his presence.

"I never loved Don the way a woman should love the man she marries." It was easy to bare her soul when she focused on her art.

"Why did you stay with him?"

"Guilt. And for the kids' sake." The pencil froze against the paper and she stared into space. "And I grew accustomed to his paycheck. The big house. Vacations. New cars." She worked on shading the inside of the boxcar.

"You aren't the first woman who's wanted better and you won't be the last."

"I wanted the perfect life." She set the pencil aside and looked Jackson in the eye. "And the need for perfection carried over to my artwork. I lost confidence in myself, so I made up excuses for not drawing."

"Because you felt guilty for marrying Don for the wrong reasons, you punished yourself and stayed with him."

She opened her mouth to deny the charge, but the words jammed up in her throat. "When my father-in-law passed away and Shirley moved in with us, I tried harder to ignore my unhappiness. I focused on the kids and their school activities, college visits and proms. But the hollow feeling in the pit of my stomach never went away." She pressed her hand against her midriff. "It took Don filing for divorce to make me see the truth."

"Are you more content now that you're focusing on your art again?"

"I'm happier than I expected to be. The parts of me that have been dormant for so long are slowly coming back to life and I feel more energized than ever."

"Where do you go from here?" he asked.

"I don't want to map out my future again. I want to learn to be content with not knowing where the road I'm traveling will take me."

He eagle-eyed her sketch. "The boxcar looks like a living, breathing entity now."

"Exactly." She ran her fingertip across his lips. He had the most beautiful mouth, but she'd never tell him, because it would embarrass him. Instead, she said, "You're amazing."

"After the other night, I've been waiting for

you to tell me that." He grinned, and she punched his arm playfully.

"You've always gotten my art." And he'd always gotten her.

He tugged on a strand of her hair. "Maybe we're rushing things."

"You think so?"

"You're not officially divorced."

"True." As much as she'd enjoyed rekindling the flame with Jackson, she wasn't ready to make a commitment to anyone but herself. The fact that he understood proved how well he knew her.

He cupped her cheek and stared into her eyes. "For now we'll settle for being friends."

"Friends with benefits or just friends?" She quirked an eyebrow.

"Just friends." He motioned to the sketch. "Grab your stuff, and I'll take you home."

"What's going on between you and Jackson?" Abby waltzed into the break room Saturday afternoon at the Buy & Bag. Katelyn was seated at the table, her feet up on a chair, sketch pad in her lap.

"Nothing. Why?"

"Dad said Jackson skipped his AA meeting yesterday and stayed awake until all hours of the night working on a car."

A week had passed since she and Jackson had visited the railroad tracks and decided to remain friends without benefits. They'd seen each other once—when she'd walked out of the grocery store, his pickup had zoomed past on the street. She thought he might give her a lift home, but he'd only waved.

She was both relieved and disappointed that they weren't sleeping together. "Jackson and I aren't fighting, if that's what you're asking."

Abby didn't look convinced, but she dropped the subject. "I could use your advice."

"Sure," Katelyn said, her attention on the portrait she'd begun drawing yesterday.

"My boss called."

"How old is your boss?"

"Steve's thirty-seven." Abby pulled out a chair at the table. "Why?"

"You've never mentioned him before, but you sounded excited when you brought him up just now." Katelyn smiled. "You have a crush on him, don't you?"

Abby looked away and opened her locker. "The company has a strict policy against dating coworkers."

"He's not your coworker. He's your boss."

Abby sighed. "Okay, fine. He's handsome. And brilliant."

"Divorced?"

"Never been married."

"Is he dating anyone?"

"No."

"Do you catch him watching you when he thinks you're not looking?"

Abby sucked in a quick breath. "Yes."

"You're pretty and smart. Any man in his right mind would have snapped you up before now, but I bet you're holding out because you want to be with Steve."

"If we date, one of us would have to leave the business."

"So quit. Find a job somewhere else and go after the man you want to be with." A long time ago Jackson had made Katelyn happy, and then she'd traded up for Don. What would have happened to her and Jackson if she'd returned to Little Springs after college? Would he have stopped drinking? Would she have kept drawing all these years?

"I've worked hard to climb the ladder at Milligan Natural Gas. I don't want to start at the bottom somewhere new," Abby said.

"You said you wanted kids."

"Becoming a mother shouldn't mean I have to give up my dream career."

"You're right," Katelyn said.

"Being part of Steve's team makes me happy. I miss the work and I miss him."

"You're in a tough spot," Katelyn said.

"Steve wants me to lead a new PR campaign." She offered a shy smile. "I don't like bragging, but I'm really good at what I do."

"What happens if you decline the opportunity?"

"I'll get passed over when the next special project comes along."

"Then go to Dallas."

"I don't know if my dad's strong enough to be left alone."

"He's not alone. He's got Shirley."

"But that relationship ends as soon as you and your mother-in-law return to St. Louis."

"If they're still getting along by the end of the summer, maybe Shirley will invite Vern to St. Louis."

"I can't picture my father living out his last years anywhere but here. And there's Jackson."

"What about Jackson?"

"Dad's his mentor. He won't leave him high and dry."

"Jackson wants what's best for your dad. He'll find another sponsor."

"Dad's more than a sponsor, Katelyn. Jackson is like a son to my father. And I can never repay Jackson for being there when my dad fell off the wagon after my mother died."

A noise sounded outside the break room. Abby poked her head around the doorway. "Walter's coming." She turned back to Katelyn. "Any chance Shirley would consider relocating to Little Springs?"

Good God. "No."

"That's what I thought."

"Go to Dallas, Abby. At least for a few weeks. Jackson and I will keep tabs on Shirley and your dad."

"A few weeks would give me time to develop a campaign. Then Steve could take over if I have to return."

Hopefully that wouldn't be the case and Abby could remain in Dallas.

"Since when did fifteen-minute breaks become thirty?" Walter asked when he entered the room.

"Katelyn's on her lunch break, and I quit," Abby said.

Walter frowned. "Why? What happened?"

"It's time for me to return to Dallas." Abby slipped off her smock and tossed it into her locker. "Thank you for allowing me to work here while I was in town. I'd have gone crazy without something to do every day."

"What about giving your two weeks' notice?"

"I'll work more hours until you hire someone to replace Abby, and you don't have to pay me overtime," Katelyn said.

"Thank you." Abby hugged Katelyn. "It's been fun working with you. Tell Layla I'll give her a call before I skip town." Abby left through the back door.

"I can ask Birdie to cover Abby's hours," Walter said.

"I'll do it." Katelyn wanted her mother to enjoy the rest of her summer, and if she and Jackson weren't spending all their free time together anymore, then she needed to keep busy.

"Did you see this?" Walter pulled a yellow flyer from his pocket and handed it to Katelyn.

She unfolded the paper. Her mother's band was performing tonight at Doris's house. "I guess I know what I'm doing later."

Walter pointed to her sketch. "What are you working on?"

She turned the paper toward him. "Doris Clemmons." Ever since she'd helped the old woman find the aloe vera juice in the store, Katelyn had wanted to draw her face.

"I never noticed her eyes before. Is she always in that much pain?"

"She injured her back years ago." Katelyn studied the face on the paper. "But despite her pain, she manages a smile for everyone."

"I'll need your help up front for the rest of the day." Walter left the break room.

Katelyn set her charcoal pencil down and studied her work. She'd left town believing the only images worth drawing were beyond the boundaries of Little Springs. Why had it taken her so long to realize that it wasn't places that had stories to tell, but the people who lived there?

CHAPTER TWENTY-SIX

When Katelyn came around the side of the house, she ran into Shirley on the back porch.

"You put in a long day at work," her mother-in-law said.

"My dogs are barking." Katelyn climbed the steps and then sat in the chair and parked her feet on the porch rail. "Where's my mother?"

"She's at Doris's."

"Why didn't you go with her?"

"Vern's picking me up. We're going out to dinner before the concert."

It was already six o'clock. "What time is he supposed to get here?"

Shirley fussed with the buttons on her blouse. "Soon."

For all Katelyn knew, Shirley might have forgotten what time Vern told her to be ready and she'd been waiting on the porch all afternoon. "You two are spending a lot of time together."

"I'm not the one sneaking through town at dawn after spending the night with an old boyfriend."

No way did she want to discuss Jackson with her mother-in-law. "What's going to happen between you and Vern when we return to St. Louis?"

"I'll be back here to visit again."

Katelyn's mouth dropped open. "But you hate Little Springs."

"*Hate* is a strong word. I prefer St. Louis, but this town has a few things going for it."

"Like what?"

"Sadie's hair salon." Shirley pointed to her head. "She does a better job on my hair than Pam ever did."

"What about the lack of fine dining?" Katelyn said.

"I don't know why everyone likes Ginny's pies. I've had better."

"Besides not having a decent restaurant, you don't fit in with the ladies around here," Katelyn reminded Shirley.

"It's true that I have more class than the members of the ladies' society, but I'm willing to overlook that and call them friends."

Katelyn had never imagined she'd see the day her mother-in-law called women who ate Tombstone frozen pizzas her friends.

Shirley took a deep breath, then exhaled loudly. "The ladies I socialized with in Kansas City weren't friends—not in any true sense of the word. They would never have accepted a stranger into their circles the way your mother and the other women welcomed me. I know I'm opinionated and that I can be difficult to get along with, but real friends put up with your faults."

"So you like being part of the Little Springs Ladies' Society."

"At our age it no longer matters what kind of car you drive or home you live in." Shirley jutted her chin. "Having said that, I refuse to give up my Mercedes."

Katelyn had never thought she'd see the day her mother-in-law defended those below her on the social ladder.

"I'm going to ask Vern to return to St. Louis with us."

"You didn't by chance talk to Abby today, did you?"

"She stopped by earlier to tell me that she's leaving for Dallas."

"Is that all she said?"

"She mentioned that Vern's never been to Missouri and would enjoy seeing St. Louis."

"Are you inviting him for a visit or longer?"

"I haven't decided." Shirley's eyes sparkled and Katelyn couldn't recall her mother-in-law acting this happy in years.

"How did Vern take the news that Abby's leaving?"

"I don't know. I'll find out soon." Shirley shifted her attention to the end of the driveway, where Vern's pickup turned in. He parked next to the Mercedes.

"Hello, ladies," he said as he approached the porch.

"Did you speak with Abby?" Shirley asked when he propped a foot on the bottom step.

"She's leaving for Dallas in the morning."

"And . . . ?" Shirley prompted.

Vern smiled. "She said I was in good hands with you."

Katelyn wasn't sticking around to watch two old people make goo-goo eyes at each other. She was halfway to the door when Vern's voice stopped her.

"Jackson's finally found a sense of peace and purpose in Little Springs, Katelyn. If you ask him to give that up, I'm concerned he'll fall back into his old ways."

The old man wasn't giving Jackson enough credit. The town mechanic was a lot stronger than people believed. "You're worrying for nothing. We're friends." She escaped inside, letting the screen door bang closed behind her.

Katelyn checked her reflection in the mirror one last time. She'd curled her hair but hated the results. She looked like a forty-year-old woman trying to pretend she was sixteen. It was time to stop using her long hair as a weapon against her mother-in-law.

The woman staring back at her in the mirror was the old Katelyn—the young girl who'd given up parts of herself when she'd married Don and had the twins. It was time to say good-bye to her.

She left the house and headed down the hill to Main Street. When she passed Mendoza Auto, the bay door was closed, but the lights were on. She hoped Jackson would come to the concert. Reflecting back on their time together in high school, she was ashamed that she'd been so caught up in her own dreams and plans that she hadn't been aware Jackson had felt like an outcast in his hometown. She turned the corner at the end of the block and saw a crowd gathering in Doris's driveway. Sadie raised her hand and waved Katelyn over.

"I saved you a seat." She patted the lawn chair next to her, then opened the cooler by her feet and offered Katelyn a beer.

"No, thanks." She wasn't a beer drinker.

"Isn't it fabulous what your mother is doing?"

"I admit Mom surprised me when she said she'd formed a band."

"I saw Birdie play once. Did she tell you that?"

"No."

"She was singing at the Hoot-n-Holler in Pecos. They closed the bar years ago." Sadie swatted at a fly buzzing her head. "Birdie was nine months pregnant with you, but she managed to hold that guitar despite her big belly." Sadie smiled. "When she sang, everyone in the bar stopped talking. Birdie's voice was like smoke—low, smooth and hypnotizing. She sang three songs, then packed up her guitar and left. Two days later she gave birth to you."

And then Birdie had stowed her dream away and gone on with life.

A commotion at the front of the driveway drew Katelyn's attention. The garage door rose and the Hot Tamales came into view. And what a view it was. The ladies wore colorful sombreros and matching red blouses with sparkly gold bell-bottom pants. Katelyn's mother wore lipstick and looked ten years younger.

"Where did they get those outfits?" Katelyn asked.

"Ginny and I helped sew them."

"We're the Hot Tamales," Birdie spoke into a microphone. "Our first number is called 'No Men Allowed.' "

"Boo!" Gary laughed.

"Behave, Mr. Gifford, or I'll escort you back to your junkyard." Harriet winked, and the audience cheered her.

Birdie strummed her guitar, and Mavis pounded a steady beat on the drums. Faye and Etta played the piano together, while Nanette clunked a stick against a wood block.

Birdie's eyes scanned the onlookers, her lips pressing into a flat line. Katelyn could feel her mother's apprehension. It was difficult to expose your soul to people, understanding that not everyone would treat it kindly. Katelyn put her fingers in her mouth and whistled. When her mother looked her way, she gave a thumbs-up.

"Men," Birdie sang, "drive women insane. . . ."

Everyone cheered, and Birdie stood straighter, her hand moving more confidently across the guitar strings.

Sadie was right about Birdie's voice—the low notes flowed from her mouth in smooth whispers that pulled the audience forward in their seats. After the second verse, Katelyn no longer heard the drums, or even the guitar—only her mother's voice reached her ears.

When the ditty ended, Katelyn stood and clapped. "You go, Mom!"

"Sing us another one, Birdie!" Gary hollered.

"This one's called 'Go Cheat with Yourself.'" Birdie's voice grew stronger. As Katelyn listened, it occurred to her that if her sixty-year-old mother could stand in front of her peers and sing, then there was no reason why Katelyn couldn't find the courage to put her artwork in front of strangers.

Halfway through the third song, Katelyn's neck itched. She turned her head, and her gaze collided with Don's. Her soon-to-be ex stood out like a sore thumb in a suit and tie. She left her chair and skirted the crowd. The spare tire around his middle appeared smaller. How long had it been since they'd seen each other? Two months? More?

She grasped his arm and escorted him behind

a tree out of view of the concertgoers. "What are you doing in town?"

"I brought the divorce agreement for you to look over."

"You could have mailed it." She hadn't planned on finding a lawyer until she returned to St. Louis sometime in August, but apparently Don was in a hurry to be rid of her.

"I also flew out here to check up on my mother, since she isn't returning my calls."

This was the first time she'd heard about Shirley ignoring Don's attempts to reach her.

"I saw the note taped to the back door," he said, "so I walked down here and followed the sound of the music."

Katelyn had left a message for Layla that she'd be at the concert. Her coworker had mentioned she might drop by to chat while Brian and Gavin went to an arcade in Pecos.

Don's gaze dropped to her left hand. "You took your ring off."

If they weren't standing in the middle of a crowd, she might fling a four-letter word at him. "Did you think I'd lament over you after you cheated on me?"

"I admit I could have handled things better."

You think? "We had almost nineteen years together and two kids. I deserve more respect than you've shown me."

He shoved a hand through his thinning hair.

"I'm sorry." He didn't sound sorry. "Since when did Birdie start singing in a band?"

"Since a couple of weeks ago."

His gaze searched the crowd. "I don't see my mother."

"She's not here." They needed to talk, but Katelyn didn't want to draw attention away from the band. "Let's get out of here." They walked down the block, and when they turned the corner, she pulled up short.

"Jackson." Katelyn introduced the two men. "Don, this is Jackson. Jackson, Don."

Neither man offered a handshake.

"I was on my way to the concert," Jackson said.

Surprised he'd decided to go, she said, "The Hot Tamales sound great."

She felt Don's fingers grip her arm. "If you'll excuse us." She walked on, Don at her side, neither speaking as they passed the Buy & Bag and climbed the hill to Birdie's house. When they reached the front yard, she sat on the porch steps. "It was rude of you to show up unannounced. You should have called before coming to town."

"So you could warn your old boyfriend?"

"We're friends." Not that she needed to explain their relationship to him. Don paced in front of the porch. The man was always moving . . . thinking ahead . . . planning. Never relaxing. He was nothing like Jackson, who found pleasure in sitting quietly and soaking in the moment. "Can I ask you something?"

"What?"

"Why didn't you tell me you were unhappy?"

"You know me. I don't like dealing with emotions."

"Your mother believes you're having a midlife crisis."

He shrugged. "Call it what you want."

"The kids phoned me. They're upset."

"I know." He pushed his fists into his pants pockets.

"The divorce might have gone better with them if you hadn't cheated."

Don stared at his shoes. "Lauren wasn't the first time, Katelyn."

Any nostalgic feelings she had left for Don or their marriage died a quick death. "How many?"

"Does it matter?"

"Yes, it matters. I gave up a lot"—of herself—"when I was married to you." At his perplexed expression, she said, "I don't intend to bad-mouth you in front of the twins, but I'm not your ally anymore. Don't count on me to encourage them to forgive and forget." It occurred to Katelyn that the only thing she could say about their relationship after so many years of marriage was that they had two great kids.

"The papers are in the rental car." Don walked away.

Katelyn followed him around the house, and they reached the driveway right as Shirley's Mercedes turned in.

"Who's driving my mother's car?"

"Her boyfriend."

Don didn't have a chance to react before Shirley got out of the car and swatted the back of her son's head with her hand.

"Hello, Mother."

"What in the world is the matter with you? I raised you better than to—"

"Aren't you going to introduce me to your boy, Shirley?" Vern stepped forward, saving Don from another wallop.

"This is my son, Donald," Shirley said.

"Vern Wilkes." The men shook hands.

"Vern's a minister," Shirley said.

"Don't worry," Vern said. "I have the utmost admiration for your mother."

Don's head jerked as if Vern had slapped him, and Katelyn swallowed a chuckle. It was about time someone reminded Don that he should show more respect for his mother.

Shirley glanced between Don and Katelyn. "Does your visit mean you two are—"

"No," Don said. "I brought Katelyn a copy of the divorce agreement, and I wanted to see how you're doing."

Shirley's lips trembled, and Vern slipped his arm around her waist.

"Everything will be okay, Mom," Don said.

"How will it be okay when you want to put me into an apartment and then forget about me?" Shirley pointed at Katelyn. "I was never in favor of you marrying her, but your wife cares more about me than you do."

"That's true," Katelyn said.

"I'm here for you, too, Shirley," Vern said.

Don cleared his throat. "I was trying to do the right thing by finding a place for you to live, but I realize now that I should have asked if you wanted to move into the apartment before I signed the lease."

"Yes, you should have."

"Do you want me to keep the apartment or break the lease?" Don asked.

"Am I welcome to live with you?"

Katelyn silently applauded Shirley for putting her son on the spot.

"I'd have to speak with Lauren first."

Shirley sucked in a loud breath. "It didn't matter what your wife thought three years ago when you invited me to move into your house."

Right now Katelyn loved her mother-in-law.

"Maybe we should discuss this later," Don said.

"I'm keeping the apartment. Vern's never been to St. Louis, and we'll be staying there this fall."

"So you two are . . . ?" Don stared at Vern.

"Your mother's a special lady," Vern said.

"I'd like to take you both out to lunch tomorrow before I fly back to St. Louis."

"We'd enjoy that," Vern said.

Don faced Katelyn. "Can I have a private word with you?"

Shirley hugged her son. "I'm glad you came."

Vern offered his hand, and Don said, "Nice meeting you."

Shirley and Vern walked over to Katelyn. "We stopped by Doris's for a few minutes. Birdie's a better singer than I thought she'd be."

Don waited until the pair entered the house before he spoke. "Mom seems happy."

"Vern's wife died this past Christmas."

"The new owners move in November first, so you have time to figure out where you're going to live and what furniture you want to take with you."

"Thanks for the heads-up."

"Melissa said she's staying with a friend in Georgia when she returns from overseas."

"Mom and I plan to meet her at Stephens to help her get settled in."

"I'd go, but—"

"You're traveling." Katelyn studied Don. The lines bracketing his mouth appeared deeper and his skin sallow. Perhaps the price of his infidelity was taking a toll on him.

"Please make time for the kids," she said. "I know they're adults now and they'll be busy with college, but don't forget about them."

"I'm not an ogre, Katelyn."

"Right now the twins think you are."

He walked to the rental car and opened the driver's-side door, then pointed to the manila envelope she held in her hands. "I didn't screw you over."

"My lawyer will be in touch." Katelyn tossed the envelope onto the porch steps, then headed back to Doris's house.

CHAPTER TWENTY-SEVEN

"Earth to Layla." Katelyn smiled at her coworker, who stared in a trance late Monday morning.

"Sorry." Layla shook her long locks. "What did you say?"

Ever since the brunette had arrived at work, she'd acted distracted. "There's something different about you." Katelyn pointed to her face. "You're not wearing false eyelashes." And she wasn't wearing as much makeup, either. Without the lashes, dark eyeliner and sparkling shadow, Layla almost looked too young to be the mother of a twelve-year-old. "What's going on with you?"

"Brian and I slept together."

"Congratulations. How was it?"

"Amazing." Layla's cheeks turned pink. "He doesn't look like the kind of guy who'd be good in bed, but . . ."

Katelyn laughed. "Does this mean you two are in a relationship?"

Layla's smile faltered. "Don't get me wrong. I like Brian a lot. He's nice and generous, and he gets along well with Gavin."

"But . . . ?"

"He's an Entenmann's deliveryman."

"So?"

"I've spent my whole adult life trying to make ends meet." She waggled a finger. "I want what you have . . . or had. A husband who makes enough money so I can stop worrying about paying my bills on time and I can buy whatever I want when I need it."

Katelyn remained silent—to accuse Layla of being ridiculous and shallow was like the pot calling the kettle black. At least Layla had the guts to admit what she wanted and not lie to herself like Katelyn had all these years. Their conversation was cut short when the doors swooshed open and Brian and Gavin waltzed into the store.

"Brian got the day off, Mom, and he's taking me fishing."

"Did you thank him?" Layla wasn't looking at her son when she asked the question. It was obvious that she wished she could go with them.

Katelyn wandered away from her register and pretended to straighten the magazine display. After Brian and Gavin left, she said, "You don't look well, Layla. Maybe you should go home." She paused to see if their boss would step out of his office. He didn't, so she spoke louder. "I don't want to catch whatever it is you're coming down with." When Layla scrunched her forehead in confusion, Katelyn signaled her to play along.

A moment later Walter appeared in the doorway. "Who's not feeling well?"

"Layla looks feverish," Katelyn said, "and pale at the same time." If her coworker wanted to play hooky and fish with her guys, she'd better act more convincing.

"I've had a headache since I clocked in." Layla rubbed her temples.

"I can't send you home. The produce truck gets here in an hour."

"I'll stock the produce between customers," Katelyn said. Good grief, it was noon and only fifteen people had been in the store since it had opened.

"I feel faint." Layla leaned against the counter and fanned herself.

"Fine. Go home and rest." Walter returned to his office and closed the door.

"Thanks, Katelyn," Layla whispered.

"Have fun and use sunscreen. You don't want to show up at work tomorrow with a tan."

Layla giggled. "Good idea."

A short while later Walter stopped at Katelyn's register. "Birdie's coming in for a couple of hours."

"It hasn't been that busy."

"She said she wasn't doing anything this afternoon."

If Katelyn had known he'd ask her mother to fill in, she wouldn't have put the bug in Layla's ear to leave.

"If you have time before the delivery truck arrives, will you fill the cigarette case?"

"Sure."

Walter walked away but stopped after a few steps. "I know Layla's not sick." He kept a straight face. "Hopefully she'll catch a fish or two."

"You're not such a bad guy, Walter."

"Does that mean you'll have dinner with me before you leave town?"

"No."

He shrugged. "Had to give it a shot."

Katelyn finished stocking the smokes right as her mother arrived. "I'm sorry Walter asked you to come in."

"I don't mind. Gives us a chance to catch up." Birdie buttoned her employee smock.

"What's Shirley doing?" Katelyn asked.

"I dropped her off at Vern's house. They're making a new chili recipe for next year's cook-off." She studied Katelyn. "What's going on between you and Jackson?"

"What are the gossipmongers saying?"

Birdie shrugged. "That you haven't spent the night at his apartment since the Fourth of July celebration."

That was true.

"And you two haven't been seen sneaking off to the railroad tracks together."

"Jackson thinks we should remain friends."

Friends who avoided each other. She'd planned to stop by the garage on her way into work today, and she swore he saw her coming and that was why he'd closed the bay door and turned off the lights.

"Is it because he knows you're leaving?"

"Maybe but I'm okay with being friends." She actually appreciated the breathing room as she adjusted to the changes taking place in her life.

"Where have you been sketching when you're not working?" Birdie asked.

"Here and there. Wherever the impulse strikes." She'd gone to the tracks once by herself, but it didn't feel the same without Jackson there.

"When I gassed up your car at the Texaco the other day," Katelyn said, "I drew the convenience store. Yesterday I walked over to Gifford's Resale and sketched the back of the building where Gary keeps all the junk that won't fit in his store. Later I sat in the park and drew Etta and Faye having tea on the porch of Mama's Kitchen."

"Speaking of drawing." Birdie walked over to the bulletin board across from the registers and took down a flyer. "Did you see this?" She held out the paper. "You should register and pay for a booth."

PECOS THIRD ANNUAL ART FESTIVAL,
SUNDAY, AUGUST 7

Intrigued, Katelyn scanned the flyer for more information. "They're charging five hundred dollars for a booth." She doubted she'd recoup the money. But it would be a great opportunity to find out if people were willing to pay for her artwork. But what if she didn't sell a single sketch or painting? "I don't have enough inventory."

"You gave up your art when you married Don. You said you were too busy raising the kids. Are you going to keep making excuses?"

Katelyn hated it when her mother was so blunt.

"Before you left for college, you would have jumped at an opportunity to show off your talent."

"I'm not that Katelyn anymore."

"I didn't believe I was the same Birdie who grew up with a guitar in her hands, but you pushed me to play again, and I discovered a lot of the old Birdie was still inside me. It's my turn to push you."

If her mother had found the courage to share her passion with others, then Katelyn could do no less. "I'll think about it."

"I thought you were taking the summer off from your job." Doris set her handbasket on the checkout counter and looked at Birdie.

"I'm filling in for Layla today." Birdie snatched the flyer out of Katelyn's hand. "Did you see this? Katelyn's entering her work in the art show."

"Your mother's mentioned your talent," Doris said.

"It's a mom's job to brag about her kid." Katelyn smiled.

"You're not getting your blueberries from Etta and Faye's garden?" Birdie scanned the carton of fruit.

"Their blueberries didn't come in this year. Faye blamed Etta for not putting enough organic matter in the soil."

While the two women conversed, Katelyn excused herself and returned to the break room. She'd call the number on the flyer, and if they still had a booth left, she'd take it and worry about what pieces to show later.

"Where are you off to this early in the morning?" Birdie asked when Katelyn waltzed into the kitchen with her purse in hand Friday morning.

"Sadie's giving me a haircut before I go into work." She grabbed a banana from the bowl on the counter. "Later this afternoon I'm heading down to the tracks to work on my drawings." She paused at the back door. "The chairwoman of the art show in Pecos confirmed that I have a booth." And despite Jackson's cold shoulder, Katelyn was counting on their special place to calm her nerves and nurture her creativity.

"That's great news," Birdie said. "If you need

more time to prepare, I'll cover your shifts at the store."

"I think I'll be fine."

"Have you told Jackson about the art show?"

Katelyn shook her head. They still hadn't spoken since she'd run into him a week ago when Don had shown up in town.

"Vern told Shirley that Jackson's been in a grumpy mood since you two spent the night together."

"Vern should be pleased. He thinks I'm a bad influence on Jackson."

"He's protective of him."

"Whose side are you on, Mom?"

"Yours, of course." Birdie winked.

Katelyn opened the screen door, then asked, "What are you doing today?"

"Gary's closing his store early and driving me over to the Shady Lady to play for a few hours."

"You landed a gig at the bar on Route Thirty-nine?"

"Yep."

"Are you and Gary . . . ?"

"Nope. He's got his eye on a cocktail waitress, and he's using me as an excuse to hang out at the bar."

"I'll try to swing by later and watch you."

"You'd better not. I want you to work on your drawings so you don't have an excuse to bail on the art festival."

"If you have the guts to sing in a bar in front of strangers, then I can find the courage to let art enthusiasts gawk at my work."

"That's my girl."

Katelyn left the house and cut through the strip mall parking lot, then crossed the street and headed toward the park and around the block to the salon.

"I'm here, Sadie," Katelyn called out when she stepped into the shed.

" 'Morning." Dressed in leopard-skin leggings and a black satin sleeveless blouse, Sadie guided Katelyn to the chair in front of the washbowl. "After you phoned last night, I browsed through my collection of hairstyle magazines and found the perfect cut for you."

"Good. I'm ready for a change."

Sadie sprayed warm water over Katelyn's head, then worked shampoo through the strands. "You know what they say about a woman who cuts her hair."

"What's that?"

"She's about to change her life."

When Katelyn had studied her image in the mirror the previous evening, she'd made an amazing discovery—the length of her hair matched the number of years she'd been married: almost nineteen inches. She'd kept her hair long because her mother-in-law hated it, but she hadn't realized the hairstyle had also mirrored her marriage—both had been in a rut.

From now on when she looked at her reflection, she wanted to see the future, not the past—a woman taking charge of her destiny and happiness.

Sadie wrapped a towel around Katelyn's wet head, then escorted her to the styling chair. "Do you want to see the photo of the haircut I have in mind?"

"Surprise me."

"I'm thinking lots of layers and side-swept bangs."

"That works as long as I don't have to spend a half hour styling it."

"You're okay with a choppy look that you can air-dry and fluff with your fingers?"

"That sounds perfect."

Sadie combed the wet mass. "I'm going to hack off your hair above your shoulders, so close your eyes if you'd rather not watch."

Katelyn kept her eyes open, her gaze following each strand as it fell to the floor.

"You need both highlights and lowlights," Sadie said.

"Don't go to too much trouble."

"This is as much fun for me as it is for you." Sadie wielded the scissors like a pro, bits and pieces of hair flying in all directions. After fifteen minutes she stood back and studied her efforts. "Perfect." Then she spun the chair so Katelyn faced the mirror.

"Wow."

"Is that a good *wow* or a bad *wow?*"

"I like that you left the bangs longer." The style didn't take any years off Katelyn's face, but the woman staring back at her in the mirror appeared confident and even a little sassy. "My head feels a lot lighter." No more weight dragging her down. *Or holding me back.*

"You'll have to tell me what Jackson thinks when he sees your new cut."

"I don't care what anyone thinks." Katelyn smiled. "I did this for me."

Sadie held a cardboard swatch of color samples in front of Katelyn's face. "I'd like to use warm chestnut along the sides and back and then frame your face with the bronze."

"I have to be at the Buy & Bag in an hour."

"Walter won't care if you're late when he sees the new you."

"He's interviewing job applicants this morning. I need to set a good example and show up on time."

"Abby should have gone back to Dallas months ago. Vern guilted that poor girl into staying." Sadie mixed the hair color and placed the bowls on a tray, then painted the color onto thin strips of hair and wrapped the strands in foil sheets. "I was having lunch the other day at Mama's Kitchen and Ginny said she thinks Shirley will talk Vern into leaving Little Springs for good."

"Would that be a bad thing if he left?" Other than Jackson having to find a new AA sponsor.

"The town will have to search for another minister. Reverend Sanders and his wife are nice enough people, but they made it clear when they filled in for Vern that they don't want to stay here forever. They want to work with a younger parish."

Sadie spun the chair and used the foils on Katelyn's bangs. "If you could talk your mother-in-law into moving to Little Springs, then Vern would return to the pulpit, and everyone would be happy."

"You'd have better luck convincing Shirley to let her hair grow long than to live in West Texas."

"Speaking of Shirley's hair . . . I've done three deep-conditioning treatments since she's been here and I have to say she tips well."

Usually her mother-in-law was stingy with tipping unless Katelyn prodded her to leave more money. "How much does she give you?"

"Twenty dollars."

Wonders never cease. Little Springs wasn't only changing Katelyn; it was working its magic on the former perm queen, too.

CHAPTER TWENTY-EIGHT

K atelyn?"

She stopped in the middle of the bread aisle when Walter came around the endcap and then put the brakes on.

"What did you do to your hair?" he asked.

Walter wasn't her therapist, so the only explanation he'd get from her was: "I decided I needed a change."

"Why did you cut off so much?"

"What's the matter? Don't you like it?"

He backed up a step. "I like it fine."

A squeal pierced Katelyn's ears and she spun. "Oh, my God, I love your hair!" Layla rushed forward. "The color's amazing. Did Sadie do this?"

"Just a few hours ago."

Layla grasped Katelyn's arm and walked with her to the registers. Walter disappeared inside his office and shut the door. "You look ten years younger."

She laughed. "I do not."

"Jackson will love it."

"I didn't change my hair for Jackson. I did it for myself."

"Doesn't matter." Layla waved her hand. "He'll still love it."

"It was a spur-of-the-moment decision." And one she didn't regret making.

"You and Jackson should go out to a fancy restaurant tonight," Layla said. "Doll yourself up and put on high heels."

"We decided that we're staying friends for right now."

"Why?"

"I need to focus on my art and helping my kids get through the divorce." And Jackson didn't trust her not to hurt him again.

"Your kids will be fine."

Katelyn agreed. Michael and Melissa were strong, independent young adults and she was confident that with time they'd adjust to their parents' splitting up.

"Any sane woman would jump at the opportunity to sleep with a handsome man after her husband cheated on her with a younger woman."

"I don't know that she's younger."

Layla wrinkled her nose. "They're always younger."

"I want to focus on me and . . ."

"And what?"

"Look, I care for Jackson, but if I'm going to be with him, then I need to be sure it's for the right reasons."

"I'm not following."

"I don't want him to be my rebound guy."

"A girl's gotta do what a girl's gotta do to survive."

"Maybe, but Jackson and I are different people than we were all those years ago." Katelyn rearranged the display of candy bars at the checkout but stopped when she saw her work buddy staring into space. "What's the matter?"

"It's what you said about being different people. The more I hang out with Brian, the more I feel like I'm losing the old me." Layla shrugged. "This morning I walked right past the mirror without checking my reflection."

"You aren't wearing as much blush anymore." And Layla had toned down her bright lipstick.

"Brian said I was even more beautiful without makeup." Layla's cheeks turned pink.

"Does this mean your feelings for him are deepening?"

"He's the nicest boyfriend I've ever had." A deep sigh escaped her.

"What is it?"

"I wish Brian wasn't so content being an Entenmann's deliveryman."

The doors whooshed open, putting their confession session on hold.

"Good morning, Harriet," Katelyn said.

"Ladies." The older woman picked up a handbasket, then turned toward the registers, her gaze focusing on Katelyn. "You cut your hair."

"Do you like it?" Katelyn asked.

313

"It's very becoming. What does your mother think?"

"Mom hasn't seen it yet."

"And Jackson?" Harriet asked.

"He hasn't seen it, either." She steered the conversation in a new direction. "Everyone loved the Hot Tamales."

"I'm trying to convince the band we should go on the road," Harriet said. "Except for your mother, they're all too lazy."

Katelyn smiled. "Do you need help finding anything?"

"No, dear, I'm fine." Harriet walked off, veering toward the produce section.

"Back to you and Brian," Katelyn said.

Layla took a deep breath. "I don't want to give Brian the impression that anything lasting will come of our relationship."

"What if you fall in love with him?"

"It won't happen." Layla's chin jutted. "My life has been nothing but hard work, hard times and a whole lot of regrets. I'm not going down that road again."

"Gavin's not a regret."

"I know. I'm thinking about what's best for me and my son."

"I thought Gavin liked Brian."

"He does. And Brian treats him well, but I don't want my son to grow up and become stranded in this town like me." She sniffed. "I need to find a man who can give me and Gavin a better future."

"So you're choosing money over love?"

Layla frowned. "You did."

"Take it from me—what we *think* is best for us doesn't make it true."

"Even though your marriage wasn't perfect, you and your kids had everything you wanted and needed."

But Katelyn's abundant life had come at a high cost—her happiness.

"Are you doing anything after our shift this afternoon?" Layla asked.

"I'm taking my sketch pad down to the railroad tracks. Why?"

"You want to draw at the lake with me, Brian and Gavin?"

"Why would you want me to tag along?"

"I need a second chaperone. Last time I sent Gavin home early and went back to Brian's place with him."

Katelyn laughed.

"Please?" Layla's puppy-dog expression swayed Katelyn.

"Fine. But I'll need a ride to the lake."

"I have an errand to run when I leave work. I'll ask Brian to pick you up after his last delivery."

"What time will that be?" Katelyn asked.

"Probably around five thirty?"

"Sounds good."

The rest of the day passed quickly and when

Katelyn returned to her mother's, she changed clothes, grabbed a snack and went out to the front porch to work on the painting she'd begun last night. As was her habit lately when she focused on her work, she lost track of time.

"Hey, Katelyn." Brian Montgomery came around the side of the house and stopped in front of the porch. "Birdie said you were out here."

"I'm working on a painting to enter in the Pecos Art Festival."

"Mind if I have a look?"

"If you promise to act surprised in front of Layla at the art show."

He climbed the steps and peeked over her shoulder, then sucked in a quick breath. "She's beautiful."

"I wanted to paint her without the false lashes, lipstick and glitter eye shadow."

Brian looked mesmerized. "Who's she staring at?"

Katelyn hadn't finished the sketch, but the scene she'd committed to memory was the afternoon Gavin and Brian had come into the store and announced they were going to the lake, and Layla had pretended to be sick so she could go with them. "She's looking at you."

Startled, Brian gaped at Katelyn. "I want to buy the painting."

"As long as I can display it at the festival. A Sold ribbon might drum up interest in my other pieces." She put away her paints and moved the easel inside, then grabbed her sketch pad and pencil. "I'm ready."

They walked to Brian's pickup in the driveway and got in.

"I realize you only started working with Layla this summer." Brian glanced across the seat before pulling away from the house. "I thought maybe she might have confided in you."

"About what?"

"Me." His neck turned red. "I feel like Layla's holding back on me." He merged onto the highway. "She said it was over between her and Gavin's father, but I'm worried that she still loves him."

"There's isn't anyone else, Brian." Except a phantom white knight. "Layla's moved on."

The frown line between his eyebrows vanished. "Then I wish she'd tell me what was bothering her."

Money. But it wasn't Katelyn's place to say.

Ten minutes later he pulled into the mobile home park where Layla rented a single-wide, and asked, "Will you keep our conversation between us?"

"My lips are sealed."

"Isn't it beautiful out here?" Layla sat next to Katelyn on the rocky shore of Catfish Bay.

"I'm glad I came. Seeing the lake again

reminds me of how much my dad loved his job."

A late-afternoon breeze blew the pungent smell of algae and decaying oak in Katelyn's face and brought back fond memories of her father—a man who had lived and breathed nature and never needed an alarm clock to wake up before dawn to go to work. Unlike Katelyn's mother, who hit the snooze button more than once before she crawled out of bed to get ready for her shift at the grocery store.

"Were you close to your dad?" Layla asked.

"When I was little, I'd tag along with him to the lake and play in the sand or collect twigs."

Layla's attention remained on Brian and Gavin, where they stood knee-deep in the water, casting their fishing lines.

"What about you and your father?" Katelyn asked.

"I've only seen photos of him. He left a few months after I was born." Layla picked up a stick and drew in the sand. "I hate that history repeated itself with Gavin's father." She studied the heart she'd made. "I thought a lot about what you said earlier today. That we don't always know what's best for us."

"Take my advice with a grain of salt. I've made plenty of mistakes in my life." Art was like oxygen and for years she'd been cutting off the air supply to her brain—was it any wonder she second-guessed herself?

"I want to give Brian a real chance, but . . ."

"You're afraid of getting your heart broken?"

"Not me. I'm a big girl. I worry about Gavin. He'd never forgive me if I hurt Brian."

"Even when your intentions are honest and sincere, there's still a chance you could end up with regrets." *And lose yourself in the process.*

Each time she opened her sketch pad, Katelyn was uncovering bits and pieces of her old self. But after she'd ignored her creative side for years, the process was like unearthing fossils—brushing away one grain of sand at a time.

"Gavin's got a fish on his hook!" Brian's shout carried across the water.

Layla scrambled to her feet. "Thank you, Katelyn."

"For what?"

"For making me see that my priorities are screwed up." She smiled. "I'm done waiting for some rich guy to make my life easier. I don't know if Brian's *the one,* but I'm ready to find out." Layla ran toward the water, her laughter floating in the wind.

Katelyn flipped the page in her sketch pad, eager to capture the trio. Her pencil raced across the paper as she drew Gavin's grin after he held up the fish. Brian's proud expression as he placed his hand on the boy's shoulder. Layla's soft smile when she walked through the water to join the pair.

Katelyn committed their images to memory—later she'd fill in the finer details of the scene. For now she watched the story unfold before her. Gavin spoke; then Brian's head fell back, his deep laughter rumbling through the air. Layla slipped her hand into Brian's. Gavin dropped the pole with the fish still on the line and all three dove forward to retrieve it, their legs tangling as they tumbled into the water. The pole forgotten, the trio laughed and splashed one another. Gavin returned to dry ground, but Brian caught Layla's hand and held her back. He stared into her eyes, and Katelyn's heart pounded when she recalled the heated look Jackson had given her as he'd led her into his bedroom on the night of July Fourth.

It was time to pay the mechanic a visit.

Monday morning Jackson lay on a creeper beneath Doris's classic 1978 Pontiac Trans Am, searching for a leak. The older woman didn't drive the car anymore, but she'd found a wet stain on the garage floor and wanted Jackson to check the engine. If he had the money, he'd offer to buy the car from her, but he had his hands full paying the monthly mortgage on the garage. He checked the fuel pump, and sure enough, that was the source of the leak. Easy fix.

A movement out of the corner of his eye caught his attention, and he turned his head toward the street. At barely eight a.m., Katelyn parked a lawn chair beneath the oak tree in front of Mama's Kitchen. She opened her sketch pad, then stared at the garage for a long moment before the pencil in her hand moved across the paper.

They hadn't spoken since he'd run into her and Don at the Hot Tamales concert, and then he'd regretted insisting they remain friends—it had been a knee-jerk reaction in an attempt to protect himself from her leaving him behind again when she returned to St. Louis.

He'd thought about calling her but had come up with a hundred excuses. Twice he'd walked to the Buy & Bag only to chicken out and return to the garage. Now it was the end of July and Katelyn would be leaving in a few weeks and who knew if she'd be coming back? He had no idea what the future looked like for them or even if they had a future together, but he didn't want to make the same mistake he'd made in high school and let her go without telling her what she meant to him.

Wait a minute. Something was different about her. *Holy* . . . "Ouch!" He swallowed a curse after he sat up and banged his head. He rolled out from beneath the car and climbed to his feet. His long strides carried him across the street. He stopped in front of her chair. "You cut your hair."

A smile flirted at the corner of her mouth and a sharp pain spread through his chest. God, he'd missed her. "Why?" He'd liked her hair. Liked how soft it had felt sliding through his fingers.

The long strands had reminded him of the young girl who'd been the only bright spot in his otherwise sucky adolescent life.

"I needed a change."

What did that mean? She'd cut her hair after they'd slept together. After her ex had shown up in town.

She set the pencil on the pad. "If I'd known chopping my hair off would get you to notice me, I'd have done it sooner." Her expression softened. "I've missed you."

He backpedaled until he could no longer smell her perfume. "I didn't know if you and Don had decided to get back together."

"I never would have slept with you if I had hoped to reconcile with him."

He rubbed a hand down his face. "Would you like to come with me when I visit my mother on Saturday?"

Katelyn's eyes widened. "How come you didn't tell me that your mother is back in your life?"

"It happened a little while ago," he said.

"I'd love to meet her."

He couldn't stop staring.

She tilted her head. "What's the matter?"

"Nothing." He spun and made a beeline for the garage. He knew why he didn't like her shorter hair even though it looked great on her. The new style meant she'd finally let go of her past.

And he was a part of her past.

CHAPTER TWENTY-NINE

I'm glad you finally came to your senses and cut your hair, but all those layers look messy. You should have gone with a sleek bob." Shirley climbed the front porch steps Wednesday evening and sat in the rocking chair Birdie had purchased with some of her birthday money.

"I finally cut my hair, and I still can't please you," Katelyn said.

Shirley let the subject drop. "Birdie said Melissa's back in the States."

"She called a few days ago when she made it safely to Sara's home."

"Sara?"

"Sara Kerns. She's one of the incoming freshmen who went on the trip. Her family owns a horse farm in Georgia, and they invited Melissa to spend a few weeks there."

"That's nice."

"Don's going to be out of the country in August when school starts, so Mom and I are planning to meet Melissa at Stephens to help her move into her dorm. You're welcome to join us."

"You and Birdie should go and spend time with her."

Katelyn was surprised her mother-in-law turned down the invite.

Shirley pointed at the easel. "I had no idea you were this good." Shirley was a pro at giving backhanded compliments.

"I can't help feeling that there's something missing."

"The wrinkle across the bridge of her nose. It shows up when Layla smiles."

"You're very observant." Katelyn added a tiny crease in the skin between Layla's eyes, then examined her work with a critical eye. "Perfect." She wiped the tip of her brush on the paint rag. "You've had lunch with Vern five days in a row."

"Is there something the matter with that?"

"Do you ever run out of things to talk about?"

"We haven't so far."

Katelyn prodded her. "You both live very different lives. I didn't expect the two of you to have anything in common."

"He took Elaine to a symphony once, because she'd never been."

"So he's cultured?"

"A little."

"What about politics?"

"We've agreed to disagree."

"Let me guess." Katelyn laughed. "Vern's in favor of expanding social programs to help the needy." Shirley was in favor of the needy helping themselves.

"Robert never cut a single piece of fruit during our marriage, but you should see the fancy way

Vern carves a watermelon." Shirley was smitten with the minister.

"What's his house like?"

"Traditional. I offered several suggestions on updating the decor."

Shirley wasn't a great cook and she detested cleaning, but she had a keen eye for decorating. Still . . . Katelyn doubted Vern had been receptive to changing his home after his wife had passed away less than a year ago.

"Vern said Jackson invited you to visit his mother."

"We're seeing her this Saturday."

Shirley picked at her nails—a nervous habit Katelyn had picked up on when she'd first met the woman years ago. "What's the matter?"

"I have a confession to make."

This ought to be interesting. "What's that?"

"I didn't go to Jackson's garage to ask about an oil change for the car."

"I figured you didn't."

"I went to warn him away from you."

Katelyn set her paintbrush aside. "Why?"

"I'd hoped there was still a chance you and Don might reconcile."

"And now . . . ?"

"I realize what an ass my son has been."

Katelyn smiled. "Divorce doesn't bring out the best in people, but you shouldn't worry about Don. He'll be fine."

"I'm not worried about him. He'll get what's coming to him eventually. It's you I'm worried about."

"Me?"

"Jackson's not good enough for you." Shirley held up her hand when Katelyn opened her mouth to insist her opinion didn't matter. "I realize you grew up in Little Springs, but you left this town and bettered yourself. The last thing you want to do is go backward in life."

"If that's true, why are you interested in Vern?"

"My situation is unique."

There were always two standards—one for Shirley and one for everyone else. "How is your relationship with him different?"

Shirley clasped her hands tightly and stared at the porch floor.

As Katelyn had always suspected, her mother-in-law was afraid of being alone.

"I'm going to ask Vern to come back to St. Louis with me." Shirley looked Katelyn in the eye. "Before you accuse me of using him, you should know that although he's not a man I would have associated with when I was younger, I like him very much, and I believe he'd make a nice companion."

"It doesn't bother you that he's a recovering alcoholic?"

"It's not something I plan to broadcast to people."

"Is he willing to sell his home in Little Springs and move into your apartment with you?"

"I haven't asked him to move in with me. I want him to see St. Louis first."

"What if he doesn't like the city?"

"Then I'll spend more time with him in Little Springs."

"I can't picture you living here permanently."

"The people are entertaining."

Oh, brother.

Shirley got up from the chair. "Your mother is a little unpolished, but underneath her ugly capri pants and T-shirts is a sensible, clever woman."

"I'm sure Mom would be pleased to know you approve of her."

"If you inherited even a smidgen of Birdie's common sense, you'll realize Jackson isn't the right man for you. He'll hold you back."

The only person who had held Katelyn back all these years had been herself.

A horn honked, and Shirley said, "That's Vern."

"Don't forget your purse." Katelyn peeked through the window. "It's sitting on the coffee table."

Shirley entered the house, and Katelyn watched her through the window, making sure she found the bag. When she backed away, she caught her reflection in the glass and plucked at her bangs.

As she stared at her likeness, she realized that

the old Katelyn—the one who'd second-guessed herself—had been replaced by a new Katelyn: a woman ready to take risks with her art. Ready to take her life in a new direction.

A woman not afraid to fail.

"Next week you and your sponsor will spend the majority of the time evaluating your progress with the twelve steps," Vern said. "Let's bow our heads."

After he recited the Lord's Prayer, the AA members folded their chairs and stacked them against the basement wall. Jackson stood by the church doorway and waited for Vern to say good-bye to each member.

"Thought you'd be the first one out the door," Vern said.

It was no secret that even after three years Jackson wasn't comfortable at the Friday meetings. "I'll walk you home," he said.

"Shirley's picking me up"—Vern checked his watch—"in an hour."

They left the church and turned the corner at the end of the block. Vern's house sat across from the town park. "Have you talked to Abby?" Jackson asked.

"She left a voice mail message." He snagged Jackson's arm and they stopped walking. "Is she checking up on me?"

Abby had phoned Jackson three times in

the past two days, because her father hadn't returned her calls. "She wants to make sure you're okay."

"Why wouldn't I be?" Vern grumbled beneath his breath.

"Abby's happy to be back at work," Jackson said. "She's dating her boss." Layla had caught him up on Abby's life after he'd run into her at Mama's Kitchen that morning.

"Abby's coworkers don't know about her and the boss," Vern said.

"If you want, I'll drive you to Dallas so you can check this guy out."

"And embarrass my daughter?" Vern chuckled. "I'll think about it."

"You've adjusted really well to Abby's absence."

"I'm not proud that I begged my daughter to stay with me after her mother passed away."

"She'd do anything for you." Jackson slowed his steps when they reached the park. He motioned to the bench near the flower bed and they sat. "You haven't acted this happy since before Elaine became ill."

"Shirley keeps me on my toes." Vern frowned. "What is it you want to talk to me about?"

"What happens when Shirley leaves?"

"She asked me to go to St. Louis with her." Vern glanced at Jackson. "I told her I'd think about it."

"You should take Shirley up on the offer."

"You told me I needed to return to the pulpit, and Reverend Sanders expects me to take over services in October."

"The town can find another minister. Besides, you can preach the word of God in St. Louis if you decide to move there permanently."

"What about you?" Vern asked.

Jackson scowled. "You're not worried I'll start drinking again, are you?"

"No, but—"

"No buts, Vern. You've had my back since before I opened the garage. As much as I appreciate all you've done for me, it's time you put yourself first. I'll miss you, but I won't fall apart if you leave town."

"I didn't think you would."

"Yes, you did."

"Maybe a little." Vern scuffed the toe of his shoe against the grass. "What are my chances of talking Shirley into moving here?"

Jackson laughed. "Zero to none."

"That's what I was thinking."

"What about a compromise?" Jackson asked.

"Compromise?"

"Spend the summers in St. Louis and the rest of the year here."

Vern rubbed his chin. "I'd have to see if Reverend Sanders would be willing to fill in during the summer."

"If he can't, then the town will find another minister to take over for three months."

"Elaine's only been gone—"

"Elaine would want you to be happy."

Vern dropped his gaze. "I know she would."

"Promise me that if you stay in Little Springs, it's because you want to and not because you're worried about me."

Vern place his hand over his heart. "Whatever I decide will be best for me and no one else."

"Good." Jackson checked his cell phone. "You'd better get going. You've got a half hour to spruce up for Shirley."

When they reached his house, Vern said, "I'd need someone to run the AA meetings if I go to St. Louis."

"I'll step up." He meant it. Conducting the meetings would help him become more comfortable opening up to people. "See you later."

After Vern closed the front door, Jackson walked off, wondering if he asked Katelyn to stay in Little Springs, what the chances were of her saying yes.

CHAPTER THIRTY

A knock sounded on Jackson's apartment door early Saturday afternoon. His nerves had been stretched taut since he'd woken in the morning, because he knew Katelyn was tagging along with him to visit his mother. He removed the pie from the fridge, hoping his mom wouldn't be disappointed—Ginny had been under the weather yesterday and hadn't baked any peach pies, so he'd settled for lemon. When he opened the door, Katelyn nodded to the pastry box.

"Usually a guy gives a girl flowers on a date, not a pie," she said.

He struggled to keep a straight face. "It's not for you."

"Oh."

He stepped outside and then motioned for her to precede him down the stairs. He followed, his eyes glued to the swish-sway of her fanny. "What are you wearing?" he asked when they reached the pavement.

She plucked at the blue floral material. "Palazzo pants. They're comfortable."

"I like the way they show off your ass."

Her laughter settled his nerves. "One out of two isn't bad."

"What do you mean?"

"You don't like my haircut, but you like my pants."

He led the way to his truck, then held the passenger-side door open and waited while she secured her seat belt before he handed over the bakery box. After he got behind the wheel, he started the engine and flipped on the air conditioner. "You caught me off guard."

She brushed her bangs out of her eyes. "I don't care what anyone thinks of my new hairstyle. I like it."

"It's nice." He stared into her eyes. "But seeing you in short hair made me realize that we can never go back to the way things were between us."

"Did you think we could?" she asked.

He backed the truck away from the Dumpster. "I thought we could forget the past twenty-some years and pick up where we left off."

"But we're not the same people."

"I know." He squeezed the steering wheel, grappling with how to explain his fear of being left behind again.

"I'm ready to move forward with my life, but that doesn't mean you can't join me." Her lips flirted with a smile. "That is, if you want to hitch a ride with someone who doesn't have a clue where she's going."

"Getting lost can be fun." He turned onto the street and headed south out of town.

"How come you didn't talk about your mother when we dated?" she asked.

"It was bad enough that people gossiped about my dad's drinking."

"How did you and your mom reconnect?"

"I found out she and her husband had been in a car accident when a rehabilitation hospital in San Diego contacted me. My mother was ready to be released, and they wanted to know if I was coming to get her."

"That must have been a shock."

"The accident killed her husband and left her paralyzed from the waist down," Jackson said.

"That's terrible. Did you know she'd gotten married?"

"Nope."

"So you two have made amends?" Katelyn asked.

"I wouldn't say that." His mother had never asked for his forgiveness and he'd never offered it. "We don't talk about the past." He shrugged. "She needed help finding a place to live. The guy she married left her well-off. Money isn't an issue."

"That's fortunate for her."

"We decided it would be best if she moved to Odessa so I could check on her. She rents a guesthouse on a property outside of town."

"Have you thought of moving her to Little Springs?"

"Her doctors are in Odessa, and it would be

difficult to find visiting nurses willing to make the drive to Little Springs." Even though he'd allowed his mother back into his life, Jackson wasn't comfortable around her and he liked keeping some distance between them.

He turned on the radio and focused on his driving—the stretch of I-20 between Little Springs and Odessa was known as Armadillo Armageddon. He'd be lucky if he didn't run over one of the stupid pests. Thirty minutes later he parked in front of the rental house.

"Does she know I'm coming?" Katelyn asked.

"Yes." He got out of the pickup, then opened Katelyn's door and took the bakery box from her. When they reached the house, he knocked instead of walking in. "It's me, Jackson."

"Door's unlocked!"

"You first." Jackson opened the door.

Katelyn wasn't sure what a woman who'd abandoned her child would look like, but the frail, petite mother with salt-and-pepper hair didn't appear strong enough to hurt a fly.

"Mom, this is my friend Katelyn. Katelyn, this is my mother, Nicole Parker."

"Nice to meet you, Mrs. Parker."

"Call me Nicole."

"Ginny ran out of peach pies." Jackson set the bakery box on the kitchen counter. "I brought you a lemon instead."

"Thanks, honey."

Honey. The endearment sounded natural and spontaneous, as if the woman had called her son that for years and not only when he'd been a little boy.

"Sit down." Nicole waved them to the couch in front of the window. "Jackson tells me you and he dated in high school."

"We did," Katelyn said. "Then I went off to college in Columbia, Missouri."

"I understand you're a very good artist."

Katelyn flashed Jackson a smile. "I'll find out how good I am when I show my work at the Pecos Art Festival."

"My husband was creative. He used to make furniture out of old car parts."

"Jackson's father?"

"No. Ken, my second husband," Nicole said.

Katelyn listened as mother and son talked about the weather and Mendoza Auto. The pair didn't act as if they'd reconnected after years of no contact. Maybe they were putting on a good show for her. Or maybe ignoring the past was the only way forward for them.

Nicole pushed her wheelchair closer to the coffee table. "I can't remember where Jackson said you live now?"

"St. Louis," Katelyn answered.

Nicole's gaze dropped to Katelyn's bare ring finger. "Will you be moving to Little Springs after your divorce?"

Surprised Jackson had told his mother so much about her, she said, "I'm not sure, but I haven't ruled it out."

"And I hear you have twins."

"Michael and Melissa. They'll be freshmen in college this fall."

"And your soon-to-be ex-husband . . . what does he do?"

"He works for a company called NicorTrune."

A knock interrupted Nicole's interrogation. Jackson answered the door, then said, "I'll be right back."

"That's Joan," Nicole said. "Her husband isn't very handy, and she asks Jackson to fix things when he visits."

Katelyn watched the pair through the window. Joan smiled at something Jackson said, and she winced when the little green monster pinched her.

"Do you care for my son?"

Startled, Katelyn said, "Pardon?"

"I sense Jackson has strong feelings for you."

"We have a special history together." Katelyn wasn't comfortable with Nicole's nosy questions, and didn't feel the woman had a right to ask them.

Jackson's mother must have read her mind, because she said, "I hurt my son when I left. That's something I have to live with, but it doesn't mean I don't care about him." She narrowed her eyes. "I don't want you to hurt him."

If Nicole knew how badly Katelyn had hurt her son years ago, she'd run her over with the wheelchair. But how could Katelyn promise *not* to hurt Jackson again when she had no idea what a future for them looked like? "Why did you leave Jackson's father?"

"Ricky was never going to stop drinking." Nicole's chin jutted in the air. "He didn't hit me, but he threatened to, and I knew if I stayed, it was only a matter of time before I got a black eye."

"Weren't you worried that he'd abuse Jackson after you left?"

"No. He never yelled at our son. Half the time he didn't even know the boy was around." She straightened her shoulders. "I gave Jackson forty dollars and told him that if things got bad, he could buy a bus ticket and leave town."

Leave town to go where? Katelyn clamped her mouth shut, afraid she'd say something she couldn't take back.

"My son was better off staying behind where he had a roof over his head and food on the table."

Katelyn's throat grew tight as she envisioned a miniature version of Jackson pleading with his mother not to leave.

"I begged him not to turn out like his father." She expelled a deep sigh. "But he ended up like Ricky—an alcoholic who works on cars."

"There's nothing wrong with being a mechanic."

"It's an honest living, but he won't ever be able to afford luxuries."

Nicole sounded like Shirley. "Luxury is overrated." If anyone knew that, it was Katelyn.

"I'm sure you don't believe I have a right to ask anything of my son." Nicole wiped a tear from the corner of her eye. "I realize every visit is a gift from him that I don't deserve."

Katelyn was spared from responding when the front door opened and Jackson walked in. "I fixed the leaky spigot on the side of Joan's house."

"Cut us a piece of pie, will you?" Nicole asked.

"Sure."

"I'll help." Katelyn joined him in the kitchen, eager to escape Nicole's scrutiny.

The visit lasted a half hour longer, and then Jackson said, "I need to get back to the garage."

"It was nice meeting you, Nicole." Katelyn flashed a quick smile, then slipped out the door, allowing Jackson a moment of privacy with his mother.

"You hungry?" he asked after he climbed into his pickup and they drove off.

"Not really." Was he looking for an excuse not to take her home? "Shirley's out with Vern, and Mom's over at Etta and Faye's, helping them with their garden. We can talk at the house."

Jackson turned on the radio and they listened to country music on the way home.

Little Springs would always be Katelyn's

home, but this summer the town was beginning to feel a lot like a place she belonged.

When they reached Birdie's, she poured glasses of iced tea and they sat on the back porch.

"Katelyn?"

"Yes?"

"Did Don try to talk you out of signing the divorce papers when he came to town?"

"No. We're both ready to move on."

"For what it's worth . . . I wish things would have worked out for you two."

She studied Jackson. "You really mean that."

"Your happiness has always been important to me."

"I'm working on it." She bumped his shoulder. "Same goes for you."

"I'm working on it, too."

"You know what would make me happy right now?" She turned her head toward him.

"This?" He leaned across his chair and brushed his lips over hers, but the moment he deepened the kiss, a horn honked.

Birdie had horrible timing.

CHAPTER THIRTY-ONE

Katelyn walked into an empty kitchen Sunday morning to find a fresh pot of coffee and a note from her mother.

> Helping Doris clean her house after church. Tell Walter I'll come into the store later this afternoon.
>
> Mom

Katelyn glanced out the window. The Taurus was gone, but Shirley's Mercedes sat parked in front of the storage shed. She poured herself a cup of coffee, hoping the caffeine would charge her batteries. She'd had trouble sleeping last night, thinking about Jackson's mother. She couldn't imagine how difficult it had been for him to allow Nicole back into his life after she'd been AWOL all these years.

He's letting you back into his life after you left him.

Jackson could be very persuasive, and Katelyn had known that if she waited to break up with him until she went home from college for the holidays, he would have changed her mind.

The back door opened, startling Katelyn out of her trance. Shirley waltzed into the kitchen with her blouse buttoned crooked, her hair messed up and no lipstick. Katelyn struggled not to laugh when she said, "Your sandals are on the wrong feet." A horn honked, and she looked out the screen door. Vern was dangling Shirley's purse out the window of his pickup. "You forgot your purse."

Shirley returned outside, and Katelyn spied on the two lovebirds. Vern wouldn't let go of her purse when Shirley made a grab for it, and she giggled. A minute later she climbed the porch steps and entered the kitchen.

"Did you stay the night at Vern's?"

"We didn't do anything bad."

She'd like to know Shirley's definition of *bad* but didn't ask.

"Sit down and I'll pour you a cup of coffee." Katelyn removed a mug from the cupboard, filled it to the brim and then joined Shirley at the table. Her mother-in-law's gaze pinged around the kitchen, landing everywhere but on Katelyn. "You must have done something sort of *bad*"—Katelyn stared at Shirley's feet— "unless your disheveled appearance is the result of being mauled by a feral cat while you went for a morning walk in your rhinestone sandals."

"Don't you dare say a word to anyone. Not even Birdie." Shirley sipped her coffee. "Vern and I got to talking last night and time slipped

342

away from us. I didn't want to disturb you and your mother, so I slept at his house."

Katelyn had to ask. "In his bed?"

Shirley scowled. "No, in the guest room."

"Who crawled in with who?" Katelyn couldn't help but laugh. "Women your age still have sex, you know."

Shirley went to the pantry and confiscated a box of Entenmann's donuts. "It was the most romantic night I've experienced in I can't remember how long."

Katelyn grinned over the rim of her coffee cup. Did Shirley even realize she was eating junk food?

"Vern makes me feel young." A dreamy sparkle filled her mother-in-law's eyes. "I've felt so old since Robert died." She shook her head. "When Vern looks at me, I swear he sees the young girl I once was."

Katelyn waited for her to finish the pastry, then asked, "What are your plans for the future?"

"Vern's returning to the pulpit."

"He's not traveling with us when we leave Little Springs?"

"I won't be going back with you," Shirley said. "Vern and I plan to visit St. Louis in September so that I can arrange to have a few of my belongings shipped here."

"You're moving to Little Springs permanently?"

"We'll spend the summers at my apartment

in St. Louis and then the rest of the year here."

"It's probably a good idea to keep the apartment in case you go stir-crazy in Little Springs," Katelyn said.

"I'm keeping the apartment so the kids have a place to stay when they visit their father or friends in St. Louis."

"That's very thoughtful, but will management allow them to be there when you're not?" Katelyn pictured the twins having wild parties in the apartment.

"Don said I'm allowed to have guests as long as they're eighteen or older."

"I'm sure he'll have room for the kids wherever he ends up."

"Michael and Melissa may not want to stay with Don and that slutty girlfriend of his."

Katelyn grinned. *Lauren* was in for a big surprise when she discovered what kind of baggage Don came with.

"I never believed you were good enough for Don." Shirley shook her head. "I always thought my son would marry a wealthy girl from a prominent Kansas City family. A girl who lived in a beautiful home. Who knew how to dress and accessorize and was no stranger to spas and beauty salons. I never imagined he'd choose a girl from a little backwoods town in Texas whose mother worked as a cashier at a grocery store and whose father spent his days trekking through the woods."

Considering the source and the lens through which Shirley viewed the world, Katelyn didn't take offense at the insults. "I'm sure it was a shock."

"There is a bright side to Don divorcing you."

"What's that?"

"I'd never have met Vern or your mother's friends if my son had decided to keep you around."

Katelyn left the table and dumped the remainder of her coffee down the drain. "I can't believe I almost didn't bring you home with me this summer." She turned away from the sink. "So when's the wedding?"

"I'm not marrying Vern."

"But—"

"It's too soon after his wife died."

"You're probably smart not to rush into anything." Katelyn was happy for Shirley and admittedly relieved her mother-in-law had someone else to latch onto. "I've got to get ready for work."

"Where's Birdie?"

"She's helping Doris clean her house before she clocks in at the grocery store this afternoon."

Shirley stood up. "Vern's making dinner for me tonight."

"If you keep sneaking in after curfew, you should have your own set of keys to the house."

Shirley ignored the suggestion and walked out of the room.

Katelyn checked the clock. She had an hour to get ready for work, and if she hurried, she could steal a half hour to work on another painting.

Layla waved her over as soon as Katelyn walked up to the registers late Sunday morning.

"What's going on?" Katelyn asked, noticing the sparkle in her coworker's eye.

"Brian and I talked last night, and we both agreed that we wouldn't date anyone else."

"So it's official—you're in a relationship?"

Layla smiled.

"What made you decide to give Brian a chance?"

"He may not be Mr. Moneybags, but he works hard and my son is at the age where he needs a male role model in his life."

"So you're dating Brian because of Gavin?"

"Gavin's a big part of why I'm giving this relationship an honest chance, but last night when I told Brian I dreamed of being a massage therapist and working in an upscale spa, he said he'd keep an eye on Gavin if I wanted to go back to school."

"That's great. Are you thinking of moving in together?"

"Brian says we should, but I don't want to rush things. Tomorrow I have an appointment with an admissions counselor at the community college in Midland to find out what kind of financial aid I qualify for."

"I'm excited for you, Layla. I hope things work out."

"I heard you went to see Jackson's mother yesterday."

"It was awkward meeting her for the first time."

"Didn't you already know her?"

"Jackson's mother left town years before he and I dated."

The doors opened and a family of four walked into the store, grabbed a cart and headed to the produce section.

"What about you?" Layla asked. "Are you and Jackson officially in a relationship?"

"We're taking things one day at a time like you and Brian." She'd hurt Jackson once before because she'd wanted to go off and find herself. The last thing she cared to do was inflict another wound when she was still searching for answers.

"I wish you'd move back to Little Springs," Layla said. "Even though you're older than me, I think we could be good friends."

Katelyn laughed. "We get along well, don't we?"

"And"—Layla spread her arms wide—"when Abby visits her father, the three of us could plan a girls' weekend and go somewhere."

Walter's head popped out of his office. "Layla,

would you take inventory in the health-and-beauty aisle?"

"Sure." Layla removed the handheld computer scanner from beneath her counter. "Are you nervous about the art festival next Sunday?"

"A little."

"You should ask for a couple of days off this week so you can get ready for the show."

"My mom offered to work some of my hours, but she's having fun with her music and I don't want to bother her."

"Walter hired Harriet's niece, Kim. She starts tomorrow, and he said she's looking for as many hours as she can get. I bet she'd take a few of your shifts, and I can work overtime."

"Thanks, Layla. I'll talk to Walter before I leave today."

"Brian's coming with me to the festival. He says he might buy one of your pieces."

And Katelyn knew exactly which one he was interested in.

CHAPTER THIRTY-TWO

The Pecos art show was in full swing by noon on the first Sunday in August. Katelyn's booth sat smack-dab in the middle of the town square. She'd been hoping for a spot near the sidewalk, but her late entry had landed her in a maze of stands.

"How's it going?" Birdie held out a bottle of water she'd purchased from a food truck.

"Thanks." Katelyn waved to the canvas over her head. "It was nice of Vern to let me use one of the church tents. It feels more like a hundred degrees out here than the ninety the weatherman forecasted."

"I ran into Shirley a few minutes ago. She and Vern will be by after they grab a bite to eat." Birdie picked up an empty soda cup from the ground and tossed it into a nearby garbage can. "Is Jackson coming?"

"I don't know."

"You didn't invite him?"

Katelyn shook her head. The art festival was a larger event than the Fourth of July celebration in Little Springs, and she didn't want to pressure Jackson into coming when she knew he'd feel overwhelmed by the crowds. "Did you check out the pottery booth near the entrance?" Birdie asked.

"I bought one of her flower vases and put it in the car." Katelyn moved the folding chair in the corner over. "Sit down."

Birdie turned sideways on the seat so she could people-watch. "How's Harriet's niece working out at the store?"

"Fine, I guess." Katelyn had met the twenty-one-year-old earlier in the week. "She and Layla get along great."

"Why's that?"

"They both love talking about the latest hairstyle and makeup trends."

"Does Walter know I'm going back to St. Louis with you in a couple of weeks to help Melissa move into her dorm?"

"I told him, and he's fine with it now that he hired Kim."

"I've been thinking," Birdie said, "that I might switch to part-time when I come back."

"That's a great idea." Katelyn paused when a couple stopped to view her work, but they moved on before she had a chance to initiate a conversation with them. "I'd be happy to help you make ends meet, Mom."

"I can still manage on my own," Birdie said. "I make more money in tips playing at a bar for three hours than I do standing at the register for eight."

Katelyn hugged her mother.

"What was that for?"

"I'm excited that you're performing again."

"And I'm proud of you"—Birdie pointed to the artwork on display—"for believing in yourself."

An older couple approached the tent. The gentleman pointed to the painting of Mendoza Auto that Katelyn had made from the sketch of the building. "Is that a 1978 Pontiac Trans Am sitting in the bay?"

"It is." Katelyn had painted Jackson standing next to the car, staring out the bay door as he wiped his hands on an oil rag.

"That garage is in Little Springs, isn't it?" he asked.

Birdie jumped into the conversation. "It used to be Al's Auto. Then Jackson Mendoza bought the business."

"My father took our family car there when I was a kid. I remember sitting on that bench outside the door and waiting."

"The detail is lovely," the wife said.

"You don't have a price on the painting," he said.

"I'm not sure if it's for sale yet." It was difficult to put a price on her memories of hanging out with Jackson at the garage after school.

She wrote her cell phone number on a piece of paper and made a mental note to look into ordering business cards. "If you have a photo of your old family car, I'd be happy to paint a picture of the garage with that vehicle inside."

"That would be nice, Roy." The woman looked at Katelyn. "We'll be in touch."

As soon as the couple walked off, Birdie said, "What's wrong with you?"

"What do you mean?"

"You worry that no one will want to buy your art—then when someone comes along ready to pay money for one of your pieces, you can't pull the trigger."

Katelyn was rescued from responding when a woman in a blue-and-white polka-dot dress and matching hat stopped at the booth. "Hello," Katelyn said.

"Is this your work or are you the artist's representative?"

"I'm the artist."

"Sonja Doyle." The woman fished a business card from her purse and handed it to Katelyn, then leaned forward and peered at the scrawled signature across the bottom of a drawing.

Katelyn had signed all the pieces as Katelyn Chandler, because Katelyn Pratt was not and never had been an artist.

"I manage a gallery in Dallas and your charcoal sketches intrigue me." The woman smiled. "Do you have a card?"

"I'm sorry." Katelyn hated looking unprofessional. "I'll write my contact information on the back of your card." Katelyn scribbled her name, her cell number, email and the words *charcoal sketches*.

"I'll be in touch." Sonja Doyle moved on to the next booth.

Birdie whistled. "An art gallery. That's big-time, daughter."

"We'll see if she reaches out to me." Katelyn's heart thumped heavily with excitement and the possibility of having her work find its way into a gallery.

"I need to stretch my legs," Birdie said.

"Thanks for being here with me today, Mom."

"I wouldn't be anywhere else. I'll try to send some business your way." Her mother walked off and a moment later, Katelyn heard her say, "Be sure you check out the paintings and sketches in that booth. She's a local artist."

Local artist.

If Katelyn decided to stay in St. Louis, she'd have to first find an apartment or a home to rent. Then, second, she'd have to figure out what to draw. She doubted people who lived in the Midwest would want artwork highlighting small-town life in Texas.

"Katelyn!" Shirley and Vern zigzagged through the crowd.

"How was your lunch?" Katelyn asked.

"We had barbecue, but it was too smoky for my taste." Shirley pointed to a piece behind Katelyn. "That's Sadie's beauty shop."

Vern moved closer to the charcoal drawing. "Is that you sitting in the chair?"

Shirley slipped on her glasses. "That is me!"

Katelyn had captured the scene in the beauty shop the day Sadie had cut Shirley's hair.

"They look like a pack of hyenas ready to pounce on their prey." Vern's smile turned into a grimace when Shirley elbowed him in the side.

In the drawing, the members of the ladies' society were gathered around the styling chair, each of them examining Shirley's new hairdo.

"Are you upset that I did a sketch of you?" Katelyn nibbled her lip.

Shirley shook her head. "I love it."

"Then I'll get it for you. I've been trying to think of something to buy a woman who has everything." Vern grinned at Katelyn. "Will you put a Sold sign on the picture?"

Shirley beamed. "I think it should hang on the wall inside Sadie's beauty shop."

"If it makes you happy, sweetheart," Vern said.

Sweetheart? The perm queen was no sweetheart.

"Vern will settle up with you at home," Shirley said.

When had Katelyn's childhood home become her mother-in-law's?

Shirley took Vern's hand and they walked off. Katelyn sold one more item—a Fourth of July scene at the town park—then sat by herself for over an hour before Layla and Brian showed up at the booth. A pang of envy caught her by surprise. She wished she could spend the day looking at art with Jackson. "Are you two having fun?"

The couple exchanged a smile. "Has anyone bought your work?" Layla asked.

"Vern's buying the beauty shop picture, and I might be doing another painting of Jackson's garage for a man and his wife." She looked past the lovebirds. "Did Gavin come with you?"

"He stayed the night at a friend's house." Layla nudged Brian. "What are you staring at?"

"You." He pointed to the easel in the corner.

"Is that me?" She walked closer to the painting. "It's sold. Who bought it?"

"I did." Brian put his arm around her. "I'm hanging it in my bedroom."

Layla's cheeks bloomed pink.

Brian spoke to Katelyn. "We'll be back later to get the painting." The pair left, stumbling when they tried to kiss and walk at the same time.

A few minutes later Jackson showed up at the tent. Even though he smiled, his stiff posture said he wanted to be anywhere but standing in the crowded town square. Katelyn wrapped her arms around him and pressed her nose to his clean-smelling T-shirt. "Thank you for coming."

"How's it going?" he asked.

"Brian bought the portrait of Layla."

Jackson's attention swung to the painting of

Mendoza Auto. He stared at it for the longest time, then looked at her, his eyes shimmering with an emotion she couldn't identify. "Is that how I look to you?"

"If you mean I see a confident, strong, self-assured man, then the answer is yes."

He swallowed hard. "Can I get you something to eat or drink?"

"Thanks, but I'm good."

"I'll be back at the end of the day to help you take down the tent." He disappeared into the crowd. She hadn't expected him to show up at all today, and his support meant the world to her.

An hour before the festival ended, the judges made the rounds, viewing all the entries. Like the other artists, Katelyn hoped one of her pieces might catch the eye of a judge. Winning a ribbon would go a long way in proving that she wasn't deceiving herself into thinking she had talent. The art gallery manager's interest in her charcoal sketches had been an unexpected bonus and Katelyn would have to ponder long and hard about what she wanted for her future.

She moved the easels out of the shadows, then crossed her fingers behind her back and pasted a confident smile on her face when the judges stopped at her booth.

CHAPTER THIRTY-THREE

"Do you want to grab a bite to eat to celebrate your first-place ribbon?" Jackson stopped the pickup at a red light in downtown Pecos.

Katelyn had been floored when the panel of judges presented her with a Best-of-Show ribbon for the painting of Mendoza Auto. "Since my mother hauled my artwork home in her car, we can do anything you want tonight." When Jackson didn't crack a smile at her suggestive comment, she suspected there was something other than celebrating on his mind.

"Let's stop at Sonic and get our food to go," she said. "We can eat by the tracks." The one place she and Jackson had always been able to talk freely.

She closed her eyes and breathed deeply. She was tired, but her fatigue had nothing to do with standing on her feet all day—she'd grown accustomed to that working at the Buy & Bag. Her weariness was the result of the anxiety that had been steadily building inside her as she'd prepared for the art show. Not knowing how her work would be received had tied her stomach in knots, but when the judges had placed the ribbon on her painting, the ball of stress had unraveled, leaving her with a peaceful, hopeful feeling.

In an attempt to lighten the mood, she said, "Why do you think they picked the Mendoza Auto over my other pieces?"

His gaze swung to her mouth. "The sexy mechanic in the sketch swayed them."

Katelyn laughed. "I bet you're right."

They stopped at the fast-food restaurant and ordered foot-long chili-cheese dogs, French fries and sodas, then left the town of Pecos. When they approached the outskirts of Little Springs, Jackson took a different route along a farm-to-market road, then drove half a mile before veering onto a dirt path and stopping.

"Whose property is this?"

"It's the south side of O'Malley's land. The house has been vacant for years. After O'Malley passed away, his kids tried to sell the place, but the bank ended up with it."

"With Catfish Bay close by, I'm surprised a developer hasn't bought the land and turned it into an RV park."

"It's too close to the tracks."

"I wouldn't mind hearing a whistle or feeling the ground shake every day." The noise had always reminded her that there was a big world outside Little Springs waiting to be explored.

When they got out of the pickup, Jackson lowered the tailgate. Before Katelyn had a chance to climb up and sit, he hoisted her into the air and set her on the edge. "You're still a lightweight."

"I'm twelve pounds heavier than I was in high school. I think you've got bigger muscles, that's all." She divvied up the food.

"The sky's clear. We should see the stars tonight," he said.

"We spent a lot of time down by the tracks before I left for college, but we weren't stargazing."

"I was too busy trying to get into your panties to care about watching the sky."

She smiled. "Your eyes were my downfall."

"What do you mean?"

Katelyn popped a fry into her mouth. "For a guy who doesn't care to discuss his feelings, your eyes do a lot of talking."

"You do a lot of talking with your mouth, and I don't make fun of you."

She caressed his cheek. "You never pushed me into having sex. You always let me set the pace."

"You were worth the wait."

"It took you thirteen seconds to answer me when I said I was ready." She laughed. "I thought you'd gotten cold feet."

"I wanted it to be good for you." He crushed his food wrapper into a ball.

"We never spoke about it, but was I your first?" she asked.

"No."

After all these years, a marriage and two kids, Katelyn still felt a tiny prick of jealousy. "Who was she?"

"I only knew her first name. Annette was at a house party I went to in Midland. We made out in one of the bedrooms. Never saw her again after that night."

"I'm glad you were my first." She rested her head on his shoulder and sighed when his fingers toyed with the ends of her hair. Don had rarely touched Katelyn's hair—not even when they'd made love. "I can't believe how fast this summer has gone by," she said.

"You didn't get here until the middle of June."

"Jackson."

"What?"

"I admire you for checking up on your mother. It can't be easy."

"It takes too much energy to hold a grudge."

"I wish I hadn't sent you a breakup letter."

After Katelyn had told Jackson she'd accepted the art scholarship from the University of Missouri, she'd felt him pull away from her—not physically, but emotionally. Maybe he'd known all along, despite her protests and assurances, that when she left town, she'd never return.

He pushed off the tailgate, paced several yards away, then faced Katelyn. "I wanted you to pursue your dream," he said, "but at the same time, I wanted you to want me more." He'd almost driven to Missouri and begged her to give up her scholarship and return home with him.

As if she stood in a real-life painting, the sun

sank behind the horizon, leaving her swathed in a purplish glow.

"I didn't break up with you face-to-face," Katelyn said, "because I knew you would change my mind."

"Would you stay now if I asked you to?" Jackson watched her struggle with the question, mesmerized by the way her eyebrows moved across her forehead. He'd been drawn to Katelyn because she hadn't tried to conceal her feelings from him. She'd always given her emotions free rein and had never worried about the consequences. But a lot of years had passed them by, and she wasn't the same girl he'd dated in high school. The decisions she made about her future would impact not only her but also her children.

"I've finally started sketching again, and if I'm going to give myself a chance to see where my art can take me, then I need to be in the right place."

"You had offers to buy your paintings today." He closed the distance between them, stopping in front of her. "We don't have to rush into anything. We can take it slow."

Katelyn's face twisted in pain. "You don't get it."

"Help me understand."

"I've had to face some hard truths with my divorce."

"Like what?"

"That my marriage was supposed to feed my creativity, and instead it stole my confidence and nurtured self-doubt."

"Do you still have feelings for Don?"

"No," she said with conviction.

"Are you afraid I'll start drinking if things don't work out between us?"

She dropped her gaze. "The thought has crossed my mind."

"I was drinking before you left for college, and I would have continued drinking even if we'd stayed together." He inched closer. "I'd like to believe that if our relationship hadn't ended, I'd have eventually given up booze, but I doubt that would have happened."

"Vern seems to believe differently. He warned me away from you."

Jackson grasped her arms and waited until Katelyn looked him in the eye. "I am the only one who has control over my drinking. It's taken years for me to admit the truth, but I've accepted responsibility for the path I chose in life and I'm at peace with that."

"I want to believe you, Jackson."

"I'm not asking for any promises. I'm not asking you to marry me or even for us to move in together. I'm asking you to think about staying in Little Springs and seeing if what we have together is better than what we have alone."

She played with the collar of his T-shirt. "You've helped me reconnect with my creative side, but I'm terrified that if things go south between us, I'll lose that burning desire to sketch again."

"You can't lose what's been inside of you your whole life, Katelyn. Maybe I helped bring it out. Maybe being back in this town, reconnecting with your mother, working at the grocery store or spending time at the train tracks has helped you recapture your yearning to draw, but don't believe for a minute that I, this town or anyone else has the power to rob you of your passion."

"What if there's another place that inspires me to do better work? How will I know if I don't search for it?"

Jackson's stomach bottomed out. His gut told him that Katelyn wasn't worried as much about finding that perfect place to nurture her creativity as she was about trusting him.

Ignoring the stinging pain of his chest splitting wide open, he cupped her cheek and said, "What I want most is for you to be happy, so go search for that perfect place." He pressed a gentle kiss on her mouth, then took her hand. "C'mon. I'll take you home."

The drive into Little Springs was the longest four minutes of Jackson's life.

"Good morning," Walter said when Katelyn walked into the employee lounge Monday morning.

"Am I late?" She stowed her purse in the locker and slipped on her smock.

"No, I wanted to congratulate you on winning Best in Show at the art festival."

"Thank you."

Walter frowned. "You don't seem too happy about it."

"I didn't get much rest last night." Her sleep had been disturbed by dreams of riding a train traveling too fast for her to jump off.

"At least one of my workers is in a good mood today," he said.

Kim wasn't scheduled to come in until this afternoon, so he must be talking about Layla. "What's going on?"

"Layla hasn't stopped smiling since she clocked in an hour ago."

When Walter stared expectantly, Katelyn asked, "Did she say why she's happy?"

Walter beamed. "I told her I'd work around her schedule if she went back to school this fall so she didn't have to look for a new job."

"That was nice of you."

"Speaking of schedules . . . when's your last day?" he asked.

"Mom and I planned to leave next Thursday or Friday."

"With Birdie going to part-time, I may have to hire another employee." He rubbed a hand down his face. "What about you?"

"What about me what?" she asked.

"Are you coming back to Little Springs after you help your daughter get settled in college, or are you staying in St. Louis?"

"I haven't decided."

"If you do return, you're welcome to work here as often or as little as you want."

"I appreciate the offer."

"I'm stocking shelves today," Walter said.

She followed the boss to the front of the store, but before Katelyn and Layla had a chance to speak, Ginny wheeled her cart up to the register.

"I ran out of flour and sugar this morning while I was making pies." Ginny stacked the baking supplies on the counter. "I'm stocking up, since it's on sale this week."

"Did you leave any on the shelf?" Katelyn laughed.

"Nope. I cleaned you out."

"I'll let Walter know." Layla went to search for the boss.

"Any chance they'll build a Costco around here in the future? That's the place to buy in bulk," Katelyn said.

"By the time they do, I'll be too old to drive."

"Walter appreciates your business, Ginny." Katelyn glanced over her shoulder when she heard the front doors open. Brian entered with his dolly and Layla met him at the door. He followed her to the cigarette case, where they chatted while she stocked the smokes.

"What's going on between those two?" Ginny inserted her credit card into the payment machine.

"They're officially boyfriend and girlfriend," Katelyn said. Walter approached the register and she said, "Would you help Ginny load her bags into her car?"

"Sure." Walter pushed the cart toward the exit, and Katelyn heard Ginny say, "You're helping me because you want a free pie."

Walter chuckled. "Am I that transparent?"

Katelyn averted her gaze when Brian leaned in and kissed Layla. Once he'd wheeled his cart away and disappeared down the aisle, Layla approached the register. "Did Walter tell you that he's working around my school schedule?"

"He did."

"He asked me if I knew your plans for the future."

"I honestly don't know."

"Did Jackson ask you to stay?"

"Yes."

Layla's eyes widened.

"We're taking it one day at a time like you and Brian."

"But how can you do that if he's here and you're in Missouri?"

"I don't want to talk about it." Katelyn winced when Layla took a step back. "I'm sorry. It's that

I don't like thinking about the future. It makes me anxious."

"Boy, do I get that." Layla lowered her voice. "I'm worried I'll screw this up with Brian."

"How so?"

"He's such a responsible guy, and he treats Gavin like a son."

"And you're concerned because . . . ?"

"What if I grow bored with our relationship?"

Katelyn could never imagine herself growing weary of being with Jackson. "What if you don't?"

"I keep telling myself that if things don't work out, at least I gave it a try." Layla shrugged. "All these years I had my sights set on finding a wealthy guy so I could live on easy street, and I end up falling for a deliveryman."

"Sometimes what we think we want isn't what's best for us."

"I thought about your situation," Layla said. "You married for money and look how things turned out." Her tone softened. "You lived in a big, beautiful house. Traveled all over the world. Never had to worry about how to pay the bills, and your kids had the best of everything, but your marriage didn't last."

"No, it didn't."

"After I began dating Brian, I told myself to live in the moment and that the future would take care of itself, but you know what?"

"What?"

"I realized there's more good in life than bad and it took Brian to make me see that." She smiled. "I'm a better person when I'm with him."

Jackson's face flashed before Katelyn's eyes. He'd supported her dreams and encouraged her to chase after them. He'd always believed in her. It was Katelyn who'd lost faith in herself.

CHAPTER THIRTY-FOUR

"Mom! What did you do to your hair?" Katelyn hugged her daughter in front of Wood Hall on the Stephens College campus, the third Saturday of August. "Do you like the style?"

"I love it." She gave Katelyn a second hug. "You look younger."

"And you look older." Melissa's suntanned skin glowed. Where had eighteen years gone? The little girl who tripped over her shoelaces had grown into a lovely young woman right under her mother's nose.

"You're not going to cry, are you?" Melissa smiled.

"Don't be silly. I missed you this summer."

"I missed you, too. I took a ton of photos from my trip abroad and uploaded them to my computer. We can look at them later tonight." Melissa glanced around. "Where's Grandma Chandler?"

"Talking to the girl by the fountain." The student handed Birdie her guitar and a group gathered around to listen to her play.

"Grandma's going to embarrass me." Melissa covered her face with her hands and peeked through her fingers.

"You might be surprised," Katelyn said. "Grandma Birdie plays in a band now."

"Dad said they're called the Hot Tamales."

"And Grandma Birdie sings on Friday nights at a local bar."

"I guess it's cool to have a grandmother who's a musician." Melissa frowned. "If she's performing in front of people, she needs a hipper wardrobe. Capri pants went out of style before I was born."

"Shirley offered to buy her a pair of dress slacks and a silk blouse, but your grandmother refuses to give up her Buy & Bag T-shirts." Katelyn caressed a strand of her daughter's long brown hair. "I'm glad I was able to meet you at school and help you move in."

"Dad's been acting weird since he told me about the divorce. I think he knows I'm mad at him, because he cheated on you."

"Give it time and things will get better between you."

"I know, but is it okay if I'm mad at him for a while?"

Katelyn wished she could protect her daughter's feelings. "Of course you can be angry at him, but never forget that he loves you." Katelyn motioned to Birdie. "While your grandmother's putting on an impromptu concert, why don't you introduce me to Sara's parents? I'd like to thank them for inviting you to stay at their home this summer."

"They want to meet us later for dinner."

"Sure, that sounds nice. Grandma and I are staying through Monday. I want to see if you like your classes and professors."

"I only have two classes on Monday, so we can shop if you want to. Dad gave me a credit card to use this semester."

It figured Don would try to *buy* his kids' forgiveness.

"I'll pay for a pair of Rockies jeans and a rhinestone cowgirl shirt for Grandma when she sings at the bar."

"Good luck convincing her to wear them." Katelyn pointed to the building where her daughter had been assigned a dorm room on the second floor. "What do you want to do first?"

"I guess haul my stuff upstairs. Then we can organize it all."

Katelyn and Birdie had flown into St. Louis two days ago and had loaded Melissa's belongings into Katelyn's SUV. After eight trips up and down the stairs, they had all her daughter's belongings in the room.

"When is"—Katelyn glanced at the name on the door—"Kristin getting here?"

"Tomorrow. She texted me this morning and said they had car trouble in Kansas City."

"Where's Kristin from?" Katelyn asked.

"Nebraska." Melissa fell across her bed. "Mom?"

Katelyn sat in the chair and propped her feet on the desk. "What?"

"Dad told me about the guy you dated in high school."

"Jackson?" She hadn't expected Don to mention her old boyfriend to the kids.

"Is it true that you and Jackson are getting back together?"

"Did your dad tell you that?"

"Grandma Pratt did. I called her last week to talk about my trip abroad."

Shirley must have forgotten about the conversation; otherwise, she'd have told Katelyn.

"You're not going to marry Jackson, are you?"

"I have no plans to marry anyone." Not yet. Maybe never. Katelyn considered changing the subject, but she didn't want any secrets between her and the twins. "Jackson and I have been on a few dates."

"Is it weird seeing him after all these years?"

"Kind of. He's the same and yet different—like me."

"Are you moving back to Little Springs?"

"If I do, would you visit me during holiday breaks and your summer vacation?"

Melissa nodded. "You wouldn't expect me to hang out all summer, would you? There's nothing to do there."

"Where do you want to spend your summers?"

"Grandma Pratt said I could use her apartment.

I'd be able to hang out with my friends, and Dad would be around if I needed anything."

"As long as you get a job, I think that would be okay. Grandma Chandler and I can fly to St. Louis to visit you, too."

"I guess that would work."

Katelyn was impressed that Melissa was taking her parents' divorce in stride. "Have you talked to your brother lately?"

"He bragged about getting As in his summer-school classes."

Katelyn laughed. "When are you two going to stop competing with each other?"

"Never. We made a bet our first semester."

"What's that?"

"Whoever earns the lowest GPA has to wear one of Grandma's Buy & Bag T-shirts to class for a week."

"Ouch."

"Hey, Mom? Is it true that Grandma Pratt's boyfriend is a minister?"

"Yep."

"Is he nice?"

"Very. And he puts up with Grandma, so that makes him even more special."

Melissa hopped off the bed, opened a plastic bin and began putting her toiletries away. "How's Grandma's memory?"

"About the same. She still forgets where she puts her purse, but Vern looks out for her, and since she's been spending time with him, she's in a much better mood."

"Grandma mentioned that she and *Vern* want to visit me Labor Day weekend."

"I'll make sure to remind Vern in case Grandma forgets. Shirley would enjoy showing him around her alma mater."

"How much do you want to bet Grandma puts money into my expense account?" Melissa grinned.

"I'm sure she will, so use it wisely." Katelyn pointed to the end of the bed where a framed photograph of Greece rested on the mattress. "It's a beautiful shot. Did you buy that abroad?"

"I wanted something to remember the trip by." Melissa opened a bin of clothes and put the outfits on hangers. "Grandma Pratt said there's a lady who's interested in showing your work in an art gallery."

"Grandma sure had a lot to say when you talked to her last."

"Wasn't she supposed to tell me?"

"I was hoping to keep it a surprise until this weekend."

"Tell me what happened."

"I entered my work in the Pecos Art Festival and a painting I did of the auto body shop in Little Springs won Best in Show."

"Seriously, Mom? That's so cool."

Melissa and Michael knew Katelyn had

attended college on an art scholarship, and they'd seen her doodle on her sketch pad, but she hadn't discussed art with them.

"How come you never said you started painting again when we talked on the phone this summer?"

Mostly because she feared she'd fail. "I thought I wanted to draw again, but I hadn't done it in so long that I didn't know if I still had the passion for it."

"What do you mean?"

"I wasn't sure I believed in myself and my talent." It had taken courage to display her work for people to critique.

"So what happened with the lady from the art gallery?" Melissa asked.

"She's interested in my charcoal sketches. I'm hoping she wants one of them for her gallery."

"I'm proud of you, Mom." Melissa pointed across the room. "Do you think you could do a drawing for that wall? It would be neat to have something my mother made hanging in my room."

Katelyn's heart swelled with love for her daughter. "I'll surprise you." She spread her arms wide. "We'd better get busy if we're going to meet Sara's parents for dinner in a few hours." She opened another bin of clothes and put those in the dresser. "By the way, Grandma Pratt has a new hairstyle also."

"Maybe I should cut *my* hair."

Katelyn studied Melissa's long tresses and saw her younger self in her daughter. All through high school and college, Katelyn's long hair had been her identity, her security. Then after she married, she'd used her hair as a shield against Shirley's disapproval of her. "I think your hair is perfect."

"Mom? Are you and Dad going to be okay?"

"We'll be fine, honey. The only thing you need to worry about is your schoolwork and enjoying your first year of college."

Melissa smiled. "Okay, I will."

"Pinkie swear?" They curled their pinkie fingers around each other's, and at that moment, Katelyn knew everything was going to be okay.

"You got a minute?" Vern walked over to the couch in the garage and sat.

"Be right with you." Jackson typed on his laptop. "I've got to place an order for a part."

"I can come back later."

"Done." Jackson's gaze collided with Vern's expressionless face. "What's the matter?"

"Nothing. I stopped by to see how you were doing."

"Where's Shirley?" Jackson asked.

"I dropped her off at the beauty salon. She spends more money getting her hair done than any other woman I've known."

Katelyn and Birdie had left for St. Louis the

previous week, and Shirley had remained behind. Since Vern worried about her staying alone in Birdie's house, he'd insisted she sleep in the guest bedroom at his place. "How are things going with you two?" When Vern didn't answer, Jackson walked over and sat next to his mentor. "Is everything okay?"

"Fine." Vern's gnarled fingers pressed against his slacks, bunching the material over his thighs.

"You're worked up about something."

"Have you and Katelyn made any plans for the future?"

"The only plan we have is not to have a plan." He wanted Katelyn to come home for good, but he refused to pressure her. Her happiness filled him with a sense of peace and rightness, and he wasn't going to do anything to jeopardize that.

Vern scowled. "Didn't you ask Katelyn to stay?"

"I told her to do what's best for her." If she came to the conclusion that he and Little Springs were best, then he'd grab hold of their future together with both hands and never let go.

"And if Katelyn doesn't come back, you're going to be okay with that?"

"Yep." He wasn't fooling himself—it would hurt. Probably a lot. "I'd rather Katelyn be happy without me than unhappy with me."

"If she doesn't want to live here, then sell the garage and go be with her."

"We're not teenagers anymore, Vern." He spread his arms wide. "I'm doing what I love." Running the garage and working on cars made staying sober doable. "Katelyn deserves a chance to live her own dream." With or without him.

"I don't want you to have regrets," Vern said.

"You've changed your tune about Katelyn. When she first arrived in town, you weren't happy we were spending time together."

"I shouldn't have interfered."

Jackson rubbed a hand down his face. He didn't want to argue with the man who'd helped him do something worthwhile with his life. "Did you tell Abby you're driving to St. Louis with Shirley in September?"

"Abby wants us to stop in Dallas on the way. She's got plans for us to meet her boss at some fancy restaurant."

"Shirley will like that."

Vern stood up. "It's official. I'll resume my church duties in October."

"The congregation will be happy to hear that."

"And I'm asking Shirley to marry me once I speak to Abby about it."

"What about Shirley's son?"

"I'm not worried about Don's approval. According to Shirley, he's on her shit list." Vern smiled. "Her words, not mine."

"I'm happy for you, Vern."

Vern's mouth curved in a sad smile. "Elaine

was a quiet, peaceful woman who shared her love of God with me. Every time I walk into the church or open my Bible, I feel her presence." He straightened his shoulders. "You told me Elaine would want what's best for me, and I believe that now."

Vern needed to take care of people. He'd watched over his parish for decades. He'd encouraged Jackson the past few years and he'd stayed by his wife's side as she battled cancer. It was natural that he'd gravitate toward Shirley, who'd need him more as her memory grew worse.

Vern clasped Jackson's shoulder. "You know you're like a son to me."

"And you're the father I'd always wished for." When Vern's eyes lit up, Jackson swallowed hard. He should have told the old man more often how much he meant to him.

Vern walked out of the garage. A moment later, Jackson heard the Mercedes drive off. He went back to the Civic in the bay and lifted the hood. Fixing cars was something he could control, and he needed to keep busy so he wouldn't think about Katelyn and whether she'd come back to Little Springs.

And to him.

CHAPTER THIRTY-FIVE

This was it?

Jackson sat in his pickup across the street from Katelyn's home in St. Louis and stared at the house. A Sold plaque had been slapped across the realty sign in the front yard, and an SUV was parked in the circular driveway.

He hoped he wasn't making a mistake by driving up here without an invitation, but when Birdie had stopped by the garage after Shirley and Vern had taken off for Dallas and had given him the painting of Mendoza Auto that Katelyn had left behind for him, he'd needed to speak with her—in person.

All those years ago he'd believed Katelyn had ended their relationship because he'd been damaged goods and unlovable. Something had to be wrong with him if the only two women he'd ever loved—his mother and Katelyn—had left him behind.

His drinking had grown worse, and he'd roamed from job to job. There were months when he'd laid off the booze, and other months when he'd fallen into a dark hole and hadn't remembered how he'd crawled out. Then one morning he'd woken with the worst hangover ever and decided to give up alcohol. Just. Like. That.

It wasn't long after when Vern talked to him about AA, which Jackson hadn't believed he'd needed. But he'd screwed up the courage and gone to a meeting. Then another. And another. It had helped knowing there were others struggling each and every day like him.

Then Vern had cosigned the bank loan so he could buy the garage. No one had ever before done anything like that for him. He'd finally had a chance to do something positive with his life, and he hadn't wanted to let Vern down, so he'd cut himself off from others and avoided socializing except for the AA meetings. Then his mother had come back into the picture. He'd considered ignoring her—payback for all the heartache she'd caused him—but he hadn't, because he'd needed to prove to himself that she no longer had any power over him and that nothing she did or said would make him want to take a drink. But it wasn't long before he'd been tested again when Katelyn returned to town and made him realize that cutting himself off from people had only made him weaker, not stronger.

Vern had helped him understand that he was the only person responsible for his drinking, and Katelyn had made him acknowledge that only he could give himself permission to take risks and live again.

It was time he began doing the things he wanted to do and not the things he thought he should do. Go where he pleased. Be with the people he cared about. And do it all without taking a drink.

If he didn't believe he deserved anything better than what he had right now, that's all he'd ever aspire to.

And that wasn't good enough. Not anymore.

He walked across the street. No matter how he tried, he couldn't picture Katelyn living in a house like this. He rang the bell. After a full minute, he knocked. When no one answered, he turned the knob, and the door swung open. He stepped inside and blew out a quiet breath. The furniture was gone, but it didn't take much for Jackson's imagination to picture the opulence that had once filled the spacious home.

A thud above his head drew his gaze to the ceiling. He climbed the stairs to the second-floor landing, where the soft strains of country music escaped from the room at the end of the hall. He paused in the doorway. An empty moving box was tipped on its side in the middle of the room beneath a crystal chandelier. His gaze shifted to the fireplace, where he envisioned Katelyn sitting in front of a roaring fire on a cold evening.

"Jackson?" Katelyn walked out of the closet. Her white T-shirt was covered with dirt smudges. Her face was shiny with perspiration. Her hair limp.

She looked beautiful.

Her mouth curved in a sassy smile. "If I'd

known you were in the neighborhood, I'd have put on makeup and done my hair." She rubbed her hands on her jeans. "You're a long way from home."

"I needed to tell you something."

Her attention swung to the box on the floor. "You could have called."

"I wanted to see you." *Make sure you were okay.*

She shoved her hands into her back pockets and shifted from one foot to the other. Maybe she felt as uncomfortable as he did in her bedroom.

"I'm sorry there's nowhere for you to sit."

"That's okay." What he'd come to say wouldn't take long, but he hesitated in getting to the point. "Do you need help packing the rest of your things?"

She shook her head. "I'm almost done."

A glint in the carpet caught his eye. He walked over to the fireplace and picked up a shard of glass, then looked at Katelyn.

"I threw a wine goblet against the fireplace the night I read Don's breakup letter." Her gaze softened.

"For what it's worth, Katelyn, I'm sorry you have to go through this."

"I know."

He set the sliver on the mantel. "You have . . . had a beautiful home."

"I did."

Standing next to the fireplace, he could see into the master bath. There was an obscene amount of marble everywhere—floors, shower, bathroom counters. "Will you miss this house?"

"No." She walked past him and stared out the French doors, which opened up to a balcony. "After everything that's happened this past summer, the house feels different. Claustrophobic. I'm not comfortable here." She shrugged. "I never was."

"Birdie gave me the painting of the garage."

"This time when I left, I wanted you to have something nice to remember me by."

His pulse skidded to a halt. "So you've decided you're not coming back?"

"I haven't made up my mind about anything yet."

Maybe he still had a chance.

"Sonja Doyle, the manager of the art gallery in Dallas, wants two of my charcoal sketches."

"Which ones?"

"The Fourth of July celebration in the park and my mother's birthday party at Doris's."

"That's great," he said.

"Sonja gave my name and number to a friend of hers who manages a gallery in South Carolina. He called yesterday and asked me to send photos of my work."

"Your dreams are finally coming true. I'm happy for you." And he meant it.

"I couldn't have done this without you, Jackson."

He had to touch her. He closed the distance between them and brushed his fingers across her cheek. "I want you to know something."

"What's that?"

"You did the right thing when you broke up with me after you left for college."

"How can you be sure?" Tears filled her eyes.

"Don't cry, Katy." He expelled a long breath. "If we'd stayed together, my drinking would have become an issue, and I'd have always worried that you'd leave me for someone better down the road."

"If I'd stayed, maybe I could have saved you."

"That stuff happens in fairy tales, not in real life." He took her hands in his. "I want you to believe that I'm going to be okay with or without you." He held her gaze, letting her stare into his eyes so she'd see the truth.

"What matters most to me," he said, "is your happiness. You were happy this summer when you were sketching. I want you to feel free to come and go in Little Springs and not have to worry about me or my feelings. We can be together or we don't have to be. I'm happy in Little Springs running the garage. And I'll still be happy doing that whether you're there or not. Whether we're more than friends or not."

"So what are you saying?" she whispered.

"There's room for both of us in Little Springs if that's where you want to be. The town might not look like much to outsiders, but it's in our hearts. It's where you found your passion to draw. And it's where I found the courage to stay sober."

Her teeth worried her lower lip. "If I come back, I can't make any promises to you."

It took more strength than he'd imagined to force the words out of his mouth. "I'm not asking for promises." More than anything, he wanted her to give him . . . them a second chance, but the only way to show her he meant what he'd said was to prove he could be happy without her.

"I'll think about it," she said.

Jackson's heart beat steadier than it had in years. He nudged the box with the toe of his shoe. "You sure you don't need help hauling anything out to your car?"

"I'm sure."

He walked to the bedroom doorway, but stopped when she called his name.

"Jackson." She smiled. "Thank you for coming."

He'd chickened out of going after Katelyn when she'd left for college, and he wasn't making the same mistake again. "Take care of yourself."

"Hey, watch that hose, kid!" Jackson yelled at Gavin, who was spraying the high school girls instead of the soap on the car. He smiled when a petite blonde smacked Gavin upside the head with a soapy sponge.

"I think my son has a crush on Jennifer," Layla said, walking over to Jackson. "I can't thank you enough for letting us use your business for the soccer team car wash."

"Happy to help the kids earn money toward their new uniforms." Brian had asked Jackson for help with the fall fund-raiser, and he'd said yes, looking forward to an opportunity to engage socially with others.

"Have you heard from Katelyn?" Layla asked.

He shook his head. They hadn't spoken since he'd left St. Louis three weeks ago. It was the end of September, and he had no idea when or if he'd hear from her. He and Katelyn might never get a do-over, but he'd always be grateful for the time he'd spent with her during the summer. Because of her, he'd begun letting people into his life again.

"How are your classes going?" he asked Layla.

"Who told you I went back to school?"

"Birdie." He grinned. "She stops by the garage every now and then to complain about the new checkout clerk Walter hired."

"Sharlene wouldn't be so bad if she'd stop complaining about her husband all the time." Layla waved her hand. "I won't lie. Going to school while working is difficult. I don't know what I'd do if I couldn't depend on Brian to keep tabs on Gavin."

"He's a good kid."

"I know. I'm lucky to have him." She pointed down the street. "Walter's bringing his car in. I better tell the boys not to mess with my boss." Layla walked off and Jackson went into the garage to find more dry towels and caught Shirley snuggling with Vern on the couch.

"They need sign spinners to stand on the corner. Why don't you two make yourselves useful?"

"Maybe after our break," Vern said.

"You've been sitting around since you got here."

The couple had returned to Little Springs a few days ago after secretly getting hitched in Dallas. Birdie hadn't figured out how Vern had overcome Shirley's reluctance to marry, but neither of them was spilling the beans. Sadie had thrown a reception in her beauty shop for the couple this past weekend, which Jackson had attended. He'd hoped Katelyn would return for the celebration, but he'd been told that she'd already flown to South Carolina to meet with the owner of an art gallery when she got the news, and that Shirley's son hadn't shown up because he'd been overseas on business.

"Is Birdie here?" Shirley asked.

"I haven't seen her," Jackson said. "Vern, if you fetch the outdoor cooker from the church, I'll send Gavin over to the store to buy burgers and dogs. We can charge a buck apiece and give the money to the soccer team."

"Great idea." Vern popped off the couch, but Shirley caught his arm. "That's too much of a bother. Let me write a check for the uniforms."

Vern coaxed Shirley to her feet. "Don't be a party pooper." The older couple left the garage and Jackson took more towels out to the boys, thinking he'd be up until dawn doing laundry after the fund-raiser.

When Katelyn arrived at her mother's in Little Springs, no one was home. She left her SUV and the U-Haul trailer she'd towed across three states parked in the driveway, then walked around to the front yard, where she spotted all the activity taking place at Mendoza Auto. When she reached the bottom of the hill, she noticed the posters advertising a car wash.

She strolled along Main Street, taking in the scene. The Hot Tamales had set up their band beneath one of the church tents and were playing an Elvis song. Shirley and Vern danced to the music. Brian and Layla were kissing in the shadows on the side of the garage. Ginny was guarding her pies on the bake-sale table. Sadie braided a teen's hair while a group of young girls watched. A car turned into the garage and the boys waved the driver forward. The older man had barely gotten out of the front seat before

Gavin sprayed the hood with water. And right in the middle of all the chaos, Jackson stood grilling hamburgers and calling out food orders.

Katelyn soaked in the homecoming scene. She hadn't told anyone of her decision to move back to Little Springs. After Jackson had left the house in St. Louis, she'd cried. An ugly cry—the kind where snot poured out of her nose and her eyes swelled shut. No matter how hard she'd tried, she hadn't been able to shove her feelings for Jackson or the memory of their relationship into a quiet corner of her heart and then shut the door on it. For good or bad, her creative energy would forever be tied to him and this place. It had taken a lot of courage to accept the truth—that the only way to fulfill her dream was to go back to the future she left behind.

Katelyn had always blamed Little Springs for holding her back. But this town and all its inhabitants had nurtured her passion for drawing. The young girl had left the small town, but the small town had never left the girl.

Jackson glanced up and she knew the moment he saw her—the burger on the end of the spatula dropped to the ground at his feet.

He set the spatula aside and walked toward her. They met in the middle of the street. The commotion around them went on: kids shouting and laughing, Birdie singing, Vern and Shirley dancing, Layla and Brian kissing.

Walter conversing with Gary. Ginny serving a slice of pie to Jackson's mother, who sat in her wheelchair, watching Sadie style the teens' hair.

"You're back," he said.

"For good."

"And us?"

"I can give you one day at a time."

His mouth widened into a smile. "I can do one day at a time."

"Are you available to help me move into my new place next week?"

"What new place?"

"I bought the O'Malley house by the railroad tracks."

"No kidding."

"It's a fixer-upper, but we could work on it together."

"I'd like that."

Katelyn wrapped her arms around his neck and released a heartfelt sigh when his lips brushed hers and a locomotive whistle drifted in her ears.

The train had been a driving force, moving Katelyn through the stages of her life. If she hadn't left Little Springs, she would never have understood that her artistic ability was deeply rooted to this special place and the people inhabiting it. As long as she followed the tracks, the train would always lead her down the right path.

ACKNOWLEDGMENTS

Special thanks to editors Danielle Perez and Sarah Blumenstock for your expertise in fine-tuning and polishing Katelyn's story. Thank you to the fabulous team at Berkley—the copy editors, the publicists and the members of the art department who helped bring this book to life.

To my agent, Paige Wheeler, thank you for your guidance and brainstorming help from beginning to end on this project. I appreciate all the support you've given me through the years.

To my author assistant, Denise Hall, who has been a huge supporter of my books through the years, your encouragement and friendship mean the world to me.

Last, I want to thank my husband, Kevin, for putting up with the crazy hours that come with my job. My children, Thomas and Marin—I'm so proud to be your mother. The world is a better place with both of you in it.

QUESTIONS FOR DISCUSSION

1. As a teenage girl Katelyn couldn't wait to escape the small town of Little Springs, Texas, and only later in life does she realize that the one place she thought would stifle her creativity actually nurtured it. Did you have similar thoughts when you were Katelyn's age? Later in life, did you end up back home or have you made a new home somewhere else? How does where a person is from impact where he or she will go in life?

2. Katelyn's relationship with her mother-in-law is trying, to say the least. How would you characterize their feelings toward each other? Use specific examples from the book to illustrate your points. How does their relationship change throughout the story? Do you have a good relationship with your mother-in-law (if you have one)? If not, what do the two of you disagree about, and how do you handle those disagreements?

3. Katelyn doesn't regret choosing to be a stay-at-home mom and raise her children, but her divorce does wake her up to the realization that she's lost part of her identity and that she set aside her aspirations when she decided to put her family first. Many women feel the same way when they marry and have children. Have you ever forgotten what you believed in? What you stood for? What was important to you? If so, how did you find your way back? What are some ways a wife and mother can put herself first without feeling guilty?

4. Growing up, Katelyn watched her mother and father struggle financially and she knew she wanted a different lifestyle for herself. But what does "having it all" mean? Is it different for each woman? And what kind of a price does it come with? What price did Katelyn pay for having it all?

5. Katelyn's impending divorce makes her face painful truths about herself and her marriage. We've all made decisions we regretted, but have you ever suffered through the consequences or stuck by your decision even when you knew doing so would make you unhappy?

6. Birdie admits that she was jealous of Katelyn's artistic talent, because her sketches reminded Birdie of her own lost dreams. Do you believe it's possible for a mother to be both proud and jealous of her daughter?

7. Getting involved with an old flame can be exciting and scary at the same time. What are some of Katelyn's biggest concerns about getting involved with Jackson again? Why is Jackson leery of getting serious with Katelyn? Is he nervous about getting his heart broken a second time? Are you satisfied with where their relationship stands by the end of the book?

8. If Katelyn had stayed behind in Little Springs and continued dating Jackson, do you believe his drinking would have sabotaged their relationship? Do you think that by the end of the book Katelyn has enough confidence in herself and her dreams to continue pursuing her artistic passion? Or do you think that she will revert to her old ways? Use specific examples from the book to illustrate your points.

9. It's not uncommon for a woman to change her hairstyle after going through a major life change such as a divorce or the death of a loved one. What do you think made Katelyn decide to finally change her hair? Have you ever made a drastic change to your appearance and if so, what was it? Did it make you feel better? More empowered? Or did you regret it?

10. Katelyn made a lot of excuses for not drawing while she was married and raising her kids. What kinds of excuses have you made for not doing what you love to do? What steps could you take to foster your talents or reach your goals?

11. The train is an important symbol in Katelyn's life. When she stands still and watches the fast-moving locomotive blow past her, it represents the powerful energy that drives her hectic world. What are some other things the train symbolizes to Katelyn aside from her life's journey? What object best represents the path your life is taking?

12. Sadie's beauty salon, like many salons, is more than just a place to get your hair done. It's an important place of social interaction for the Little Springs Ladies' Society. What's the biggest lesson Shirley learns from the matrons of Little Springs? Do you believe that Shirley has truly changed and grown over the course of the book or do you think that she will revert to her old ways?

Dear Reader,

Life is hard. And if we're being honest here, then it's okay to admit that like Katelyn we've all gotten lost at times. We're so busy trying to survive day to day that we can't see beyond the here and now. Usually it's not until we face an unexpected crisis that we wake up and realize life is passing us by and some of the promises we made to our younger selves have gone unfulfilled. It's often heartache that makes us pause and examine our lives—how far we've come, how far we have to go and the future we left behind.

Only we can determine if what we left behind is the *something* that's still missing from our lives. Whatever we learn, we should use the information to live a fuller life or simply appreciate the life we have a little bit more. And if we discover that it's time to let go of those promises, that's okay, too. Because when it's all said and done, life is all about the journey and not so much the accomplishments.

Marin Thomas is the award-winning author of more than twenty-five novels, including the Cash Brothers series and *The Promise of Forgiveness*. She currently lives in Phoenix, Arizona.

Books are produced in the United States using U.S.-based materials

Books are printed using a revolutionary new process called THINKtech™ that lowers energy usage by 70% and increases overall quality

Books are durable and flexible because of smythe-sewing

Paper is sourced using environmentally responsible foresting methods and the paper is acid-free

Center Point Large Print

600 Brooks Road / PO Box 1
Thorndike, ME 04986-0001 USA

(207) 568-3717

US & Canada:
1 800 929-9108
www.centerpointlargeprint.com